JOPHIEL'S SECRET

Marrow Publishing
Jophiel's Secret
By Johanna Frank

ISBN: 978-1-7777317-5-5 Paperback
ISBN: 978-1-7777317-6-2 eBook
ISBN: 978-1-7777317-8-6 Hardcover
ISBN: 978-1-7777317-9-3 Audio
Fiction/Fantasy

Acknowledgments:
Damonza – cover design and interior formatting
Kathleen Costello – copy and line editing
Family and Friends – encouragement extraordinaire

JOPHIEL'S SECRET

JOHANNA FRANK

A Lifeline Fantasy Series by Johanna Frank

The Gatekeeper's Descendants, Book #1
Jophiel's Secret, Book #2
Kasartha's Tour, Book #3, *Coming next and going back in time*

Same great characters. Stand-alone plots.

Jophiel's Secret is a work of curio-fiction fantasy, combining everyday living with the whimsical. While a few theological underpinnings are at work throughout the story, many are fantastical, born of pure imagination.

For my mother,
who for a time was shoeless,
and always said,
"You can bet your boots; He's real."

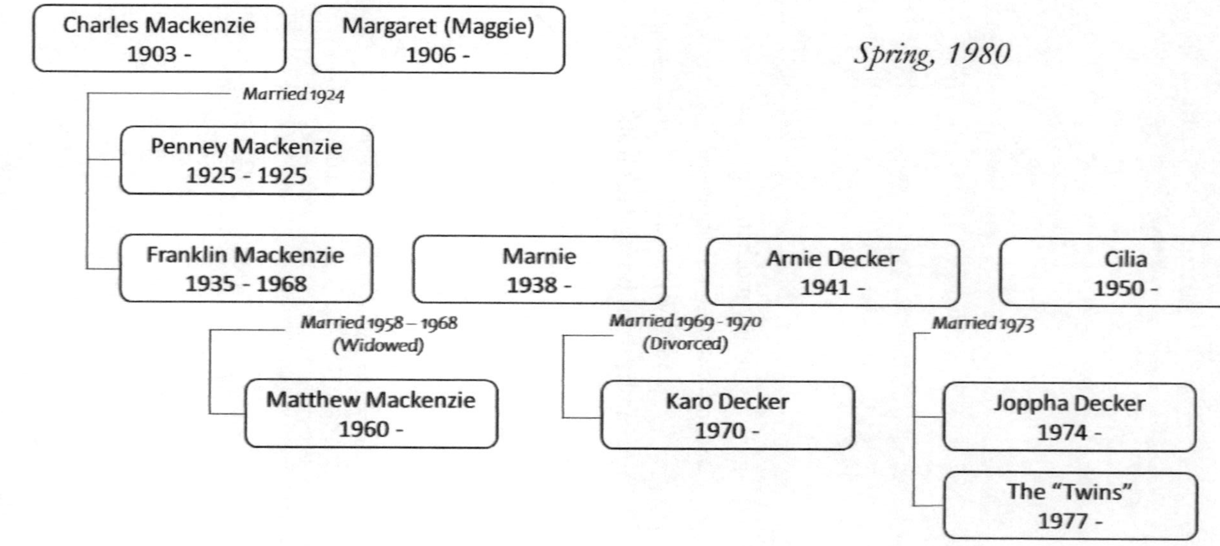

Spring, 1980
Charles Mackenzie
1903 -
Margaret (Maggie)
1906 -
Married 1924
Penney Mackenzie
1925 - 1925
Franklin Mackenzie
1935 - 1968
Marnie
1938 -
Arnie Decker
1941 -
Cilia
1950 -
Married 1958 – 1968
(Widowed)
Married 1969 - 1970
(Divorced)
Married 1973
Matthew Mackenzie
1960 -
Karo Decker
1970 -
Joppha Decker
1974 -
The "Twins"
1977 -
x

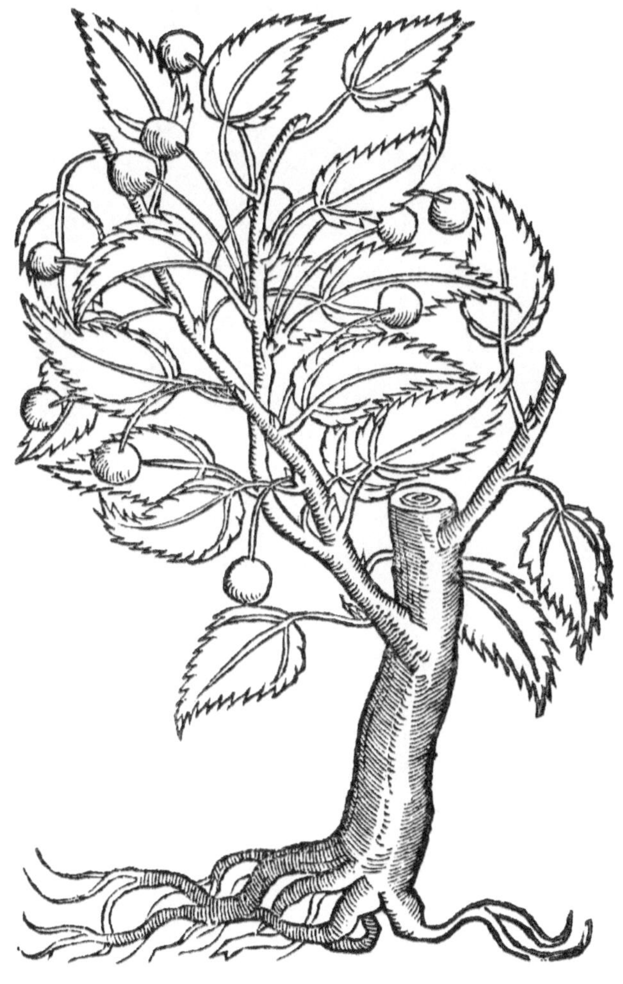

CHAPTER ONE
CHERRY STRUDEL

In the Outer Courtyard of the Kingdom

ONE MORE RUNNING scissor jump. *Goodness, Mother, will you be surprised when you see me!* A graceful landing on both feet and then up again, airborne, straight through the gate and into the outside world—the Kingdom's Outer Courtyard. The place where she grew up from childhood. A couple more sprints to drain the day's nervous energy, then she scampered into a squat. Here, in a patch of lavender, she would watch and wait.

Pipiera's mother was due to arrive.

Papah, the man who had pretty much raised her, was nowhere in sight. Unusual, since he was the Head Gatekeeper and rarely left his post for any length of time. *He can't be far,* Pipiera figured. *I know he wouldn't miss this for anything…he knows how I've ached for decades; this reunion means everything to me.*

Legs stretched out, leaning on her elbows, Pipiera admired

the wide and majestic horizon, a familiar view that shaped her very existence. A shoreline crested with incoming waves, one after each, powerfully pulling through galaxy upon galaxy, dutifully bringing forth Arrivals from a faraway world, a place the Authoritarians called Earth. A place where she had lived once herself, some years ago, for a mere number of days. The Outer Courtyard was the final stretch of the journey. Arrivals would be gingerly delivered in front of Papah's gate, the Kingdom gate, their delivering wave then taking a deep and gracious bow before gently melting into the ground.

Soon, Mother will come over that horizon, riding on a wave. I will meet her. It shall be grand!

Thankful she wasn't late, Pipiera closed her eyes and let the gentle breezes push her bangs back while she drank the day's aroma, each day different, each day healing. Today's a mixture of citrus and vanilla. She checked the delicate package tucked close to her body, secured by her left elbow. The baked strudel filled with plump cherries hadn't leaked inside its wrapping and didn't appear squished. *A little miracle,* she thought, given all her excited jumps. Well, not too squished, anyway.

Pipiera knew little about her mother, but one thing the ancestor aunties, Serena and Alexien, had told her was a story about their generational line's crazy love for cherry strudel. Pipiera wondered if they had made the story up simply because it was Serena's favorite thing to bake. Besides, who could resist the flesh of the Kingdom's own vibrant selection of sweet, red cherries enveloped inside Serena's hand-stretched layers of paper-thin dough? It was perfect for kicking off a homecoming celebration.

But never mind that—far more splendid would be the long-awaited moment when Pipiera could meet the eyes of her mother. A new page written; instead of sadness and grief, Pipiera imagined joy and happiness. Instead of a story wrapped in a blanket of blackness, her mother could glow freely with abundant light. *I simply cannot wait for you to hold me, Mother. We will never be separated again. Ever.*

The excitement of it all was excruciating. Yet a haunting rush of anxiety coursed through her veins; she couldn't place her finger on any cause for worry. *Surely Mother will arrive at this gate.* Her emphasis on *this*.

This moment was far too precious not to share.

"Now, where is he?" Speaking to her host of lively purple lavender, Pipiera looked around. No Papah Megalos. "Surely, he knows what today is!" Jumping up for a better scan—it was habit—she placed one hand on her hip and buckled her lips, toes dug into the soft vegetation. "Papah…*where* are you?" she sang at a pitch only her own ears could appreciate.

Though momentarily absent, Megalos had held his prestigious role for well over 300 years. Head Gatekeeper for the Kingdom. Pipiera was proud of the work he performed day in, day out, greeting and processing Arrivals. Sometimes having to turn them away. Rebels, of course, were mostly to blame for that. Of more personal importance, Megalos was Pipiera's outright favorite relative. Adopted relative, that is—there is quite a story behind the adoption. Another day for that tale. All that mattered now: Pipiera adored Megalos and Megalos adored Pipiera.

Roly, Megalos's faithful second-in-command, emitted a quick hello-nod her way. As much as Pipiera wanted desperately to inquire just where in the blazes her Papah 'Megs' was, she decided that wasn't such a great idea. Interrupting while gatekeepers are in the midst of processing Arrivals was never a good idea. Chuckling, she recalled the few instances when she had marched over and demanded attention at the most awkward of times. *Oh dear,* she shook the memories away. Not funny then, quite laughable now. *I've grown,* she applauded herself. She would have to wait for him, too.

Still searching for Megalos, Pipiera noticed both aunties, Serena and Alexien, sitting themselves down at a picnic table in the citizens' waiting area. She bolted over to join them, nearly dropping the strudel.

"Oh, good. You *are* here," Serena said with zero excitement.

Why the somber tone? Pipiera wondered. *There was no reason for that, not today.* "Of course! Where else, for the Kingdom's sake, would I be? Mother is about to arrive." Pipiera held up the wrapped package with both hands. Well, that got a slight rise of a smile from Serena. Though not from Alexien. *Something's up. Something's wrong.*

Pipiera slipped her legs under the table and settled in. "What's going on?" she eyed the pair, one at a time, not liking the face either had composed. Then her heart sank, pulling her shoulders with it. "No. Don't tell me. She's not coming." Pipiera curtly tossed the wrapped strudel onto the table, cherry guts seeping out.

Dismayed, Serena pulled the package together while Alexien appeared to contemplate an explanation. This day was, in fact, a long-awaited one; the arrival of a family member always was. Completing an Earth tour and returning home? Well, that was something to celebrate.

"No, Pip, that's not it. Maggie will arrive as scheduled." Alexien's voice was dry.

Pipiera exhaled sharp and quick. *Whew.* She took an inhale and looked behind her toward the horizon, where soon her mother would roll in along with one of the Kingdom's escorts. *Toward me. Toward the next forever phase of our lives.* Not sure what the aunties were bothered about, Pipiera wasn't about to let them ruin this moment. *My moment. No, I won't allow anything to interfere. Whatever they are upset about, they will have to deal with on their own.*

She glanced toward the gate. Still no Megalos. Small groups of gathered citizens were excitedly chatting at other tables, waiting for their own loved ones to arrive, all under a myriad of grapevine archways and large blooms of climbing white roses.

Her attention resigned back to the aunties. "Oh, what then? Come on, tell me."

Alexien was the wise and cautious one, at least according to Pipiera. Serena was the creative, scheming one, always having something new and fun up her sleeve. The aunties had taken Pipiera under their wing once she herself became a citizen. They were ancestors, great, great, many-times ancestors, and they, too, had been adopted into a line of descendants now belonging to Megalos. They were all one family now.

Alexien spoke slowly as if the words were painful. "It's — *Jophiel.*"

Serena's mouth twisted about. She was the one who would blurt everything out and then some. But at this particular moment, it seemed she preferred to hold her tongue. Rare.

"Serena?" Pipiera probed. Alexien remained seriously quiet.

This can't be good. It was automatic, Pipiera's fingers clasped in time to catch her chin. *No, please, King, let my Jophiel be alright.*

"Well," Serena tilted her head, readying herself to spill. "There *is* good news. He's coming home early."

"What? No! He can't come home early. I mean, of course, I would like that. But no, he's got plans, I'm sure of it. He wouldn't have taken a journey without a purpose, I mean, or without a major goal at heart. Why can't he stay longer?" Thoughts racing in circles like a wild rabbit trapped inside a cardboard box, Pipiera continued to blurt out questions as though her aunties were in charge, as though they would have some answers. "Is he hurt? In trouble?" Both hands slapped the table, giving Alexien a jolt. "What and why? Why does the King want Jophiel home so early!?"

Having been somewhat afraid of what Pipiera's reaction would be, Alexien and Serena shook their heads in unison, simply acknowledging her rant.

Ugh. Pipiera hated when they did that, the unison part. Catching her own attitude in the look of caution in the eyes of her aunts, she gave herself a scold. "Trust the King," she whispered softly.

The aunties heard the murmur and nodded, again in unison.

Scratching the back of her head, she twisted about to check on the horizon. It was a legitimate way to stall the discussion—was her mother coming yet? *Nope.* Agitation got the better of her. "Where's Papah Megs, anyway?" *I need him right now.* Her Papah Megs could always put things in the proper perspective, the Kingdom's perspective.

Alexien glanced toward the watch post that towered above the Kingdom gate. Atop it was a room, a humble room with not much but an ornate wooden bench that Papah liked to sit upon when he needed to contemplate. A single window provided a view of the entire horizon, so careful watching never ceased.

"He's up there. With Aivy. I suspect she's telling him to expect Jophiel soon." Alexien employed her voice of wisdom. Aivy was the Kingdom's transition agent, in charge of the list: the list of all scheduled arrivals. "We thought you could be happy for Jophiel, to know he would soon be on his way. And besides, all journeys have purposes and goals, no matter their length. *You* better than any of us know that, Pip."

Jophiel and Pipiera had a history. They met a mere six years earlier when Pipiera had been elected to take part in an intervention, her one and only mission. He had been the assigned escort to ensure that her travels to and from Earth were free from danger. During it all, they bonded. Supportive and special to each other. Jophiel was now on an Earth tour himself.

Pipiera calculated. He would be six years of age by now, still a boy. A young boy with the gift of intelligence beyond his years, she was sure of that. *Even so, what purpose could he have possibly accomplished?* She pushed the somber dispute down, hard. Though the aunties were right, she should know better than anyone that the length of a tour was not a key measurement.

A dewy wetness soaked her lashes. "I am. Happy for him. Don't get me wrong; I can't wait to see him. It's just…just…"

Alexien interrupted, "We know, Pip. And we get it." Her counseling tone conveyed an understanding. Neither Serena nor Alexien wished for Jophiel to come home before he could accomplish his tasks and build the character he was meant to build. Serena leaned forward and grabbed Pipiera's elbows, eager to share something else.

Alexien placed a hand on Serena's back as though to caution her words.

Pipiera leaned in. *Might there be a scheme of some sort? Leave it to Serena.* "I'm listening."

"Risks," Pipiera could barely hear Alexien's voice. "Mind the risks."

So, there is a plan!

Serena's telling face, her mouth twisting all about, eyes artfully churning to a squint, invited Pipiera to lean in even closer.

Whatever it is, it looks like these two might not agree. Pipiera leaned in closer anyway.

"Okay," Serena started. "Three things. You'd have to go now. And I mean now. And you must stay there, like, be an earthling and all, not just coming and going. You'd have to stay there for awhile, maybe even the entire summer. Secondly, you cannot use any powers—no disappearing and reappearing, don't go floatin' about or anything; you mustn't raise any suspicion."

Pipiera's back stiffened as she pulled away. "Me? Go there? Stay there? What? *Why?*"

Before she could reject the plan resolutely, Serena injected with term number three.

"And most of all, Pip…are you hearing this? Most of all, do not—and I mean *do not*—create close relationships. No one must discover just who you are. You've a job to do. Get in, stay the course, get out. One summer at most. That's it."

Is she serious? Pipiera examined the faces of her two aunts. Dead serious, both of them. "Am I missing something? Why would I need to go *there*? Besides, my mother is about to arrive." Totally baffled, she cast a firm, "No way!"

Her knee banged the underside of the tabletop but didn't slow her from making a stand. She would have walked away,

but these women meant so much to her. Those two words—
"No way!"—wavered visibly inside the airspace of the three
women, churning into a circular motion, rotating the tension
until it simulated a fierce column, a whirlwind of sorts. They
all watched as it darkened, a soft light growing from its inside.
Then it all disappeared.

Pipiera sat back down. She admired and trusted her
aunties. But their suggestion that she needed to go to Earth
for the summer, pretending she was an earthling? And all of
this right out of nowhere?

Serena rested her head on the table, hands covering her
short, brunette curls.

Alexien offered a resolution. "It's okay, Pip. We really
didn't think you'd be up for it. It's a far-fetched plan, anyway.
We simply couldn't come up with anything else." She then
glanced again at the tower room. Pipiera figured it was her way
of suggesting the deal for Jophiel to end his Earth-journey at
such a tender age and return to the Kingdom was being final-
ized at that very same moment.

"My mother," Pipiera bullied her defense. "You think I
could leave now? Now that I've waited so long for her arrival?
I've been preparing for *so* long for this moment. You're both
crazy. Seriously!"

The aunties remained quiet, eyes cast downward to where
the whirlwind vision had come and gone.

"You'll have your mother forever when she arrives. Jophiel
won't get another chance. You know that. One Earth-journey
per person…" Pipiera could see that Serena really was serious.
And persistent.

Alexien interrupted, "Unless, of course, we cause a commotion, an unofficial interference, a mission."

"Unofficial?" Pipiera gasped. "Uh, you remember how I fumbled the last one?" she added.

"No, no…Pip, it all ended well. There was no fumbling. All ended well, remember?" Alexien was being encouraging.

Shifting her seating direction, Pipiera nodded hesitantly. That one and only mission she had taken was something she'd rather forget—except meeting Jophiel, that is. She thought about Alexien's words for a moment. *She's right; it did end well, I suppose.*

Pipiera pushed her back up tall to begin a line of questioning. "Let me get this straight. I'd be a real person, a human earthling whilst there?"

"Just for the summer," Alexien said.

"I have it all figured out," Serena added in a tone full of hope.

"I need more details."

"You'll get them. We don't have time right now," Serena replied.

"Pipiera, dear, you literally must leave now. Now, before Megalos comes down those stairs and out of his tower. We need to tell Aivy and him that you've already left to help young Joppha. They'll *have* to pause his return then," Alexien explained.

"Well, no, they don't." Pipiera was pretty sure they didn't.

"Megalos will insist they wait if it's *you* who went," Serena pleaded. "He'll fight and plead with the Authoritarians. They'll *listen* to him." Alexien moved in closer. "Pip, it *has* to be you."

Oh, I get it now.

Pipiera knew Papah always gave in to her. And though this unofficial plan of her aunties' felt wrong, helping her friend Jophiel, whom she promised to watch over, felt so right.

"Jophiel did say in a letter that he took the Earth-journey knowing he had me to look out for him. What would he think if I disappointed him?"

The two aunties nodded, signaling agreement, in unison. But then Serena crouched low. "Psst, we gotta go. Now! C'mon."

Pipiera scanned the horizon. No Mother.

"C'mon!" Serena grabbed Pipiera's elbow and pulled her off the picnic table. "Alexien will stay behind. She's gonna tell them you've jumped in the main tunnel, all distraught and determined-like. You left to help Jophiel. But we must get a head start!"

Pipiera choked. That tunnel. The last time she jumped in, it was a nightmare. Terror. Trauma. The very reason she'd sworn to herself she'd never go on another mission, despite any promptings from that Intervention team. She had adamantly rejected their repeated invitations to join their group. Though with those words, 'but it ended well,' ringing in her ears, her nod was slight and just enough for Serena to grab her elbow and pull her along till they were both sprinting in the direction of the main tunnel.

Pipiera glanced behind. A leaky strudel on the table, no mother on the horizon, and an absent Megalos to guard the gate. She kept running, though she wondered why. Two people she loved so dearly were about to meet: her adopted Papah Megs and her earthly mother, Maggie.

And I won't be there for the celebrated moment. King, I pray I'm doing the right thing!

CHAPTER TWO

GET HER ON THE TRAIN

MEGALOS STOOD, ARMS crossed, chest puffed. "He really wants him home early—the King wants Jophiel back now?" Megalos cast his eyes away from his tower room window to focus on the beloved half-pint, vinegar-filled visitor standing in front of him. Aivy, who really was half the size of Megalos by height and even three times narrower by width, wasn't the slightest bothered by the annoyance Megalos filtered into the tiny room.

"Yes," was all she said, as she had already said enough. Aivy was a Kingdom transition agent, one of the best. In fact, she led a whole host of transition agents, which pretty much meant when someone was on the schedule to arrive home, back from their earthly tour, then she most assuredly knew about it. She herself prepared the daily arrivals schedule, complete with precise measurements of time, all based on information that came straight from the Authoritarians, which, of course, came straight through from the King himself. Many details had to be worked out as adjustments and changes happened all the time. It surely was a living schedule and a lively job—one she found quite satisfying most of the time. This particular moment, however, was one of the odd and unusual awkward times. She had even admitted it.

Megalos breathed in heavily and let his heavy shoulders slump in concert with the exhale. That was Aivy's cue—he's considering her proposal. She touched his lower arm gently, which was now hanging lazily by his side. "She's gonna be okay. I promise."

'She' was Pipiera, a most adored, officially adopted, great-times-a-few-granddaughter to Megalos. More than that, they were friends. Dear friends. Aivy had just talked Megalos into concurring with a plan, one that required Pipiera to leave the safety of the Kingdom for a mission where she could integrate as an earthling into the daily life of another descendant and future head gatekeeper for the Kingdom, Matthew Mackenzie. Oh, she could never be harmed—well, not truly harmed—because she was a Kingdom citizen, of course. She could, however, be quite traumatized by the process. Earth was a tough place more often than not, and even the slightest of visits can cause lasting damage. Megalos shivered at the thought of his Pip going back for a mission.

He reiterated Pipiera's role as he understood it. "All she's gotta do is *influence* Matthew."

"I would say, *inspire*, but yes, Megs, that's it!" Aivy held her head and hands high like it was a simple cheesecake kinda job.

"What if she fails? What if Matthew doesn't take the bait? What if he can't, in turn, influence Arnie Decker? And what if Arnie, in turn, doesn't, in fact, become the light and strength for that whole community? What then? It sounds like a long shot to me. A strange girl coming into town, just showing up like that."

"We'll take care of the details, I promise you," Aivy's head cocked to one side. That was her empathic pose. She knew just how much Megalos would concern himself the entire time Pipiera would be away. But Megalos wasn't fully convinced, and she could see he was starting to walk back, away from the plan.

"What if he recognizes her?! Have you even thought about that? This won't be her first visit. Don't play the fool with me, Aivy. You know he's *already seen* her!"

"He won't recognize her. Most likely, anyway." Aivy felt the heat coming directly from his face to the top of her head. "Look, he may find her *familiar*. But he won't recognize her. That's simply not possible. Besides, we are counting on that familiarity. We need Matthew to let her into his life, and fast. We only have two months. And having a *familiar* attraction is helpful."

"Two months?" Somehow that part of the plan had been skipped in its presentation.

This time it was Aivy who needed to take a step back. She breathed in and exhaled, too, with her own shoulders slumped, her face turned upward to his.

"No." He continued, "I'll agree. I already said it. But one week max."

"Megalos. You're being impossible. Whip up. Five weeks." Aivy pushed her head high. She was in negotiating mode now.

Megalos didn't like this. A few more quibbles, then the two shook hands and agreed on exactly twenty-one days, though Megalos knew full well the length of time would be precisely what was required, not a day more, not a day less. Their agreement was truly pointless.

Megalos stepped up to the single window and took in the sweeping view of the grand horizon. So magnificent. The real purpose, though, for his peek was simply to check on the activities around his gate. He smiled. Roly, his number-one assistant, was managing the Arrivals and their processing just fine. He thought of another question before Aivy could slip away. "How, for goodness' sake, will you even convince Pip to take an assignment, anyway?" He chuckled, thinking that'd be the showstopper. The Interventions Desk has been inviting her involvement for the past five years, to which Pipiera denied any and all interest in the opportunities.

"Oh, I've got a little plan for that." Aivy was back to her chirpy little self, practically singing the words. "I've already set my idea in motion."

"Huh?" It was most definitely a cross tone. "You already moved forward? Without my concurrence?"

Aivy knew she'd have to respond fast and get out of there. "Unofficially, of course. I simply let some information leak— like, err, Jophiel's possible premature return."

Megalos was astonished at this tidbit of information. Aivy had broken a rule. The arrivals schedule is never to be shared with Kingdom citizens until it is authorized for such. "Aivy, have you lost your mind?"

Aivy twisted her body about and pursed her lips. "It had a purpose. And…I think it worked. You see, I leaked to Serena. *And…,*" Eyebrows arched high, she checked his face, presuming he would know where she was going with this. "Well, you know Serena and Alexien and Pipiera were all out there in the waiting area moments ago." She pointed out Megalos's window toward the picnic tables. "And look! Now, only Alexien is there."

A horrified wash fell over his face. "I almost forgot!" Megalos exclaimed. "Isn't Maggie arriving today? Now, in fact? Huh! She's been waiting for this moment for so very long. I can guarantee she won't be going anywhere, not when her mother is about to arrive."

A sly look came over Aivy's face; she stepped aside so he could have a look-see out the window himself. "Well, Megs, she wouldn't miss that moment for anything, *unless,* of course...,"

"Unless, of course, she's slipping away to help her friend Jophiel." He sighed. "You got me."

As Aivy bounced her way out the door and down the staircase leading to the Kingdom's Outer Courtyard, Megalos called out one last instruction, "At least get her on the train route. You know how badly her trip in the travel tunnel went the last time!"

CHAPTER THREE
A FALLEN STRANGER

In the Town of Havensight, May 1980

PIPIERA REGARDED FOUR walls, examining each, one at a time. Yellow-gold paint. Oddly shaped shadows cast from a glass sphere hanging above her. A single window positioned high, a mere few inches from the ceiling, and a fully-armed, green plastic chair beneath. Double-paneled blackout curtains. An oversized armoire for her sparse belongings. She would spend an entire summer here in Havensight and this room would be home base.

She sniffed the air. Something stale and water-logged lingered. She flicked a switch; not much light. She rubbed a curtain panel between her fingers; flower prints would have been nicer. A loud, hollow bang echoed from somewhere inside a wall; cold air whistled and blew fiercely from a vent into the already-chilled room.

"Get settled." Her voice was as commanding as it was sarcastic, though no one was around to hear. "Just how does one get settled?" She tossed her peach fedora hat onto the bed. She followed next, jumping onto the perfectly dressed mattress and settling into a cross-legged position, deciding to review Serena's instructions once again. *Get it right. Do not deviate,* echoed in her head. *Rules, rules, rules. Yeah, yeah, yeah.*

A soft knock tapped on the door as it cracked open enough for the landlady to peek inside.

"May I come in?" Mrs. Damien said as she slipped into the room anyway. "Are we getting settled?"

Pipiera smiled at the tall lady with the humpback and expectant expression.

"Yes, Ma'am."

"Oh, so wonderful to have you. I'm not used to another female in the house. I've only one son, so if there's anything you need, anything I've forgotten, do tell."

"Thank you, Mrs. Damien."

It was too early; Pipiera didn't know what she might need. She caught the gleeful curve on Mrs. Damien's lips turn upside down as her eyes stopped abruptly at Pipiera's feet, all packaged up tightly inside shiny new three-inch-platform shoes. Though fashionable, according to Serena anyway, Pipiera wondered if it was their mucky residue on the bedspread that Mrs. Damien didn't like.

"Um," the lady spoke quietly. "We usually don't allow exterior footwear on our beds."

"Oh!" Pipiera jumped off the bed. "I'm so sorry; I'm not used to wearing shoes…er, I just forgot. Silly me." She hoped her blushing didn't give her away. Was that even possible, that someone might catch on that she had simply injected into an Earth form temporarily? A fraud, some might even think.

"It's okay, dear, not to worry." She paused before adding,

"Now you know. Supper is at five, but there's plenty of time before that to show you around the kitchen. Just make your way up." Then away she went.

"Show me around the kitchen? Whatever for?" Pipiera wondered what room and board really meant. Was she not supposed to have her meals made? Might she have to make her own, or worse, *theirs?* She plopped onto the bed again, mud-caked shoes included. "Serena! I need more details! And why am I in a basement?"

The door propped open again. "Did you say something?" Mrs. Damien hadn't gone far and now here she was again in the room with a disheartened look on her face. *She really doesn't want my shoes on the bed.* Pipiera jumped up again, "I'm sorry."

The discouraged Mrs. Damien mumbled that her son, Emerson, would be home later and he would be happy to show her around town. "I think you two will get along just fine," she snapped, vacating the room, leaving a slightly unpleasant odor behind while closing the door with an abrupt shut.

Oh, fiddle ducks. Pipiera flopped onto the bed once again. She freed her toes from the harsh shoes that suddenly weren't feeling so lovely, only heavy like cement blocks weighing her down. She pulled out the oversized Kingdom manual Serena had camouflaged as a hard-covered textbook entitled *Eldercare* and opened it up. Leafing past the "Mission" and "Helpful Hints" sections, she went straight to the largest part of the book: "Rules - Read and Report Daily." One bullet point midway down the page stuck out in particular: "Be kind and polite—do not stir up any negative emotions unless absolutely necessary to complete the mission."

Well, off to a good start. Not!

She flipped over to the mission checklist. Spotting a pencil on the floor underneath the armoire, she thought of a better idea. *Hmmm, what would I like to do now that I am here?* She pinched herself and giggled her way out of a bad mood. "I've wondered my whole life what I missed. Now's my chance. Adding a few things of my own surely won't do any harm."

Pipiera had indeed had her chance at an earthly tour more than several decades ago. It was brief, very brief. She had passed away at only a few weeks old. To have this chance, to be on a mission as a human for an entire summer—what an amazing opportunity! She scribbled furiously.

"Ride a bicycle." *A definite list item. Run into the watery waves that melt into the sandy shore. Yes!* "Jump waves." *I wonder what it's like to sit in a classroom. I bet much different from the hall of awareness in the Kingdom. I should visit a forest, talk to the trees, the flowers, the birds.* "Forest walk." *That ought to be lovely.* She sighed at her next thought. *At last, long last, to spend time with my Earth-father.* "Father." Now, that one was already on her mission list. In fact, there were many rules surrounding the expected time she would spend with Charles, what she could say and more about what she couldn't reveal: notably, who she, herself, really was. *Another rule.* She got busy creating a long list of things she wanted to do, figuring the summer would not only fly by but would be so much fun.

Pipiera kept coming back to Jophiel. "Best of all, I plan to tease the dickens out of you, in your little Joppha form! Now *that* is gonna be so amazing." Her head fell backward, plopping into and displacing an assortment of crocheted pillows.

She remembered the first time she met him. Jophiel. A majestic height well over twice hers, at least; his powerful wingspan impressive beyond measure. Eyes like blue sapphire, and that crooked grin. She even loved the remembrance of his scolding and jabbing. And now, Jophiel had taken on the challenge, from Kingdom escort to the most treacherous of all: an earthly humankind tour. As much as Pipiera knew, Jophiel was the sole reason for her visit, an unsanctioned mission as it was. *Curious and stubborn I bet he is, even as a youngster.* She chuckled at the naming upon his earthly birth, Joppha, though the precarious scenario of the present triggered a sigh. They would cut his fate determination short unless she could change something. As to what that was, she hadn't a clue; she believed she had all summer to figure that out. She had to admit to herself that her admiration for Jophiel was great. Otherwise, how could she possibly let herself be talked out of being present at her own mother's arrival? Heaven forbid.

"Forgive me, Mother! But I promise, you *will* understand," she whispered upward.

CHAPTER FOUR
JOPPHA'S GATE

J OPPHA SAT UP tall, eager and anxious. His neck arched to see out the backseat window. The driver, his favorite babysitter and best uncle ever, pulled the old Impala toward the curb, angled in, and slid it back. The car ticked, clacked, then gave a huge, chugging exhaust. Joppha giggled. "Sounds like it farted."

"Just for you, buddy," Matthew chortled.

"Nice work, dude," Emerson, also in the car, chimed in. He was truly impressed with his best friend's parallel parking job.

Matthew smirked at Emerson and, while at it, looked back and winked at a wide-eyed Joppha.

"That's it. That's the bus station, Jopphie. *The* gate to the world."

Joppha had never been out of Havensight in the entire six years of his life. The small camping tourist town was his entire world. His favorite outing was to the pebbly beach west of town, where, with the careful guidance of his parents, he would jump the waves.

His fists pressed firmly into the ripped foam padding of the back seat, his little arms straightened to hold him up so he could get a real good look. Mouth gaped open, he scanned the long, wide building and its centered, revolving doors, people coming and going carrying suitcases of all colors and sizes. He blinked a couple more times before returning the gaze that his 'Uncle' Matty cast upon him. "Can we go in?" he asked, with a voice an even higher pitch than normal.

Given their age difference, Joppha's father, Arnie Decker, insisted his son refer to Matthew as uncle. Since Joppha's birth, Matthew had, in fact, become part of the family and using the uncle label provided a simpler reference than *your stepsister's brother.*' Fewer questions.

"Like, look at everyone else. They're just walkin' in. No guard or anythin'." Joppha exclaimed. It surprised him that there was nothing to stop all those people from entering. "Why ain't there no gatekeeper?" he asked.

Emerson and Matthew caught each other's eyes and shared some silent chuckles. It was just another 'J.S.'—a Joppha saying, when he says something bizarre, yet sometimes perfectly logical. Though sometimes a handful, and sometimes his super-sensitive nature drove them around the bend, Joppha could always make the boys smile.

Emerson turned to face the backseat, where Joppha was fully absorbed with the goings-on. "Now, why would the bus station need a gatekeeper, Jopphie?"

Joppha mumbled a response, annoyed with the supposed near-grownups in the front seats of the car. "A new world should be clean," he announced with a six-year-old's sense of knowing.

Matthew smiled, "Right, buddy." Matthew knew just how serious Joppha was about his own logic and respected the little guy's infectious imagination. "So, uh, Jopphie. Is it *safe* for us to go in?"

Joppha pulled out a couple of plastic toy soldiers from his pocket. With one in each hand, it appeared a tête-à-tête was called for in order to decide. Joppha lifted his head and nodded. "Yeah, it's okay, they're gonna watch out for the enemy; we just gotta be careful." He added a fierce whisper of caution, "Don't think it's a joke."

Emerson cracked into a laughing rage and play-punched Matthew on his forearm, "Ooh, be careful, Matty, boogey-man's gonna getcha."

Joppha tucked the two soldiers in his pocket and crossed him arms. He didn't like Emerson much.

"So, let's go." Lifting the mood, Matthew reached both arms over to tickle Joppha's sides, shaking him into a roaring giggle. "You and Emerson get out here. I'll boogie to the parking lot and meet you inside. Laura's bus isn't due for another fifteen, anyway."

"Yeah, bud, we'll sneak past the guards and check out the surroundings!" Emerson teased some more.

Joppha shook his head. *You guys know nothin'.*

The threesome was there to pick up the woman Matthew often referred to as the love of his life—to be—one day: Miss Laura, Havensight's summer school dance teacher, only child of longtime residents, Mr. and Mrs. Bing, admirer of Matthew since grade eleven, and now in the ten-percent club of Haven-sight's population to have earned or be actively working on a university diploma. An unofficial club, of course, as no one ever really counted. Laura had completed the final exam of her first year just that morning and would at this very moment likely be rounding the bend following an arduous, five-hour, two-transfer tour home.

Emerson and Joppha headed toward the building. Joppha insisted on being alone in one of the revolving door wings. Waiting patiently, Emerson agreed and let three people with large suitcases pass through first.

"Okay, go now," he urged Joppha.

It didn't take much urging, Joppha jumped in, huge grin included. That is, until the door jammed for no apparent reason.

Panicked, Joppha glared back at Emerson, who was still outside. "I can't breathe! There's no air in here." The palm of his hands flattened against the door, attempting to push the door back the way he came in. "Get me out, get me out." His little fists pounded on the glass.

Emerson could see the redness literally rise from young Joppha's neck up to the top of his head, till a blush was visible even through those boyish blonde curls. He did his best to stifle and cover up a laugh, but the more Joppha was terror-stricken, the more Emerson cracked up.

A high-pitched, airy sound caught the attention of Emerson and several bystanders, followed by an official-looking guy in a dark-blue suit, gold buttons and a cap. Pulling a whistle out of his mouth, he motioned for all to stand back as he forced the stuck door to release and revolve once again.

Once free of the door, Joppha took a run for it. Embarrassed, yes, but mostly angry at Emerson Damien. *Some friend he is. I'm telling Uncle Matty.* Like a captive escaping his captor, he ran.

It was a long, wide hall filled with rows of grey metal waiting room chairs, ticket counters, and big television monitors bolted up high. The super-shiny floor was slippery, but Joppha kept running. He passed crowds, bumped into people, even pushed some kids out of his way.

Ducking inside a book retailer, Joppha dove behind a tall magazine rack, its looming shadow providing much-needed refuge. *Emerson, you nincompoop,* he silently accused his attacker, and he felt his heart thump like the beat of a trap drum. Fast. Bouncy. Repetitive.

A glimmer of light fell from the ceiling, spotlighting a magazine and grabbing the boy's attention. The warm, inviting photo on the cover depicted a forest of odd yet strangely familiar super-tall trees with gnarly roots amidst a soft blanket of petite and colorful flowers. Each trunk and branch creatively ornamental, full of truly artful twists. All branches curved and wound inward toward each other, forming a canopy ceiling for a single happy picnicker sitting below it. Silver birds perched upon nearly every branch, camouflaged aside white flowering buds, their beaks tucked inside their wings as if they knew someone were watching, memorizing the view. Joppha was truly amazed. He had seen that place before, been there, he was sure of it. *I know that place. I know it!* He couldn't read the headline, only a few words: *heaven…back…testa-something.* Joppha grabbed the magazine off the shelf, rolled it up and tucked it as best he could into his left suspender, then pulled his sweater vest over top. He had never, ever taken anything that wasn't his, but this was different. He needed to have that photo. It somehow made his very existence feel unconditionally safe. That need for an assured feeling had been festering and growing over the past six months. The battle his toy soldiers fought daily to protect him was never-ending. The enemy was no joke to Joppha.

The precious magazine would become to Joppha a hidden gem, a scroll he would guard as though his life depended on it. He looked around cautiously, as though the entire world—well, at least all the people in the bus station—would now be after him. "C'mon, let's go," he whispered to his precious package before slinking out of the store and farther on down the hall. He would find a new place to hide and keep away from Emerson till Uncle Matty would come and save him.

CHAPTER FIVE
JOPPHA GOES MIA

MATTHEW ARRIVED INSIDE the bus terminal to find a panicked Emerson and no Joppha.

"It's not my fault, I swear!" Emerson grabbed Matthew's forearms and shook him silly. It was quite the greeting. "Ya gotta believe me."

"Whattaya mean? Where's Jopphie?" The swoosh of the revolving door behind him continued aggressively. It didn't take Matthew more than a few seconds to realize Joppha had taken off, bolted to hide and be alone somewhere. He often did that. *Oh, I knew I shouldn't have brought him.* "You need all eyes on that kid; you know that, Em!" Matthew's voice cracked. He had a bad feeling.

Joppha was super-smart, super-mature, and supersensitive. Moments like this took Matthew's mind back to images of Emerson's taunting in their high school days. He, himself, had endured the cruelty of being mocked by Emerson. In fact, 'my worst enemy' would have been how Matthew described him back then.

Emerson still liked to mock and make fun, and poking fun remained, to some degree, part of the friendship between the two. But Emerson could not seem to recognize that there is a time and place when these are not okay. Matthew knew instantly that this was the reason Joppha bolted again. It was becoming an annoying habit.

"You made sport of him again, didn't you? You know the little guy is going through a rough time," Matthew snapped while he struggled with an inability to think. *Don't panic. Stay calm.*

Shifting his weight, Emerson pursed his lips, obviously thinking about what to say, what reasoning could make sense. He managed a mumbled response: "Sorry, bud. The little dude is, like, so *touchy.*"

"C'mon," Matthew grabbed his friend's right forearm, almost lifting him off his feet. "Let's go find him."

Now technically young adults, Matthew and Emerson understood and accepted each other's many quirks. Emerson lived with and kept his mother company—who, in Matthew's view, was far too much in his face about everything.

Subconsciously, Matthew patted his front right jeans pocket before sprinting. *It's still there.* The ring. What Laura would call a pre-engagement ring. It was all the rage these days: to snag a girl and reserve her as the one you'll likely marry years later. Laura had been hinting when she left for university that she just *might* move to a bigger city, and *that* scared Matthew. *This is not how my day was supposed to go.* He was supposed to be securing his future, not chasing an emotionally charged kid around a busy bus depot.

"Which way did he go?" Matthew looked right and left and then right again. Long hallways in each direction. No sight of Joppha. "Jopphie, c'mon, where'd you go?" Matthew muttered aloud. Then he pointed to the terminal's Information Desk, and the pair darted over.

After sharing the news of a misplaced young boy and describing his height, hair color and clothing, the clerk urgently picked up a walkie-talkie to call security, though loud shouts down the hall caught everyone's attention. A round, overweight man with arms waving hollered, "Stop that thieving kid." A crowd of onlookers, although intrigued with the excitement, made no response to the repeated plea. In fact, travelers stepped aside to let the so-called thief—just a young boy—get by. Furious, the shopkeeper hollered even louder and pointed to the boy who had by now reached the furthermost exit, the gateway to the bus platform where only paid passengers could go. Once the boy could no longer be seen, the shopkeeper threw his upheld arms downward and let out an enormous and resigning, "Hummpfff, where's security when you need 'em?" before returning to his racks of books and magazines.

The clerk, annoyed, put down the walkie-talkie, "That yer kid?"

"Jopphie?" *No, Jopphie's no thief. Confused, maybe. Overly sensitive, yeah. Too smart for his own britches, for sure. But thief? No way.* The pieces didn't add up.

This time it was Emerson who did the yanking. He wrapped Matthew's left forearm with his own hands and pulled hard. "Out there. We need to get him. Before he gets on a bus or somethin'. C'mon, Matt."

Emerson and Matthew rushed toward the gate, Emerson leading the way, till Matthew caught up to take charge. Both out of breath, they were stopped from entering, the heel of a burly man's hand stretched out firmly to block them said it all.

"Nuh-uh. Need yer tickets." The deep, monotonous voice of the large ticket collector suggested he was both stubborn and bored.

"No…you don't…our boy…is in there," Matthew managed between breaths, while Emerson nodded, pointing toward the platform.

The ticket collector raised his eyebrows. Two boys—neither appearing old enough to be a parent—both claiming *their* boy was somehow on the passenger platform, expecting him to simply let them by with no ticket? He chuckled. "Now I've heard everything. Move aside." He waved them off and proceeded to collect the tickets from other folks. As three buses were leaving in the next ten minutes, a considerable crowd was forming around the gate, approaching with a polite yet distinct form of pushiness, their offensively hefty suitcases in serious play.

"A boy, Joppha, I'm responsible for him—he just got through here, not even two minutes ago. We need to get him!" Matthew pleaded to whoever would listen.

"Call security," the ticket collector yelped to the crowd's satisfaction and nodded toward a pay phone across the hall.

"Aw, forget it," Emerson announced loudly. Matthew caught his friend's wink and stepped away as if to head toward the pay phone as directed. Desperate to get through the crowds and over the turnstile, their boyish play, instinctive to both, was in action.

Emerson whipped around and crouched over, grabbing his intestines and forcing some hurling motions. A definite crowd disperser, and it worked.

Perfect.

Matthew had only seconds for his part, but mere seconds

were all he needed. He had an open space thanks to Emerson's intense distraction, and he had a target: a twenty-nine-inch, three-pronged turnstile. He readied himself, a tiny grin emerging thanks to the challenge and the adrenaline. A swift step one, then a second on his toes, he dug low into his heel and swung his arms from behind to a front block for a vertical jump. The transfer of energy took him up and over the turnstile to reach his goal: the other side, the bus platform. He scrambled up and off quickly to begin his search for Joppha. Truly, the boy couldn't have gone far.

When the ticket collector grabbed Emerson's forearm, Emerson smirked and reveled in sarcasm. "Maybe *you* should call security."

CHAPTER SIX

MILITARY FORCES ON ALERT

THE PLATFORM WAS indeed a busy place. Large passenger buses lined up neatly within the yellow lines painted diagonally on fresh asphalt. The slow hissing sound of doors opening wide, the clambering of hard-soled shoes on step stools climbing into or out of a bus, and the blast of strong, unfamiliar odors—all new to Joppha's senses. Neither he, the drivers, nor any of the luggage-loading stewards would hear the overhead speaker on account of the loud engine noises of three buses rolling in one behind the other.

"Security al... Attention all ...visors and all drivers. Watch... missing child, reported... -ing on the platform."

Joppha stepped backward until he felt the cool roughness of the building against his back. He leaned to stop the shaking. All those bodies crowding in bunches appeared to Joppha as upside down, the buses sideways. He waited for the dizziness to pass, for those somersaults in his chest to settle down. He gave the precious stolen package tucked inside his sweater vest another protective squeeze with his right arm before checking his pockets. His own private militia warned him: *be on guard.* The loudspeaker continued to blurt out its jumbled message. Wiping his forehead with a free elbow, he spied the crowds. *An enemy lurks.*

But Laura's gonna be on one of those buses. I know it, he thought.

And she was.

Joppha waved furiously, and even five bus stalls away, the beams of Laura's big smile made it all the way from the driver's doorstep to his heart. *I'm gonna marry someone like her one day,* thinking Mathew could marry Laura and he would—years later of course—marry a Laura-double. And a happy life could then exist. *But no Emerson, he's not gonna be invited to my wedding.* Right now, he had an innate instinct to protect her, to deliver her safely to Matthew. He squeezed one of his militia guys again, the one in charge. *At ease, soldier. Time to help civilians.*

Yanking on a bigger-than-her yellow suitcase, Laura made her way to Joppha. The hug was so tight, and she tussled his hair. "You've grown, my little dude!"

The heat of his blush caused him to loosen up his sweater vest.

"What'cha got there?"

He caught her eyes glimpsing inside his sweater.

"I didn't take it. It's mine."

She answered his defense with a sly look.

He stood tall and put to work his grown-up voice, the one he used when it was important to be intelligent and mature. "It's my reading materials. I got goals in life too, ya know."

Laura opened wide that big, baggy purse of hers. "Here, toss it in. It's getting all sweaty, you holdin' it like that." Laura could tell Joppha was a little skeptical about releasing the crinkled roll of magazine pages. "Hey, don't worry, it's safe with me, and I promise you'll get it back. Besides, you need both hands to carry my purse."

Joppha stared into the bag she called a purse. He had misgivings. It was never-endingly deep and mysteriously dark. *What else is in there?* he wondered.

"Jopphie, come on, you can trust me. Toss'er in, then take it. I'll carry this darn suitcase." She knew how Joppha often made life difficult on himself, always having strange and obsessive thoughts.

Craziness ensued all around. One uniformed gentleman bumped into Laura, then grabbed her shoulders to look at her squarely. "A kid is missing. Have you seen a missing kid?"

"Uh, no." She shrugged her shoulders.

The gentleman's gaze fell to Joppha. "You? You seen any kid missing, wandering around?"

Joppha shrugged as well, and the man ran off to continue his search.

Laura and Joppha watched and stood still as whistles constantly blew, causing madness among the mobs. All the passengers loaded on buses were asked to disembark. People were groaning everywhere. The platform was more crowded in every direction as the security guy and the once-bored ticket checker carried out searches on empty buses.

"That would be frightening if I had a child who got lost," Laura spoke emphatically.

"Maybe he just needed to get away, someone was like, bug'n'im," Joppha offered.

This made Laura chuckle, "Like a kid needs to get away, ha! Anyway, where would it go?"

Joppha shrugged, "I dunno. Home? I bet he just wants to go home."

Scanning the crowds, Laura scoffed, "Nah, the kid's likely just spoiled rotten, didn't get his way or something. Kids do that—for attention …or candy. By the way, where's Matty?"

Joppha heaved Laura's purse up higher against his chest, wrapping both elbows in and around the handles. "Inside," he said, shifting his weight and nodding his head toward the passageway back into the terminal. *With Emerson.* He eyed her preoccupied face; *you don't think kids have feelings? You think I always gotta get my way?* He was having doubts. Maybe he didn't need to protect her.

The platform had become shoulder-to-shoulder with off-loaded, angry passengers. With both hands clasped on her big yellow suitcase, she instructed, "Jopphie, stay close. Stay right behind me. Got it? We need to get out of here, out of the way."

Joppha reluctantly nodded at her order, though she seemed to have a question on her mind. He released an impatient, "What?"

"Uh, does Matty have something for me? By any chance? Like a *small* present?" Arched eyebrows and a sneaky sparkle in her eye transformed her face from what was otherwise grounded, mature and confident.

He shrugged and wondered. *How would I know? I'm just a spoiled-rotten kid.* He replied to her question with a simple, "Dunno." *I don't want my way; I just wanna go home. My home. My real home.* That picture on the magazine cover: he was sure he'd seen it before, been there. It was calling him. He lowered his head and remained still for a moment to allow another dizzy spell to pass.

Laura sighed and slumped in assumed disappointment.

"Yeah, sorry, kiddo. How would *you* know?" Turning, she pushed and shoved a pathway toward the entrance, not realizing that Joppha held back, choosing to contemplate his position in life rather than follow her back inside the bus station.

Realizing he had all he needed—his magazine cover tucked safely inside the sweet-smelling and ginormous purse—he decided it was time. Time to enter a new world. After all, he did already go through a gate, so it makes sense to keep going, be someplace where he might fulfill that longing to be understood.

Twisting his shoulder and elbow about, he snuck his hand into his pocket without dropping the purse. *All clear.*

Another whistle blew. The first bus was emptied, void of passengers and now security-cleared. No missing boy onboard. Its passengers now crowded tightly around the driver, waving their tickets and pushing their way up the stairs and into the bus, including a mother and two children, the young girl's hand in hers and a young boy who appeared slightly younger than Joppha directly behind. Joppha pushed his way to stand with the boy. They shared a smile, and the boy offered him one lollipop from his collection. Joppha happily grabbed the licorice one, his favorite. "We're going home," the boy said.

"Me too!" Joppha replied enthusiastically. *Hey, this is perfect,* he thought.

The bus driver waved the mother and her presumed *three* children upward into the bus and even asked others to pause so that the woman outnumbered by her young traveling companions could have some space to maneuver.

CHAPTER SEVEN
AN ENEMY ARRIVES

Seven hours later

"NO, MOM, I don't want anything." Matthew hadn't even lifted his head, leaving it lodged between his knees. If he could squish the contents out, spill the stupidness all over the floor and pounce on it for the rest of his life, he would. Joppha was missing, and it was *his* fault. He, himself, had insisted that Joppha come along for the drive to the bus station. The li'l gaffer always talked about gates and getaways and guards and so on and so on. He was an unusual boy, indeed, but so delightful, so mature beyond his years. They'd had a special relationship right from the get-go. Matthew often spent time with the boy, teaching him to catch, jumping moves and sometimes even stargazing when Joppha's parents, Arnie and Cilia, allowed it. Now, he's missing. Slipped right out of Matthew's care and into… well, who knows where he is? Matthew glanced up toward the basement window. The sun was greying. It would soon be dark. And cold. The early June evening temperatures were still dipping low. *He only had that sweater vest on.* Matthew's knees tightened the punishing grip on his head.

Marnie held the doorframe tight, unsure how to help her son. "Emerson just called. His turn with the police is done, and he's coming over. He says he's bringing his boarder, some girl who arrived today. I told him this is not a good time, but you know Emerson. I think he's bringing her anyway." A slight nod of his head gave permission to continue, this time with a whisper. "Grammie's asking for you." His head adamantly shook. "Please, Matty, she really wants to see you before… before…she's not got much time. You know that." Given the lack of response, she left her son to continue his wallow in the recreation room. She headed up the stairs to their living room, the room Marnie had converted to accommodate a hospice environment for her mother-in-law, Maggie Mackenzie.

Marnie had only met her husband's parents several years following his death. In fact, she hadn't even known they existed. Her husband—first husband, Frank—had never spoken of them and vehemently refused the topic. But since their meeting, Marnie and her two children, Matthew and Karo, had grown so very close to Maggie and Charles Mackenzie. Their grandkids were their only family and vice versa. Caring for Maggie while she weakened was the least Marnie could do, given that Maggie and Charles had moved in with her to ease the financial bleed of trying to manage a household on her wages from the flower shop where she worked.

Maggie was so proud of her grandson. She doted on Matthew all the time, even now, as she experienced confusion and weakening muscles. Dr. Bonneville had just left the house, noting that her temperature drop and diverse vitals were signals. "It won't be long now; she'll melt away into a forever sleep," was how he put it. Matthew knew this, but facing Grammie's adoration for him while he felt nothing but shame for losing young Joppha, there was no way Matthew could do it. Totally unbearable. He couldn't face her and if that meant he couldn't say goodbye, then so be it.

Matthew lifted his head to give it a break, let the blood flow in the opposite direction, the way it should—for a little while, anyway. Scanning the room, memories flooded his mind. The faded paneling, stale air, and the carpet that always needed vacuuming made him snigger. *A lot of good times in this room with you, little buddy.* His mind went back even further, before Joppha had come into his life, when his life was not so great. Recollecting an imaginary spacey, freaky-lookin' alien who used to visit him when he was down on himself. Like he was now. *Thank heavens, I haven't seen that weirdo for years.* Haunting thoughts that the guy was real still bothered Matthew to this day.

A taunting voice came straight from behind the couch. "Well, well, look at you. My, have we grown! Is that? Nooo! Peach fuzz, ha! Well, I'll be darned." Matthew felt a slapping motion across the back of his head and jumped up. *What the heck?!*

A green, egg-headed, incredibly short goon with a floppy purple hat and baggy pants stood on the back of the couch. "It's about time you thought of me again." The voice was hauntingly familiar, too familiar for Matthew's liking. "Don't look so surprised. You called me. I'm here."

"I called *you?* Pretty sure not. Get lost." Matthew shook his head vigorously. *Think I squeezed too hard; I'm imagining things.*

Just then, the doorbell rang and seconds later, Matthew overheard Emerson introducing someone to his mom upstairs. *Dang, he brought the summer boarder his mother arranged.* Matthew truly didn't feel like being hospitable; he had even sent Laura home despite her insistence that she wanted to stay for moral support. *What will Laura think if she finds out Emerson brought some curious, nosy woman over?*

"Oh, *sheee's* here?" The green goon announced his query. This startled Matthew, who was certain that the strange individual was a figment of his imagination. How could he possibly still be present? Surely the blood in his head is flowing much better now.

Emerson bolted down the stairs, a welcomed distraction.

"Hey bro, how ya doin'?" Emerson straddled across his friend and grabbed a section of the couch. The pair remained silent for several moments, the situation surreal. All they could hear was Marnie upstairs chatting with a young woman. Emerson felt he needed to explain. "She was like, adamant that she had to come. Had to be here. Like, this is okay, right?"

Matthew rolled his eyes and shrugged a shoulder.

"She was pretty freaked. She and my mom listened in on the whole interview. The police are callin' it a runaway."

"He's missing! It's no freakin' runaway."

"I know, I know. They're on it. They're gonna find him."

"He's on one of those buses. I know it." Matthew believed wholeheartedly that Joppha got onto a bus, not comprehending the consequences. "He was in one of his moods. Like *he* needs to get away from it all. He's just a kid."

Emerson nodded in agreement but argued that the police say no. "Security says there's no way he got on a bus. They made everyone get off all the buses, then checked the seats.

They say there's no way, Matt, that the kid got on a bus. He's gotta be around the station, maybe hiding out in a farmer's field or somethin'." The boys were quiet again for a bit till Emerson added some encouragement. "Arnie's still there, Matt, at the station. They'll find him. We'll all have a big fart'n laugh when they get 'im."

Matthew found Emerson's perspective annoying and irresponsible. *Gad, you don't even show remorse,* he accused silently, though a nasty look was unrestrained.

"C'mon, Matt, they say runaways come back within forty-eight hours. Why, I bet the clever kid's hitched a ride and is on his way right now. He's gonna be home and snug as a bug in a rug before ya know it. Heck, I can't even count how many times I ran away when I was his age."

Matthew pondered about a time in his own life, around his fourteenth birthday, when he had wanted nothing more than to put Havensight and everyone he knew in the review mirror, forever. After another round of silence, Matthew looked up and asked, "Do you see anyone else in this room? Like a weird, half-pint, greenish-looking guy in the corner?"

Emerson snorted, "Ha! You takin' some medication, bro? Maybe a little too much?"

The figment of his imagination gave Matthew a big smirk and a delicate wave. Matthew shut his eyes tight, hung his head between his knees, and squeezed again.

CHAPTER EIGHT

A Revelation of Sorts

PIPIERA WAS SURE her shake was noticeable; it had to be. She even heard tremors in her voice when she spoke, nearly pronouncing her temporary Earth name incorrectly. Pip-*eee*. She would have to get used to this pronunciation. Preferring to use Penney, Serena had cautioned strongly against it. Pippi was better and natural, so Pippi it was. Her temporary Earth name. *Yuk*. She didn't like it.

"And why have you come to Havensight for the summer, Pippi?" Marnie was making small talk. What else could she do, with her mother-in-law dying in the very room behind her and her son traumatized by the day's events a few short steps away in a room below?

Pipiera was standing in the Mackenzie household kitchen—as an *earthling*. They could see her, hear her, touch her and even ask her questions, like this one Marnie was posing. She could hardly believe it. *Here it comes, the answer I've been practicing the whole time since I got here.* Aivy had arranged concealed train travel instead of the travel tunnel simply to avoid the need for an escort. The train's conductor served that role just fine. She had arrived in the middle of a wheat field north of Havensight. As she exited the train, it lifted, continued around the bend farther north and vanished. Completely out of sight, without a trace. Pipiera had been careful not to bend the tall green shoots as she stepped out of the field. Many of the shoots were just beginning to flower and still held a crisp, fresh scent. Discouraged that the plants couldn't actually speak to her, she was sure they were whispering soft bellows of encouragement. Once she found her way out of the muddy field, she wandered down a country highway that led into the north section of town where the Damiens lived, the place arranged for her summer boarding. Serena had said it was an affluent neighborhood, but Pipiera couldn't tell what made it so. She had little to compare it to. Though now, across and outside the skirts of the town, she noticed some differences.

"I have come to practice eldercare in the community," Pipiera responded proudly, giving Marnie a super-large smile.

"Oh, how wonderful. Is this through a college program?"

"Yes," Pipiera continued gleefully. *Questions are going well, I'd say.* Though Marnie held a tight gaze; seemingly, she wanted more information.

"Which college program might that be? We don't have any close by. Did you get here by bus?"

Pipiera hated to lie, but there was no actual train station in Havensight, and she couldn't claim she arrived on a bus, not after that morning's events at the bus depot. She hadn't expected this question. *Think.* "I got a ride. May I see Matthew?" *Ya shoulda finished reading your bio,* she scolded herself.

"Matthew? Sure, but I just wonder, you aren't from here. How do you know my son?" Marnie, now looking suspicious, kept the questions coming. "Are you a friend of Laura's?" Karo was hugging the doorframe between the kitchen and the living room, ears tuned in sharply to the kitchen side and registering all the details, or more than likely, the lack thereof.

"Oh, uh, *Emerson* told me all about Matthew. He must be heartbroken over Jophiel…er Joppha," was Pipiera's attempt to change the topic. Marnie kept a steady eyeballing glare, rattling her even more. "May I use your wash facilities?" She hoped the wavering in her voice was unnoticeable.

"Our bathroom? Up the stairs, on the left."

Thank heavens, Pipiera felt relief. She hadn't counted on queries being so direct. It was obvious she needed to review more details for her cover story. Upon reaching the washroom, she sat upon the closed lid and pushed the summer-green curtains aside. It took only a glance out the window, out toward Warmud Street. *I'm here. I'm. Really. Here.* So amused that she wanted to pinch herself. A long exhale was welcomed. Though, along with it came an unusual and unsettling uneasiness. Anxiety, tension, excitement? So much unknown here.

A sour taste filled her mouth, followed by a series of gagging motions. Instinctively, she flipped up the lid of the toilet and experienced an urgent and natural need to bend over and retch. Unpleasant. The contents of her stomach, Mrs. Damien's so-called famous shepherd's pie, forced itself speedily out and, despite swaying motions, emptied perfectly into the ceramic bowl. *Wretched!* Pipiera leaned against the tub and cupped her sweaty head with both hands. *My King, are you trying to tell me something?* she thought, releasing a chuckle. Never had she had such an experience before. A single unused hand towel hung within her reach, a soft, white cloth with gold-embroidered initials, an F and an M. Pipiera grabbed it and wiped down her head, neck and face, smearing a bit of bright orange and a slimy green. *Carrots? Peas? Whatever it was, ugh.*

Reality hit. *Frank? Mackenzie. Frank! F. M. My brother, my dear brother, I'm in the very home you built for your family. For Marnie, for Matthew.* It was a stark reminder that she was here and she had work to do. Overwhelmed, Pipiera grasped at defining her simple priority. *Aid Jophiel. Only thing is: he's not here; he's missing.* She looked at the gold monogram and clasped it to her heart. *Frank, you love your son so much. You'd want me to help him get through this. He's blaming himself, I hear.* She thought of her brother's struggles, how he didn't get along with his parents—their parents. *Perhaps I should talk to Father, get him to release that hardness he blocked you out with. And Mother, oh Mother! Gosh, she's here. I have a chance to see her.* Perhaps Pipiera will miss her mother's arrival at Papah's gate, but at this very moment, she has an opportunity to say goodbye as Maggie leaves this Earth. The very thought put some spring into her limbs. What perfect timing! She jumped up, employed the handiest toothbrush, tucked Frank's monogrammed hand towel into her purse—another Serena-fashioned item—and down the stairs she flew.

Mother, here I come!

A hand held high, signaling her to stop at the foot of the stairs, interrupted her flight. It was Emerson's. "Not well?" he asked.

They obviously heard me, she figured. "Um, yeah, your mother's shepherd's pie."

Ignoring the pie line, he snapped at her, "We gotta go."

"We just got here…I haven't even…," Pipiera's plea was stopped short.

"Haven't even what?" He leaned in towards her and lowered his voice, "Listen, this is not a good time. I warned you before we came. My friend's in a bad way right now, and even worse, his grandmother is dying. They're all gathering around to be with her. We—you and I—*should not* be here. Come." He grabbed her hand. "Time to go."

"Can't I please see her? His grandmother. Maggie?"

"What? Why? And how do you even know her name?"

Think, think. "Eldercare is my business. This is my thing. Death and dying and the whole moving-on thing." She floated her arms in the air to dramatize her expertise. "Look, I could provide some words of inspiration, of comfort, for Maggie and for the whole family. P-l-e-a-s-e!" She fluttered her eyes at him, not even sure where that notion came from. "At least just ask Marnie if I could say a few words. This is what I am schooling for." She stood up a little straighter and held her head high. "This is why I was sent to Havensight. You don't want to ruin all the scholarly plans in place for this community, do you?" A vigorous move to stick her elbows out high with her knuckles pressed against her hips stressed the question.

"Oh." Mouth twisted in annoyance, he glanced into the Mackenzie living room, the room transformed to suit a sleep and care environment for the elderly grandparents. "Matt's mom is in the kitchen about to make some tea, so motor it into the living room and I'll talk to her. Maybe we can get Matthew up here, too. Can you do that?"

Pipiera squeezed her shoulders up, "Maybe." Happily,

she tiptoed into the living room, hoping that might somehow silence the pounding noise of the heart beating in her chest.

And there she lay, mere steps away, the mother Pipiera left behind so many years ago when she had escaped the earthly realm. Tears formed in Pipiera's eyes, her heart raced even faster, and her breathing quickened. She swallowed an emotion—had to be nerves, she figured. That feeling of impending death sickened, though the sweetness of peace took root and grew. *I can do this.*

Instinctively, Pipiera went straight to the side table, took a washcloth and dipped it in the bowl of clear, tepid water. Wringing it out, she could still feel some warmth in the cloth and gave it a triple fold. Maggie's eyes were closed, but Charles and Karo sat nearby and watched every move Pipiera made, most assuredly wondering who she was. Pipiera placed the cloth on Maggie's forehead, and Maggie groaned delightedly. Her eyelids fluttered before opening wide.

"Thank you, dear." It was a squeaky yet somewhat chirpy voice.

"Hello, Mah…Maggie," Pipiera responded.

Maggie turned her head and held her arm out so Karo could reach for her hand. After giving Charles the usual grin she reserved only for him, she fixed on Pipiera's face. *Do I know you?* was the question pierced in her eyes.

Pipiera cocked her head and soaked in the moment, wishing this wonderful creature could hear her thoughts. *Mother. How much I want to say. You can hear me and see me, but we must reserve our excitement for another day, one when you will know who I am. Assuredly that day will follow.* For now, Pipiera must answer her mother's eyes.

"No one really knows anyone, Mah…er, Maggie. At least not the full picture."

Pipiera had to bite her tongue; she had nearly called Maggie "Mother" a couple of times already.

Charles and Karo transferred their fixation from Maggie to Pipiera, no doubt with questions looming. Karo eyed Pipiera suspiciously. She stood up and headed out of the room, quite likely to find out what was taking her mother so long. If this stranger was sharing what potentially could be their last evening with Grammie and making bizarre comments to boot, surely Marnie should know about it.

Along with Karo's exit came Pipiera's chance! Only Maggie and Charles with her in the room: she and her beloved Earth parents. Alone. She leaned in close to Maggie's face, a concerned Charles leaning in as much as his aging body allowed.

Pipiera whispered, "You see, Mother, no one knows your past before this life. No one knows your future, the one that's about to come. Only a small slice of your present—and that slice is simply from another's view. No, Mother, no one really knows our true selves, not till we go home. You'll learn it all when you get there. It'll be such a celebration!" Pipiera lovingly smiled ear-to-ear.

Maggie's eyes turned glassy and child-like-wide with wonder. "Penney?" she murmured.

Charles groaned, "Huh?" He looked confused, and—dang! He didn't have his hearing aid on.

Marnie came blustering into the room, followed by Karo, and witnessed her mother-in-law attempting to caress this Pippi woman's cheek. "Excuse me, uh, is everything alright here?" Marnie glanced from Pipiera to Maggie to Charles and back to Maggie, who was simply sparkling.

Pipiera thanked Marnie and, despite her eye-rolling, told Karo it was nice to meet her, then promised Charles a visit in the very near future, before skirting toward the back door and bumping into Emerson. She grabbed his arm and directed him to the car, knowing she'd have to meet Matthew another time.

Tonight had been enough.

CHAPTER NINE
A MESSAGE FOR MATTHEW

SILENCE DOMINATED. A single lamp blared with as much heat as light. Gasping to breathe, Matthew felt his muscles contract independently, forcing him upright, his pupils slow to react. He must have fallen into a deep slumber. How could he possibly be entitled to a reprieve? Wiping his eyes with the back of his hand, he settled back down on the couch and let a load of air blow out his mouth. Not the most comfortable place to sleep, but better than the bunks upstairs where Charles napped most days. At least down here, his legs have room to stretch and his head doesn't bang on the ceiling when he sits up. He can't move out, not yet. His mother needs help financially. Not to mention help with the grandparents. When he saves up enough, he'll buy a car for himself— though his mom needs one too, he knows that. Perhaps when the grandparents die, they'll leave their savings to her—then she'll be able to pay down the mortgage and the rest of those dang old hospital bills, and he can attempt life on his own. He'd been eyeing that apartment above Hurley

Sports, where he still works as a sales cashier since graduating high school.

Matthew scolded himself for thinking in such ways. He adored Grammie and she doted on Karo and him. Granddad was the headstrong one, and sometimes hard to please, though he was ever so thankful for the care provided to Grammie. *How can I be such a jerk?* Admittedly, he felt trapped—and now, cursed.

It was all so quiet upstairs, no sounds whatsoever.

She didn't die, did she? What horror if she had. He really needed to face her, even though he blamed himself for Joppha's disappearance. If he didn't talk to her before she died, that would be two things he'd never forgive himself for.

Go see her. Now, while you can, he encouraged himself. He knew she never slept well during the nights, often hearing the household stir about at all hours.

Though each stair he climbed creaked, each step closer to his grandmother gave him an odd peace. Maggie Mackenzie embodied a loyal and forgiving love, letting others be who they needed to be. They may fall, but her love never faltered. She was approachable, and Matthew had no reason to think otherwise. He found her, head to the side, eyes open, as though she were waiting for him. Charles was snoring in the separate bed located a foot away, and his mom was sound asleep in an easy chair in the corner of the room, a flashlight on her lap.

Maggie managed a smile, followed by a wince.

"Are you in pain, Grammie? Need anything?"

She motioned for him to come closer, face-to-face, the distinctive odor of impending death between them. He held her hand in his. Fragile bones wrapped in a cool, thin layer of skin reached for his face. Might she be able to tell he'd been crying and was totally distraught? Matthew didn't know how much she knew. Did she even know Joppha was missing? How much had his mom told her at a time like this?

Like a little boy himself, he burst into a sob. "Little Jophie's missing…It's my fault…Everyone hates me…*I* hate me…I can't go on…please don't go. I need you."

Maggie shook her head slowly and spoke softly, but Matthew heard every astonishing word. "This is not who you are." Maggie winced some more, then, as though one with the universe, she gave a clear and distinct directive, "You are destined to be a great protector."

Marnie stirred and sat up. "Matty? Maggie…it's time for a dose." On autopilot, Marnie measured out a liquid of some sort in the dark as Matthew watched, wondering how she maneuvered from sound slumber to capable nurse in the blink of an eye. She was quite independent and modern, he thought, to have fought for Maggie to die at home. But she, his mother, looked weary now, too.

Once Maggie settled into a sleep, Marnie nodded an invite to Matthew to the kitchen, where they could share some quiet time together. Three thirty a.m., and they were sipping hot cocoa and saying very little. Matthew thinking about Joppha being out there somewhere, on his own; Marnie thinking about Maggie and what will happen next and how will she manage the steps Dr. Bonneville scribbled out for her. The pair realized suddenly, in the same instant, that the monotonous sound of the throat rattling had stopped. They rushed into the living room.

No vital signs. Maggie had slipped away.

Marnie noted the time and woke up Charles. Matthew went upstairs to wake Karo, who scrambled quickly to join her family, particularly to sit with and hold Grampa's hand. Marnie's hands shook as she slipped out a single instruction note from her apron pocket, read it, and gently used two fingers to shut Maggie's eyelids. Matthew had to turn away, the smell and stain of death now on him forever. But those parting words! *Destined to be a great protector? How on Earth did she come up with that?*

Five thirty a.m. The ominous hearse Marnie had called for had not yet arrived.

"Do you think Arnie might come over and say some words, a prayer, or something?" Marnie asked Matthew for his opinion.

"Oh, Mom, I don't think this is the time. He's likely up, no doubt, but he has Joppha on his mind. We shouldn't bother him with this." After witnessing a couple of sighs, he added, "No worries, Mom, the funeral home will do that. I can talk to them for you if you like." He surprised himself at this offer to be helpful, given his state of mind over the past eighteen hours. "But let's call Arnie anyway, he should at least know about Grammie, and then I can see if there is anything I can do to help Cilia and him. Maybe take over a meal? Or offer to watch the twins?"

Marnie returned the suggestion with a stern glance. She had enough on her plate right now with the situation in her living room, never mind preparing a takeaway meal her son was sure to request. Matthew lowered his head, thinking, *Yeah, right, they're not gonna want me to watch their other kids, anyway.*

He stood close by to listen in as Marnie dialed Arnie and Cilia, but all he could hear was Cilia weeping. Marnie couldn't bear to interrupt to pass along the news about Maggie. Arnie must have grabbed the phone from his wife, as suddenly he was pounding questions into Marnie's ear.

"Strange? Like what?" Marnie looked straight at Matthew. "Did you notice anything strange happen, or anyone strange hanging around watching you guys yesterday at the station, Matty? Arnie needs to know, a detective is asking."

Matthew shook his head, "Does this mean they don't think it's a runaway anymore, rather a kidnapping or something?" Marnie shook her shoulders and returned to the receiver.

"No, nothing, Arnie, I'm sorry. Maybe that's a good thing. Er, wait a minute. Might Emerson Damien's new boarder be something? She arrived yesterday, too—came here like she knew us. That was strange. And actually, she is a little strange herself. Caught her whispering really close to Maggie. Don't know why she insisted on coming over last night. Claims she knows Matthew." She turned to Matthew. "Does she? Does that girl Emerson brought over last night—do you know her?"

Matthew shook his head, *nope,* and Marnie continued giving details to Arnie to pass on to the detective. "Yes, she says she arrived yesterday—morning, in fact—and was a little evasive as to how she arrived. Okay, yes, I think so, definitely. I will. We will. If we see her or talk to her again, I'll let you know right away. Won't peep a word. Maybe this is the break you need, Arnie. If there is anything we can do, just you or Cilia give us a call." She hung up and looked at Matthew. "That little Miss Pippi was strange, wasn't she? Hmmm."

"Emerson's boarder, did *she* do it?" Hugging the doorway between the room where Charles sat by Maggie's body and the kitchen, Karo's ears hung on to the conversation, her eyes bulging with an inquisitive horror. "I knew it! She is definitely *off.*"

Matthew wondered if he should go to the Damien household to see for himself.

CHAPTER TEN
MATTHEW, MEET PIPPI

AT THE SIDE of the road, Matthew silently thanked his mother for insisting on storing that emergency jug of water in the trunk. He removed the radiator cap and carefully poured the water in until the overflow tank appeared at MAX level.

"C'mon, Betsy, I really need you today."

He leaned against the car, already warmed from the rising sun, and admired the field's waking show of blue, purple and silver spikes. Grasshoppers had threatened the crop last year, and rumor was that the farm owner threatened to plant grapevines instead. *Grammie, you'd be pleased he didn't; you loved driving past this place. Royal velvet. The best kind, you would say.* Havensight was known for its lavender aroma, and the city council rallied folks to display community-wide angst toward the farmer's quest for change, likely topping off a deal with some kind of sweetener. Without tourism, this town would suffer—and badly.

Matthew would have taken his bike if his only trip had

been to Emerson's place. He needed to see for himself what this boarder girl was all about. Fierce talk was moving around fast that she had something to do with Joppha's disappearance. But there was no time to spare for bike transportation. Matthew was on a mission. First Emerson's, then to Laura's to let her know in person about Grammie. Then to Arnie's to… well, Matthew wasn't sure what he would say to Arnie. He only knew he had to check in on him and Cilia and the twins. Not a visit he was looking forward to. Then he had to get back home to help his mom. Hopefully, Karo will have enough sense to just sit quietly with Granddad. *Likely not; she'll open her mouth and say somethin' stupid, I bet.* He slapped the hood down and continued to Emerson's place.

Mrs. Damien ran to meet Matthew, grabbing him by the arm just as he had barely managed to get one foot out of the car. She shook, her entire body jiggling like jelly, her face plump and red and sweaty. "Get her outta my house, Matt. I want her outta my sight!"

He didn't have to study her face for clues; it was obvious she was referring to her new boarder, this Pippi. He was used to Mrs. D's frequent bouts of overreacting and jumping to conclusions. In fact, it was on account of her that he and Emerson had become such good friends. Emerson needed someone to talk to without emotional outbursts and suspicious accusations. And Matthew appreciated their chats about growing up without much fatherly guidance.

Matthew wished he could command Mrs. D. to take a chill pill, but after all, this was his best friend's mother. So, he would couch it.

"Calm down. What's the skinny? Tell me."

She leaned in; Matthew leaned back. *No need to get close!*

"They think it's her. Her! And to think, I invited her into my home. *My home!*" She shook her head vigorously. "She's been lying, Matt. Lying."

He pursed his lips and waited for more. When nothing came, he pushed, "'bout what, exactly?"

She eyed her house to be sure her boarder was not peeking out any windows. All curtains seemed intact, so she went on to tell Matthew the police detectives came back, that they had arrived earlier this morning to question this Pippi, and then her. "Imagine. They questioned me. *Me?* Like, what would *I* have to do with this?"

"They're just checking under all stones and rocks, Mrs. D. Nothing to worry about. Personally, I believe Joppha got on one of those buses. And since we haven't heard anything yet, I'm bettin' he got on that 'milk run' they call 'express' to the coast."

She stepped back. "No, Matt. Emerson said the security checked every bus. Your li'l Jopphie ain't on no bus. Somebody took 'im. She's in on it. They checked every room in my house looking for him. She's hidin' 'im somewhere." She drew one eye close to his face, much to Matthew's discomfort. "She had a whole lot of mud on her shoes when she arrived yesterday, Matt. About the same time, your Jopphie magically disappeared." Straightening up her back hump as far as it could go, the large woman stood tall to deliver her concluding message, "He's hidden in a field somewhere."

"Okay, let me talk to her. I'll interview her myself." Matthew walked toward the front door as Emerson appeared in its frame, waving him in.

Mrs. D's voice trailed behind, "Don't you fall for her lies, Matt. You know she talks about you like she knows all of ya and, according to my Em, she don't!"

Warnings heeded, Matthew headed to the basement, wondering why, when this house is so very large with many rooms, they would put up their boarder in the basement? He knocked on this strange and so-called 'dangerous' woman's bedroom door. What would he say when she opened it? He hadn't a clue. Though he needed to see for himself. *Is this whole investigative business a complete circus? Joppha could be all alone sitting on a bus somewhere far away while this young woman is being falsely accused. Or am I the foolish one, and she is an incredible master at child nabbing, and to prove she's so clever, she hangs around the family so she can laugh behind their backs?* A wave of deep exhaustion struck his core. He allowed his head to drop briefly to escape the weight. He noticed his own shoes were dirty with muck. *Does that make me a kidnapper?* He chuckled at the smallness of his community. Matthew was growing more and more certain Joppha had hopped on that express bus and simply hadn't been discovered yet. The notion was in his bones.

The door creaked open no more than three inches, and the mysterious young woman also stared down at his shoes.

"I'm Matthew Mackenzie. May I come in?"

"Oh, Matthew!" The door swung open wide. She invited him in, almost as though she were waiting for him, like they were grand ol' buddies.

The room was minimal and tidy, with hardly any trace of anyone even living there. The bedspread was wrapped tightly with no wrinkles. Atop a tall armoire, a wind-up merry-go-round no child could ever reach. No clothes tossed anywhere, no suitcase to be seen, no other shoes but the ones on her feet. And no mud on them, he noticed. The chair was shoved close to the only window. He suspected she'd have to stand on it to watch the outside world, whatever there might be to see. He pondered the thought—*if she looked out that window, might she have seen me when I pulled into the driveway, heard Mrs. D. call out my name? All these claims that she knows me …is it possible she is deceitful? A fraud of some sort?*

"Do I know you?" he asked suspiciously.

She herself shifted uncomfortably at his question.

In some perplexing way, he instantly felt he actually *did* know her. She was vaguely familiar. But that was impossible.

"Does anyone really know anyone?" she replied while slipping off her shoes.

Oh please, a psychoanalyst, he thought to himself. Matthew believed he should be on guard, but his instincts tugged him otherwise. "You sound like my grandmother."

Pipiera replied with earnest condolences. She seemed genuinely sad about his loss. "The heart must endure such stabbings sometimes. Will you tell me about her?"

Her request intrigued him; it was practically a plead. And releasing this bubble of grief mounting inside would do him some good. *Some day. But not today,* he thought before looking back at the door as though he wanted to escape. *Jopphie, I get you more than you think. You just wanted to run. Be somewhere else, someone else, someone better.*

Matthew needed to ignore her request; he was there on business. He needed to get a grip. "Could we go over a few things?"

"Like?"

"Like, for instance, exactly when did you drift into town

yesterday, and how did you manage to get here? No one seems to be clear on details and…"

She interrupted abruptly. "You too? Seriously!" She crossed her arms. "Just before noon, I was given a ride by a colleague, came in through the north road, and I haven't left this house except for a trip to your house last evening. I am NOT a child thief."

Matthew held a firm stance. "Why'd you come to my house last night?"

"Because I was concerned. That's what people do, don't they? Be concerned about others?"

"Who drove you, what friend? And where is he now?"

"How do you know it's a *he*?"

"I don't. Is it? A he?" Matthew suddenly felt like a jealous husband, angry with his wife. "Look, tensions are high. I'm sorry. People are talking…they don't know you, and they think you might have had something to do with Joppha's disappearance."

She perched herself on the side of the bed. "How *did* he disappear?" Truth was, Pipiera was sick about the situation. Exactly where was her dear friend Jophiel? "Did he really run away?" She managed to bite her tongue before mentally adding, *it's not like him to do something like that. The Jophiel I know faces danger, opponents run from him!*

Matthew sat beside her. "Yup. He did. Emerson poked fun at 'im and Jopphie was Jopphie. He ran. Laura had him right there with her; he was waiting for her. Then she lost him in the crowd. So, at first, he ran away, but logically, something else *could* have happened after that, on the platform."

"He could have been taken, perfect opportunity in a crowd like that. Especially at a transportation hub. That's where abductors like to hang out. Lots of families, plenty of opportunities for crowds, confusion and distractions, fast getaways…"

"You're NOT helping!" Matthew was astonished at this woman's matter-of-fact-ness.

The pair sat painfully quiet for a couple of minutes, minds swirling silently, until Matthew spoke again. "I know Jopphie better than anyone, except maybe his parents. No, I'm not going there —this whole abduction thing. Jopphie ran. He's clever, he's sensitive, and he's determined. He got on that bus to the coast." At that, he stood up. "I'm going to figure out all the transit stops and give each and every one of them a call."

Matthew knocked his forehead with the heel of his hand, "Why didn't I think of that before?" He stood and abruptly headed out of the room without as much as a goodbye. He had a plan of action to take care of, immediately.

CHAPTER ELEVEN

PEANUT BUTTER AND TOAST

"I KNOW JOPPHA BETTER'N anyone, yeah, yeah, yeah, ha!" Pipiera mocked the notion. "Then again, I suppose you do, Matthew Mackenzie. But he was my friend first, remember that!" She was free to say what she felt; she was alone again. *Might as well be locked up.* She could hear Papah Megs's voice by simply imagining what he would say to her right now: likely something like, *dig deeper, why so bitter, Pip? What have you lost? Truly nothing, I bet.*

She crept to the window, kneeled on the chair for balance before stepping fully on it, and gently pushed the curtain aside enough to peek. Matthew's speedy getaway could have been almost heroic, but his car stalling twice as he backed up sort of dampened the effect. She witnessed him slamming his hand against the steering wheel. *Remember why you're here, Pip. To inspire.* She scolded herself for being jealous. *Matthew is out of sorts. There's gotta be something I can do to help. We both want to find Jophiel…er, Joppha.* She still couldn't picture her Jophiel a little boy. *Well, Matthew, one thing is for sure: you are so right about your little Joppha. He's anything but helpless!*

The darned vent banged so loudly it distracted her train of thought, bringing her little rant to a halt. And with perfect timing, too. Pipiera grabbed her shoes and ran out the door. If she went fast enough, she could catch Matthew before he headed down the street. Emerson attempted to block her, thinking she was escaping, given that she was a suspected child-napper and all. Mrs. Damien screamed for her son to call the police as Pipiera flung past her. Still with a firm grip on her shoes, she leaped into long-jumping mode to catch the handle on Matthew's passenger door.

Out of breath, she leaned in the window of the stalled car. "I wanna help. Let me help you." He stared, no blinking and no words. Panting, "I'll take that as a 'yes'!" She hopped into the car and leaned back, those heavy, black shoes swinging from her right hand out the window.

"You again!" Marnie was anything but welcoming to Pipiera when she came through the back door, tagging along behind Matthew. Since she'd been there last, Marnie's kitchen had transitioned into business-central for Maggie's funeral arrangements. Pipiera was thankful when Matthew changed the subject and, thus, the tone in the air. This business of being rejected as a person and accused of terrible things was wearing.

Maggie's body had been taken away, and Charles was upstairs napping in Matthew's room where his and Maggie's few remaining belongings were kept.

"That Grammie's stuff?" Matthew pointed to piles on the table.

An empty black file box sat on the kitchen chair and legal documents, brown envelopes of various sizes, newspaper clippings, an angel-winged pearl pendant, and a tiny pink bracelet were all strewn across the laminate. Pipiera picked up the pendant and let her fingers feel the delicate sides of the silver angel wings that surrounded three pearls encased in gold. *Oh Mother,* she thought and carefully returned the jewel to the table. *So precious.* Karo, in the opposite chair, reached over to pick up the tiny pink bracelet, holding it so Matthew could see. Whenever there was alarming news to announce, you could count on Karo to be eager and pleased to oblige. "Did you know Grammie had a baby that died?"

A tingling numbness shimmied its way up Pipiera's legs. She was sure blood was racing madly through her core and up her neck to blast purposely inside her head. Claustrophobic. Sweats of panic. Legs wobbly. She grabbed the backside of an empty chair as though to save her from melting into the floorboards. Questions whirled inside. *Why should a series of pink beads tied together with string arrest me so? The lettering is barely distinguishable.* It was evidence, a link to her mother and her. Proof she lived once. Here. A stark reminder once again, as though she needed it. *This is my family!*

"Darn shoes, too tight," she explained away her sweaty paleness.

As Matthew's arm reached over with an open hand to accept the clincher of Karo's news, Pipiera managed to snatch it away. Cupping the treasure with both hands and clutching her chest, tears streamed down her face, much to Marnie's discontenting cock of the eye.

Curiosity hung in the room as though a live elephant had just traipsed through.

Muscles in Pipiera's face joggled left and right, and she swallowed hard. Releasing the bracelet, she passed it on to Matthew and shrugged, attempting an excuse for what must have been viewed as inexplicably odd behavior. "I'm a sucker for sentiments." A pause. "If you'll excuse me."

She tiptoed away from the kitchen's chill and climbed the stairs to find solace in the tight and tiny corner of the washroom. She could be herself and alone there. Safe. Wedged between cool ceramics, with soft towels hanging overhead brushing her forehead softly. Still, she could overhear Marnie's scornful warning. The family trio was arguing. About her. A dose of relief prevailed when Matthew's justifications for bringing her to their home finished their debate. That was generous of him, considering she had jumped into his car without an invite.

By the time Pipiera came down the stairs, Matthew had already cleared a section of the kitchen counter by shoving a pile of dirty dishes onto the stovetop. Map and pen in hand, he was scrambling through the phone book, but he ended up tossing it onto the floor. Frustration had the better of him.

"I'm here. How can I help?" she asked, feeling like an altogether woman again and not a child. She was totally composed and ready to do whatever it was Matthew would ask of her. It was a relief to see Marnie and Karo had left the room; she needed to remain collected.

"Make notes," he instructed, and she did, each time he dialed the information operator for the number to pinpoint the security desk at every bus station along the route to the coast. Since there were well over a dozen stops, she wondered why they called it an 'express' route; it was anything but direct and there was certainly nothing *express* about it. Pipiera jotted the figures down carefully, including the area codes. A mistake would not go over well.

The rest of the morning went great from an efficiency perspective. From a results perspective, it was debatable. Matthew had spoken to every single security guard at each bus terminal along the route that he believed Joppha had taken. "He must have taken the bus on this route," he repeatedly muttered. "It's the only long hauler—a continuous loop to the coast and back. Otherwise, surely, we'd have heard by now. Other buses would have dumped their passengers, and they would have discovered him." At Pipiera's insistence, Matthew provided a complete and detailed description of Joppha's appearance: "About four feet, maybe, I think, yes; overgrown, curly, blonde hair—a cowlick-like-thing right on his forehead; chubby cheeks, they're often red, actually, and so are his ears, they go red a lot too; a stub for a nose; regular blue jeans, suspenders. Shirt? Uh, yellow, plus a sweater vest and, more than likely, sticky hands. Eyes? Uh, hadn't noticed, not sure; brown, I think. He'll run when you see him, so beware. At least I think he'll run unless he's really scared, then he might not. So, watch for him, would'ja? Yes, the police know. Here's my number…"

Pipiera hoped Matthew's efforts would work. She also hoped that by witnessing her being helpful to Matthew, his mother would stop watching her from the hallway so suspiciously.

"Matty, you haven't eaten," Marnie snipped when he plopped himself like a rag doll onto a kitchen chair. She immediately placed two slices of bread into the toaster. Pipiera found the aroma intoxicating: it summoned her senses and made her realize she needed to eat as well. All she had experienced food-wise since her subtle arrival to Earth was Mrs. Damien's shepherd's pie, and she had learned firsthand that smooshed-up peas were not to her liking. Nor over-cooked carrots, for that matter. When Marnie twisted open a large glass jar, Pipiera's stomach let out a noisy and pronounced rumble as the nutty flavors were stirred by a knife. Marnie pulled down a single plate from the cupboard and announced dryly, "Matt, you should eat now; Laura's on her way."

Uncomfortable with the waft of disguised rejection, Pipiera looked at Matthew. *Uh, say something. Quick. Help me out here, would'ja?* She thought of all the risks she had taken to help *him* several years ago, though he wouldn't know it. *Stand your ground this time,* she demanded of herself. Making swift moves to her hips with fisted hands, Pipiera pushed her head forward, eyes narrowed. *Say something.* Backing up against the counter, Matthew's face blushed as though he'd just been attacked and embarrassed. Pipiera didn't need to use her words, her look was threatening enough. A growing fierceness in her eyes said it all. *All I want is a little respect and appreciation.* It was one of those moments she wished she could reveal who she really was so they'd know the truth. *Maybe then, they'd give me something to eat, too.*

Still, Matthew said nothing.

Eyes remaining fixed on his face, she spilled a low mumble, "You haven't changed."

A loud knock on the back door cut short the tension, thankfully, for each of them. A pale, bare arm reached in, and a singing "H-e-l-l-O-oh" lingered. With black jelly shoes that matched the big ribbon in her hair and big shoulder pads that shifted somewhat as she waltzed into the kitchen, Laura swallowed Matthew with a condolence hug. Marnie gushed over how well she looked and offered some toast. Pipiera could see that Matthew was genuinely happy.

Hunger pangs rumbled again, the aroma of toast and peanut butter intoxicating. It would not be offered to Pipiera; she could tell that much. Wondering how to escape this household, at least for the moment, became her predominant thought. *Serena…what have you gotten me into?*

A noise from upstairs, a minor crash of some sort, followed by gruff mumbling, was a perfect excuse to escape. Charles. "I'll check him!" Pipiera said as she bolted up the stairs toward the distraction. She wasn't even halfway up when she overheard Marnie instructing her son that she wanted *that girl*, whoever she was, out of her house.

"I don't trust her." Marnie claimed her position, loud and clear.

"Mom, she's okay. Just give her a break."

"From what Emerson says, she could have something to do with Joppha's disappearance, Matt," chimed Laura, to which Pipiera stopped briefly to hear Matthew's simple and discouraging reply.

"Nothing's been proven yet."

CHAPTER TWELVE

I KNOW YOU

STEPPING INTO MATTHEW'S room, where Charles's distraction had churned the entire ugly mood inside-out—for Pipiera, anyway—proved to be just what was needed. Thankfully.

A tiny sparkle in his eyes, a brilliant contrast to sunken sockets. His joyful response to her entry was the fresh, uplifting breeze she needed and totally unexpected.

"You!" he grinned.

She picked his cane off the floor, the obvious cause of the crash, and placed it within his reach.

"Hey there, Mr. Mackenzie." She sat beside him and touched the back of his wrinkled hand. A gentle electrical current connected them, raising his eyebrows. *Oh, Father,* she thought. How she wanted to spill it all, to at least let *him* know who she really was. To hold him and never let go. Accompany him personally to their home, where Maggie would be waiting. She envisioned her mother and Megalos having a fun chat at this very time, this very same moment that she was sitting beside Charles, here, on Earth, in Haven-sight. *I never could have dreamed up this moment, yet, here we are,* she thought happily.

"I heard you," he said, his sparkle beamed direct at her.

"Heard me?"

"I know who you are," his smile grew enormous. His feeble arms reached over to wrap themselves around Pipiera. "You're my Penney. You're my Penney." His nose wet with sniffles, he planted his face into her neck where she held him and stroked the back of his head. A warm, never-thought-would-happen, yet long-awaited moment indeed for both. Something magical was happening. She sensed a harshness that surrounded his soul, a thickening that formed long ago from the time she left as an infant, start to melt and drip away.

As wonderful as that softening was, Pipiera acknowledged her foolishness. She'd broken a golden rule: never reveal your identity nor your purpose nor your plan. He must have heard her whisperings to Maggie. She wondered if this would be considered an interference, something that could harm the rest of his journey. Panicking, she justified her actions to herself: *that was supposed to be for Mother's ears only; she was about to leave, anyway. No harm in spilling a secret then. At least I haven't said anything about purpose or a plan. Not that I have one. A plan, that is. Does he really think it's possible I am who I am?*

Apparently, he did. Charles continued, "Your mother always talked about you like you were around. I thought her to be silly, but I went along. It felt good. But now, she's gone and you're here! You and me. We can be family again. You will take care of me, won't you?"

She moved his arms closer and clasped his hands. *Is this a competent mind?* She wondered.

He continued with a plea, "I'll buy back our house, you and I can live there, you can have your old bedroom back! I'll paint it whatever color you want. Oh, this is so grand!"

"Do you have both oars in the water?" It had slipped. *Darn*. "I mean, I'm not sure that's such a great idea."

"It is too. I want to go home, back to our house. Maggie's gone. I don't want to be here anymore." He shook his head, "They don't have time for me here. Oh, they mean well, but I wanna go back." He looked at her with eyes full of hope. "You'll take care of me, won't you?"

Pipiera swallowed hard. She knew what she had to do. "Mr. Mackenzie, I'm not Penney. I'm not your daughter. But I wish I were, if *that* helps any. And I promise to come to visit you. Here. Heck, I can talk to Mrs. Decker; maybe she'll let me take care of you. Here. After all, that is why I came to Havensight, to do eldercare." *I doubt Marnie would go along with such a plan,* she thought, *although she didn't stop me from running up the stairs to check on him, oddly enough. That was a good sign.*

"But, I heard you. You said…oh, I'm a fool," and he let go of her hands and waved her away.

She couldn't leave him like this, so hopeless and doubting himself wrongfully. She knelt down and looked up into his face. "Mr. Mackenzie, if I had the choice of any man on the entire face of this Earth to choose as a father, I would pick you. I just bet you would give me wonderful birthdays. Like ones with white, prancing ponies…and jewelry making… and special dinners…and a pearl pendant meant to be passed down." She had piqued his attention again. He looked to her as though his mind were reaching back: hopefully, she thought, to all the discussions he used to have with Maggie around the many birthdays of their passed infant child…like arranging white prancing ponies, inviting all her would-be friends to a jewelry-making party, taking her to a fancy restaurant, and best of all, passing down Maggie's mother's angel-winged pearl pendant.

He winced, eyes steadily targeted straight on the face of this mystery woman who knelt before him.

Unable to control her reflexes, she gave him a wink. "And, besides, I know what coffee you like."

He blinked before responding, "Not that percolated kind." He had caught on.

"I know, not the percolated kind. Deal? Do we have an *understanding?*"

"An understanding," he murmured, then grinned with a sideways look. He winked back and nodded.

This would become their little secret, whether true or not: Pippi was Penney, his baby girl. That in itself gave him an incredible dose of joy on this very same day, a sad day: the day his Maggie had died.

Pipiera wrapped Charles in a hug…one that an outsider might think lingered a little too long, being that they barely knew each other.

CHAPTER THIRTEEN

JOPPHA, THE JOURNEYER

On the Bus to Somewhere

IT WAS A long ride—so much stopping and waiting—hissing, then roaring—and it was getting dark. Joppha had never stayed awake so late. If it weren't for his new friend sitting next to him, he'd have fallen asleep long ago. The hum coming from the back tire well, the warm stream of air blowing in his face, and the comfort of his friend's mother in the seat directly in front were enough to make him forget about any sense of danger. It all served to keep him contented indeed. And there was no shortage of food. His friend's mother passed along scores of snacks regularly, likely to keep them quiet when the vibes of their laughter rose just a little too high. Apple slices, raisins, animal crackers, Count Chocula cereal bits, pudding pies and even some Sugar Babies candy. Joppha couldn't recall ever having feasted so well. He was experiencing firsthand one of his dad's favorite lines: "Enjoy the moment while you can, as all things come to an end, *sooner or later*."

The bus rolled into another super-sized garage, and the brakes hissed. Each time that happened, Joppha wondered whether that line of his dad's, the last part, was about to come true.

His friend's mother hastily packed up all in her sight; snacks, sweaters, toys, even the garbage. She reached back to her young son, instructing him to wake from his stupor and get his hat on. Looking up to smile at the young couple sitting behind the boys, she remarked, "Thank you so much. It was so great the boys had each other the whole ride! I don't know how on Earth I'd've kept him busy." Joppha stood to let his friend out, realizing he didn't even know the boy's name, guessing it didn't matter much now, anyway. No one seemed to notice the surprised look on the young couple's faces, as though surely no one thought Joppha was *their* son.

Like a statue, Joppha stood in the aisle and watched his comfort and safety head out the gliding door up front and into the grey street. That hollowness inside, it didn't feel so good. Several lampposts led the way for his friend and his mother and sister. *Their* path to freedom, he guessed, to take them home. If it weren't so dark, he might've gotten up the courage to go after them, walk behind for a while, like he belonged to them. Disgruntled, he chose the other direction. The tiny cubicle, a washroom, at the back. He stepped in and locked the door.

The small space offered him his own private place of comfort and safety. His curious, hungry mind swallowed and absorbed self-assuring messages. He wasn't certain he was on the right path, but he had this feeling that somehow, in some strange way, he was. Soon, too, he would be home. His real home. Although it would be lonely now for the rest of the ride, he smiled. No longer angry at Emerson, he had a purpose—a mission, even. He was going to find that place on the cover of his precious, scrolled-up magazine. *That is my home. It's calling me back.*

Allowing the somersaults in his chest to settle once again, he had an idea. A map. He needed a map. Feet sturdy on the lid of the toilet, he thrust himself up to meet the washroom mirror, pleased at how quickly it steamed up from his breath. He squeaked an outline quite efficiently using his left index finger. There it was: a single gate, a tower, a picnic table, a stick man. He added a couple of wavy lines. Even more satisfied, he pulled out his toy soldiers to study the drawing.

Some new, heavy-footed passengers boarded, causing the entire body of the bus to jiggle, displacing Joppha's balance. Falling from the toilet seat, he managed to catch the side of his head on something hard and unforgiving.

"Ouch" *Mommy!* Joppha choked silently for Cilia, suddenly needing his mother. Pulling himself up, dizzy and disoriented, he climbed back up to face the mirror, only it wasn't his reflection peering back. A tiny fracture crackled and speedily radiated outward in each direction. Joppha gasped. Was it his fault the glass was breaking? For sure he'd be in trouble now! A forehead made its way through the shards from the other side. Oval-shaped, slight green in color, the tiptop of a floppy purple hat caught in what was left of the mirror's glass.

"Now you're talking," *it* said, the ugly talking head, not wasting any time. "I've been tellin' ya, you don't belong here… finally got to ya, eh? And 'bout time, too. But why'd'ya have to go and draw *that* place?"

Joppha was fascinated. This was magic, or maybe he was in a dream. He'd forgotten about his pain and thoughts of his mother. "Huh…?" was all his young, brilliant mind could muster out, lips curved upward. Adding in, "You're pretty funny lookin'."

"Oh, come now." Gripping onto the sink handles, the character shimmied until a big popping kind of noise accompanied his final yank, and his entire body was fully exposed. Not much taller than Joppha himself, he plopped into the sink, his crossed legs spilling out. "Don't tell me you don't know me." His eyebrows twitched in pleasure as his shoulders leaned forward and *that* grin, well, it reminded Joppha of the Grinch from his favorite Christmas movie. "Surely, I am familiar!"

Joppha was fascinated, preoccupied with dozens of glass shards moving about and melting back into place, the mirror now fully restored. He picked his toy soldiers off the floor and shoved them back into the safety of his pants pockets. With no fear, he responded with a shake of his head, "Nope." Joppha had questions for this intruder but before he had even half a chance to ask anything, his body was thrusted upward. Sharp fingers jammed into his armpits, the crazy-mirror guy holding him high enough for his head to be pushed to one side against the ceiling. Scrambling for protection, Joppha couldn't reach his pockets. So he kicked and shoved, but it was of no use. His arms and legs plunged right through the intruder's body, which shook with hysterical laughter, making Joppha madder and madder. The harder Joppha kicked, the more explosive the laugh. Joppha's face got beet red and puffy, his hair soaked with sweat. Wild thumping in his chest, a pounding with no rhythm. He spat. It, too, went right through the intruder's forehead, landed with a splat, then slowly slipped off the mirror.

"Bullseye! Nice work," the intruder teased, wrapping up his fun. "Alright, alright." And he put Joppha down so the boy could shuffle his hair and clothes back into place.

"What's *your* problem? Who *are* you?" Joppha demanded, quite brave for a six-year-old. His fists remained clenched, his whole body shaking.

"Uh, just call me…um…just call me Sarthie," he said with a telling, devilish grin. "I'm a friend of your *Uncle Matty*."

"You're no friend of Uncle Matty." Joppha wiped a sweaty drop off his neck.

"Yes, I am," the intruder quibbled in return, adding a disclaimer. "Well, okay, let's just say, then, that I am a friend of a friend."

"Which friend?" Joppha, on his tiptoes, leaned into this so-called friend of a friend who calls himself Sarthie. "Uncle Matty don't know *you*, I bet! You don't look like you could even have any friends."

"Stop with the insults already, kid. Besides, *you* don't know our mutual friend. Satisfied? Now, let's get to your seat before someone steals that big purse of yours, the one you've been luggin' around like a girl. It's dangerous out there, ya know; you shouldn't trust *anyone*. Leaving that purse with all those *valuables* sitting there, right out in the open like that, somebody might grab somethin' from it. Like a *mae-gah-zeene, maybe?*"

Joppha couldn't have known this was Kasartha, a creature of sorts that his Uncle Matty had, in fact, come to know in a mysterious fashion. But what Joppha quickly learned was that Kasartha's words were confidence crushers. *How does he know I took it? Is he some kind of spy? Am I going to jail now?*

Without warning, Kasartha whirled into a spiraling array

of pale greens and yellows, coming out of it a tall, middle-aged, lanky man with a proper suit and tie, and slicked back, black hair underneath the purple hat. He grabbed Joppha's hand. "Well, c'mon, we can't be in here all night; people will talk." Out into the bus's rear corridor the two stumbled.

The bus was nearly empty except for eight to nine passengers or so, but all sets of eyes, including those of the new driver taking on the night shift, fixed upon the pair who easily passed for father and son. Apparently, there had been a great deal of ruckus coming out of that restroom cubicle.

The new driver called back, "Everything alright?" to which Kasartha joked about the room being a little tight and then shoved a guilt-ridden Joppha into his seat. The driver seemed impatient having to answer numerous calls on his CB radio about some young stowaway traveling alone, and quickly returned to his duties of getting settled in for an eight-hour shift. "Everyone accounted for here," were his final words into the radio mic before hanging up.

Joppha grabbed the bag that served Laura as her purse—why she needed such a big one, who knows? He stirred things about to have a look. *Nothing's stolen. It's still here.* He glanced up at Kasartha's face and packed the bag down, so nothing inside could be viewed.

"What'cha got in there, little man?"

"I'm not a little man," Joppha retorted. Fearful of the clearly communicated interest in his prized possession, he loosened the bag, rooted through and grabbed the magazine. He hugged it. All snug and secure.

"Let me see that," Kasartha snatched and held it high, unrolling it carefully as though it were a scroll. "Ooooh, yes! I like *that* place."

"You've been there?"

"Of course, yes; haven't you?" Kasartha may be wearing the look of a regular guy, but his devilish grin did not look normal to Joppha. "I mean, look, there's a gate, yes, and a courtyard, uhum, and a picnic table, yes, for sure I have been there! So why are you carrying this…map around?"

"I want to go there. Can you take me?" Joppha explored the notion hesitantly. *Maybe I can trust him,* he hoped.

"Why?"

"I think it's my home. My real home."

"Sure, little buddy, I can take you."

Joppha let the back of his head fall against the hard seat, his glee having gotten the best of him. *What luck! This guy shows up out of nowhere, and he's gonna take me home. I know I belong there; I just know it!* He smiled with contentment, giving a sideways glance at Kasartha. *You're not so bad, I guess.*

Kasartha returned the affectionate glance by wrapping an arm around Joppha, as a father would their child.

The driver posed another question, this time for all the folks on the bus. "Any of you good people seen a kid riding around alone here on this bus? Dumb question, but I gotta ask. Again."

The bus fell silent, only heads shaking to and fro. Kasartha shrugged a *nope* and Joppha closed his eyes and focused on his dream. *I'm going home!*

CHAPTER FOURTEEN
MEGS AND MAGGIE

In the Outer Courtyard of the Kingdom

"MARGARET MACKENZIE!" MEGALOS wrapped both arms around Maggie and leaned his chin onto the top of her head, her thin grey hairs still held in place with golden-colored bobby pins. "You have no idea…so much joy to have you back. Welcome, welcome, welcome home, Maggie." He patted her back before clasping both her hands into his and giving her palms a good look over. Obviously, he liked what he saw, as a smile spread wide across his large face. "Look, we're done here with, you know, processing and stuff. Any moment now, Aivy and Bookie will come through that gate to escort you in, but how about I take a break, and you and I chat to catch up?" He could tell her mind was swirling and needing to do some catching up on its own. "They'll come back to you soon. When you see them, I'm certain you'll remember them. There's no forgetting Bookie, nor Aivy, for that matter!"

Maggie appeared as though slathered with an artful paintbrush soaked in love and adoration. Though Megalos could see that stubborn sliver of determination, just as he had seen in her daughter, Pipiera, the day she arrived. *Oh no. Here we go again*, he thought.

She leaned in cautiously to whisper, as if she were still on Earth and others around her would never believe what she had to say, "I saw Penney." She stood back again, tall and straight.

"I know you did," Megalos responded gently. "She's with Charles and your grandson right now." Not surprisingly, she jerked back. He anticipated she'd be alarmed by this news. It's not a natural scenario. "That's what I want to talk to you about." He motioned to the picnic tables in the waiting area with one arm while the other signaled to his assisting gatekeeper, Roly, to take over.

Once settled across from her, he admired the air of amazed curiosity. It surrounded her, chasing and swirling about, a teasing dance for her senses. Her eyes followed the artful branches as they twisted into visually appealing architecture, bursting full of resplendent and showy flowers: living bouquets that she most certainly never would have seen on Earth. Her head tilted up, across, side to side, her lips never straying from its wide perma-smile position. He felt an enormous amount of pleasure simply watching her experience the courtyard. *Just wait till she goes inside*, he exulted. *She hasn't seen anything yet!* He did not desire to interrupt her senses, but they really hadn't much time. He was surprised that neither Aivy nor Bookie had arrived yet to meet her. Strange indeed, but he shook it off.

"Maggie, dearest." He reached for her hands again, though once connected, she abruptly raised hers to pull away.

"What is that?" Wiping off a red brilliance of sticky matter from her hands, she brought her nose close. "Oh my gosh, just smell that. Cherries! So amazing, and my *favorite*." Maggie couldn't help but lick a sample stuck to the side of her wrist. "Oh, my!" She delighted in the morsel.

"Evidence is what that is. Evidence that Serena and Alexien and Pipiera were all here in this very spot earlier. And..." He leaned in with his devious smile, "They brought you a cherry strudel, some of which, as you can see, spilled on the table." He roared and shook his head. "Those three! I'm telling you, sometimes I..." The blank look on her face stopped him in his tracks. "Of course, you don't know who I am speaking of, do you?" he grinned and continued. "Relatives. Well, from Charles's line, but yours, too. Pipiera...is *Penney*."

Her eyes widened. "*My* Penney?"

"Indeed," he chuckled, "your Penney, *our* Pipiera." *My Pip*, he smiled within, harboring an admitted possessiveness. His relationship with Pipiera was one he cherished ever so deeply. And this woman sitting before him was the one chosen to bring her into life on Earth so she could return and be to the Kingdom what she needed to be: a true aide to her family's line, their endurance and, in fact, their survival. A special and unique kind of hero. And now, this line of descendants was his. *Indeed, Pip, you are special. I'll take care of your mother till you get back,* he whispered within. If it hadn't been for Pipiera, his adopted line of descendants would have been cut short.

"So, what's next?" Maggie's eyes darted with energy and excitement. They reminded Megalos of Pipiera's. "Do I get to see her? Is she here then, now? Because I'm certain I met a young lady before...before—uh, you know, before I left. Was that *my daughter?* Because I'd swear it was!"

"That is exactly what I would like to talk to you about." He had finally captured the attention of every fiber that made up her being. Megalos explained it all—well, most of it, actually a tiny sliver, enough for Maggie to grasp. Surely, she would be overwhelmed with just a shred, he figured. He stuck to the basics and waited. Her response and questions would be telling enough. Will she understand? So much to grasp for a brand-spanking-new Arrival!

"*Soooo,* let me get this right," Maggie said.

She even cocks her head like Pip!

"Penney is now Pipiera. That's her Kingdom name. She came here, right here." With two index fingers, she pointed to the area in front of the gate. "She refused to go in. She was waiting for me! Right here." Fingers now pointing to the very spot at the table she now occupied. "How sweet, my baby girl waited for me. *All those years!* Can you believe that?"

Megalos nodded, and memories flooded. *Those were the days.* He dared not say it, but certainly thought it. Fortunately, Maggie continued, and he was forced to move on, away from the days of her being his little sidekick, playing in the waves and jumping over the lavender patches. Back then, whenever something disrupted his Pip's mind, she would bolt over to him. He could still hear her voice, "Papah, Papah!" It was almost always something so urgent. Well, urgent to her, because she had simply just figured something out. He beamed. *Yup, those were the days. She may have been born to you on Earth Maggie, but, I was the lucky one to watch her grow.*

"Then she did some sort of mission, you say? She came to visit me? Oh, how I wish I only knew, wish I could have seen her, known she was there, talked to her. We could've had tea!"

Megalos interrupted her, shaking his head, "No, Maggie,

that was not to be. Not then. At that moment, she needed to see you. She needed to see you were fine. You didn't need to see her then, not at that moment."

She dropped her head along with a tear, "For years, I wasn't. Fine, that is."

"I know. But let's move on, shall we?" He was gentle with his prompting, fully aware that Aivy and Bookie could be there any moment and their time, this time alone, would be cut short. "Go on," he said.

"You say she helped my grandson? I don't understand how, though. You know, by the way, that we only met Matthew once he was a full fourteen years old!"

Megalos found her expectation that he should be shocked with this news fondly amusing. "I know," was all he said.

"He's a good boy. Well, he's a man now, I should say. Gotta girlfriend and a job. He always spent time with Charles and me. Practically every day, he'd sit and we'd chat while his mom made our dinner. He listens to all that space stuff kinda news and he'd keep us posted. The boy's infatuated with the moon and the stars," Maggie claimed.

Megalos nodded and urged for more facts. What else had she absorbed from his explanation? He needed to know. A glance back toward the gate revealed Roly, busy with a group of three who had arrived together at the same time. It did appear he was managing it, given he and the threesome were joking around and carrying on with laughter. He turned his attention back to Maggie, who was deep in thought and about to speak again. He leaned in toward her, knowing she might be feeling overwhelmed. Joyous, but overwhelmed, nevertheless.

"I don't quite get just how she helped Matty?" Her eyes

were inquisitive, seeking an answer. Just how could the life of her Penney be intertwined with Matthew's?

He circled the air with brushstrokes of his right hand, "That's not important for now. Many things work together when the King's orders are to be accomplished." He urged her to continue.

"Well, Marnie always talked about the days he gave her such a hard time, but you know, we never knew him then, so…" She shrugged and let it be. "But Penney…er, Pip-i-er-a, was here to meet me? And then she had to leave…another important duty called? Can't be about Matty; he's just fine and dandy. But now that I think of it, he wasn't himself this morning…er, that day, is it still *today?*" She shook the disorientation from her head and continued. "Blamed himself for something. I can't remember what, though… Oh my, yes, that little fella, Jopphie, went missing. Matty said it was on account of him." She leaned in. "I'm sure it wasn't."

"Yes," Megalos confirmed, "Pipiera and Jopphie-*el* are friends."

"Aha!" Maggie gasped. She was catching on to these name variations. "So, she's gone to help little Jopphie, Arnie Decker's son…Jophi*el, her* friend."

"Well, and Matthew. Matthew has a job to do, and Pipiera is going to help him."

She paused for a bit. Megalos predicted she was drifting back to the fact that her daughter waited for such a long time before becoming a Kingdom citizen, that she wanted to wait for her so they could go in together. He was right.

Maggie slapped her hands on the table, "Well, I am waiting here, too. My Charles won't be long now—in fact, if you could hurry that up, I'd appreciate it. And you say Pipiera will be coming back shortly? So, I shall wait here. With you. Like she did."

Oooooh boy. He collapsed his head into his hands, elbows smooshed into the remnants of cherry gook.

"You can't explain all this to me, then tell me that once I enter that gate, I will forget all of it." Maggie was determined *and* defensive.

"Just the harmful, hurtful stuff," he mumbled.

"Well, I am going to wait." She crossed her arms and looked around. "Now tell me, where did my daughter like to sit?"

Without lifting his head, he pointed over to a lavender patch toward the wide horizon and, while doing so, caught a glimpse of Aivy standing a few feet away, arms also crossed, and not appearing too pleased.

CHAPTER FIFTEEN
CAN'T YOU REMEMBER?

In the Town of Havensight

EXULTED AND JUBILANT, Pipiera punched the air with a victory sign. *So nice when someone truly knows who you are.* A skip in her step, she had left Charles in a happy state, and she, herself, reveled in renewed hope. Slowing her movement down the stairs, she found it odd to hear dead silence in the kitchen. Particularly when Matthew's mother and Laura had so much to say, none of it particularly encouraging. Stepping into the kitchen, four pale stone faces and frozen bodies stared at her. Karo had joined them. Even Matthew looked horrified. None of them moved as she entered the kitchen, the delicious aroma of peanut butter toast still in the air, reminding her stomach to rumble.

"Whaaat's wrong?" Pipiera asked, afraid of what the answer might possibly be. *Oh no, please no, I ask you, King; Jophiel, is he okay? Is he with you? Is that what is happening right now?* "News about Joppha?" she asked meekly.

A loud banging at the front door startled Pipiera—though, she observed, not the others. Who were they expecting? At the same time, two officers bolted in the back door, practically tearing the screen from its hinges. Unnecessary. That door wasn't even locked. Soon, the five of them, Matthew, Marnie, Laura, Karo and herself, were surrounded by four uniformed officers, one with a gun drawn. The four men methodically stepped forward and circled around Pipiera, who instinctively put her hands high above her head.

A fast glance at Matthew. He looked overwhelmed. No answers came from that horrified look on his face. Nothing could Pipiera read from Marnie nor Laura's face, not even a slight bit of satisfied meanness. Karo clung to a doorframe, lips tight. *Karo? Are you responsible for this?* Pipiera could tell she was pleased with this onslaught of guard-like characters.

"Why?" Pipiera mouthed the word in Karo's direction.

The Havensight officers carried out a script as though in a play they'd performed a dozen times. "Young lady, you are under arrest." One officer kept reading from his little black book something about rights. *What could you possibly know about rights?* Pipiera mused. Another held her hands behind her back and fastened them in stainless steel cuffs.

"Do you even know my name? How can you properly arrest me?" Pipiera blurted.

"E-g-g-xactly!" Karo spewed. We *don't* know you…yet here you are. Pretending to be like…family." There was hate in Karo's pitch.

The officer yanked Pipiera's hands tighter, his way to quiet her.

"Why?" Pipiera cried, "Someone, say *something*. Tell me. Explain!"

Karo spoke confidently, "I just talked to my dad. Apparently, Joppha's been spotted getting off the bus on the coast. With—a—man. A *man* has him." She cocked her head but didn't quite have the bravery to step closer. "And you arrived with a *so-called* 'colleague,' probably a man I bet. Dropped you off north of town, you said. The same morn'in. Just *before* Joppha disappeared. Coincidence? I doubt it."

"No! No. I would never do that. He's my fr…" She almost blurted out a claim that would associate herself with Joppha, suggesting they already had some sort of relationship. Such a claim would certainly make this situation even worse.

"Your what? Your *friend?* You don't know my little brother. I don't know who you are, but you are NOT welcome here." This time, Karo stepped right up to a handcuffed Pipiera. "Trust me, I'm gonna make sure you get him back to us."

Pipiera thought of taking back the story about a friend dropping her off north of town. But what good would that do? It would only complicate things; for them it would prove she was a liar.

An officer pulled Karo back, and all Pipiera could do was hang her head. *What a mess I've made. Why did I let Serena and Alexien talk me into this?* With fallen shoulders and a mind full of regret, she was guided toward the back door by the officers. *I could be enjoying some of that cherry strudel with my dear mother right now, but nooooh. No, I am here with handcuffs on being accused of harming Jophiel when I've actually come here to help him. No wonder everyone is always so thankful when they arrive home from these ridiculous Earth-tours!*

Another glance at Matthew. *So overwhelmed.* It reminded Pipiera of that time when rebel soldiers surrounded her at the River of Times those years earlier. Matthew just stood there, the same as he is now, with a frozen and stunned face. Of course, Matthew would never remember that. It had been an event while his body lay in an unconscious state. She secretly wished he could, though. Then he'd know how she had helped him then, just like she was trying to help him now.

But then, they caught each other's eyes, just as they had that day. And as they both stared, a brief glimmer of dazzling light flashed into the room through the kitchen curtains.

Déjà vu.

Pipiera hoped that strange look on Matthew's face meant he remembered her.

CHAPTER SIXTEEN
GETTING OFF THE BUS

In a Place Called Moorelingville

"SO, WHERE NOW?" Joppha inquired obediently.

Kasartha, appearing as a tall, lanky, odd sort of a man, took Joppha by the hand and leaving Laura's big purse behind, escorted him off the bus and onto the platform of their destination: a lowly bus depot on the coast. The black of night, lit only by a large tower clock with arms signaling 1:18 a.m., was their welcoming party. Kasartha looked at his wrist where normally there might have been a watch, tsking away as though they were behind schedule. There had been so many delays, thanks to repeated searches for some missing child traveling alone.

"Where the roaring sea clashes with the land, resolving to reach some type of temporary solution, a compromise of sorts." Kasartha gestured his free hand high up, adding drama to his words, attempting to be all-knowing—poetic, even. Joppha was having a hard time keeping up with Kasartha's long strides, not to mention the meaning of these sentences. "The land wins because it stops the waters."

Joppha eyed Kasartha, wondering which one of them was he, land or the waters?

"Though, my dear friend, the waters win also, as it takes some of the land into itself."

"Huh?" Joppha asked.

Kasartha returned the boy's query with a weighty grin. "To the bog at the beach, of course. You want to go home, don't you? After all, I am your watery wave, and you, my lad, are *my* speckle of dirt."

Too weak to argue, Joppha shrugged, and the pair disappeared into the night.

CHAPTER SEVENTEEN
TO THE BRIEFING ROOM

In the Outer Courtyard of the Kingdom

"YES, I AM *all dressed up* as you say, and no, you are not coming," he chided. Hiding his impatience was never a skill Megalos got much good at. He loved Maggie dearly, but unlike Pipiera, rather than amusing herself with the astonishing scenery—the talented, orchestrated flowering plants, the curiosity of each and every Arrival—Maggie insisted on following him around continuously, yammering questions, one after the other.

"Alright, alright. I don't need a tongue-lashing! Besides, I never asked to come wherever it is you are going." Maggie cocked her head, much like Pipiera used to, and dared to ask another question, "Just where *are* you going?"

Even as Megalos resigned to a dreaded body slump, his impressive height still towered high above Maggie, though his energy drained low. *This is Pip's mother. I owe her an answer.* He clasped her hands and pondered the idea of another picnic table chat. *No time, quick and easy,* he told himself. "We're gathering. It's a meeting, Authoritarians, and all…" he sighed. "Things are not going as planned. It happens." He checked her eyes. Was she grasping what he was trying to say? Apparently not. Maggie still looked inquisitive. "*Don't worry,* we got this," was how he ended the conversation as he let go of her hands.

He headed past the picnic tables to the opening where the treacherous climb would begin, on the pathway where yielding to the supreme power is the only manner in which one could arrive at the briefing room.

"Why on Earth would there be something to worry about?" Maggie called toward him as he wandered away from her with his walking stick and those ancient-looking sandals of his. But Megalos didn't return her query nor her gaze. *She hasn't been here long enough to understand,* he thought.

"Shouldn't you at least put a shirt on?!" She hollered out one last question, another to which he provided no response.

CHAPTER EIGHTEEN

ANY OTHER SUSPECTS?

In the Town of Havensight

"THERE'S NO WAY *she's* responsible!" Matthew's steering was haphazard, his foot a little heavy. He had left in a flash immediately following the arrest by the gun-bearing gang of Havensight officers and their subsequent removal of Pipiera in handcuffs. He needed to find out why she was arrested. Was it nonsense, or was there evidence? And just who was she, exactly?

"Matt, face it. It *had* to be *her!*" Karo had jumped into the front seat, pushing Laura into the back. Both girls left a flabbergasted Marnie standing alone in her kitchen, with Charles upstairs calling down, demanding some answers to 'just what the blazes was going on down there?'

"Matt, if I didn't know better, it sounds like you, ah, *like* her?" Laura's voice was dry and slightly accusatory.

"What? No!"

"How'd you meet her, Matty?" Karo would not stop this

line of questioning, he could tell. He slammed the steering wheel and then, angrily, the brakes. They slid on the gravel at the side of the road. It happened to be the same spot his old Betsy of a car had needed fluid earlier that day. But this time, it was he who needed to cool down.

Laura stepped out of the car and slammed the door. Matthew could see her stomping away. "Just great!" He slammed the steering wheel again.

"Uh, dough-head, go after her," Karo instructed.

Matthew sat still as this Pippi creature seeped into his thoughts. *She knows something. I know it.* "I don't believe she's responsible, but I think she knows something," he confessed aloud.

"Seriously? Laura is walking away, and you are still thinking about *her*? She was arrested, Matty. Karpeeesh?"

"It's 'capiche.'"

"Aughhh! I'll never understand you."

He tapped his fingers on the wheel. *What to do, what to do.* Pressing the handle down and shoving the door outward, he heard a sigh of relief coming from Karo. He ran to catch up to Laura, who was storming away at a pretty good pace for a young woman in jelly shoes.

"Hey, wait up," Matthew called. "Please. Please, Laura!"

She stopped, shoulder pads both jiggling out of place and the ribbon that previously tied back her hair having dropped. Matthew smiled and came to his senses. *I really like her, even when she's mad like that.* He picked up the ribbon from the gravel where it had dropped and caught up to her, getting in front so he could face her.

"Laura, I'm out of sorts here. I'm sorry. Thank you for coming around, my family and I…we, we appreciate it."

He waited for a response. In return, all he received was a set of eyebrows raised higher than he'd ever seen before. *Is that a trick?* He guessed his explanation was not what she was expecting. *I'd best try again. And quick.* Her hands were now securely hugging her hips.

"What I mean is, look, I don't want you to move away." Her eyebrows shifted, but not to a pleasant kind of position, he thought. *Oops, that wasn't what she wanted to hear, either.*

Laura pushed Matthew aside and continued to storm down the town's only highway, stepping in the same direction as their car had been traveling, to the center of town, where she lived with her parents and where Karo's dad and Joppha's dad, Arnie Decker, lived. *And* where the police station's office was, where Pipiera would have been taken for questioning. Hopefully, he thought, they haven't taken her to the county's holding cells, on the outskirts of town.

Matthew chased Laura and grabbed her elbow, swinging her around. That's when he noticed her tears.

From far back, they both could hear Karo yelping out of the passenger window, "You dummy, Matt."

This made Laura laugh, and she wiped the tears off her face with the back of her hand. "She's right, you know."

"Yeah, *I know*," he humbly admitted.

"Tell me about this girl. This Pippi Whoever. How *do* you know her?"

"Look. Honestly, I met her today. Just like you. She's…" he paused, not sure how to proceed. *What is she to me?* He stepped away to think for a moment, ignorant of the glare coming from Laura's eyes. He moved back again, close, to face Laura, to ensure she heard what he was about to explain.

"Somewhere, I know her somehow, from somewhere. Like, from a *dream* or something."

Laura took two steps back, not impressed with where this conversation was going.

"No, no. Not like that!" He had caught her cold drift. "More like…a sister, an older sister from ages past, another life, even." He shook his head. "I don't expect you to understand."

She toed the gravel, the bareness of her feet showing through her jelly shoes, which were now completely covered in dust. They both watched without saying a word as her filthy shoes drew circles around and around in the dirt. Then she punched his shoulder, and he finally grabbed her close and circled his arms around her.

"I haven't even welcomed you home yet. Things got so crazy. Welcome home. I missed you." And that was true; he had.

Matthew had a sudden thought of horror: *what happened to the ring? Where did I put it?* He wanted to tell her about it and started to pat down his pockets, realizing he had slept in his clothes.

"Now what?" This seemed to annoy Laura. Some silly motion of his had interrupted their hug. And for what, a missing key or something?

Matthew felt relief when the ring's outline was still in his front pants pocket. But now was not the time nor the place. *Joppha first,* he thought.

"Look," he grabbed her forearms, "are you with me? I must find Jopphie. I'll go crazy out of my mind if we don't. No stone left turned under. Will you help me, Laura?"

"Unturned."

"What?"

"Unturned. No stone left unturned, you dummy."

He hugged her. This time they both laughed. On their way back to the car, Matthew yelled to Karo, instructing her to move into the back seat. She protested but scrambled nevertheless.

❦

The threesome parked on the street a block away from Arnie and Cilia Decker's driveway. A cruiser with a police officer munching a sandwich had the premium parking spot right out front. An empty cruiser sat in the driveway. Karo asked where all these guys had come from. Must be from neighboring towns, Laura replied. Everyone knew Havensight only had two police vehicles and no more than six officers.

Karo bolted into the house. It was her home. Her second home. In the midst of Arnie and Marnie's brief marriage, they had Karo. All this after Matthew's father, Franklin Mackenzie, the town's infamous stargazer, passed away from a two-year illness.

As for Matthew and Arnie, they had a tumultuous history, one that Matthew was ashamed of and wished he could take back. Particularly the time when Matthew's actions ended up causing so much chaos and confusion, Arnie ended up being wrongfully blamed and was fired from his vice principal job at the local high school. As for now, several years later? Matthew couldn't imagine life without Arnie. Arnie had become his father figure, and Matthew loved and admired him dearly. The idea of being responsible for losing Arnie's much-loved son, Joppha, well, that was too much to bear. Matthew wasn't sure if he could ever face Arnie again, much less right now.

"C'mon, it'll be okay," Laura gently pulled at Matthew's

arm and guided him up the cement stairwell. "We are here now. You're going in," she whispered a scold while holding open the door.

I can't. He felt uneasy. His arms, hands, legs, feet, and chest all trembled. He grabbed a side rail to keep his balance. *I can't. I lost his son. He'll hate me.* Laura held and guided him in, "It'll be alright, Matty, don't worry. We'll get all this figured out."

Laura leading the way, they entered. Knocking or ringing the bell wasn't required. Matthew often strolled in and out as though it were his second home, just like Karo. But this time, it felt like a privilege he didn't deserve. He had betrayed them. He predicted he would for sure become like a stranger, an unwanted one. Someone who will have to ring the bell and they won't have to let him in; might even close the curtains good and tight when they'd see him coming.

He barely recognized the sitting room. It had been turned into a missing child home-based office. The kitchen table had been moved into the room and held black portfolios and some communication equipment beside an oversized easel with bulleted notations.

"Maybe we'll see if there are any other suspects, or maybe even my purse showed up somewhere," Laura whispered.

But his eyes fixed on his graduation photo. It had been removed from the frame above the fireplace mantel, and his proud-as-punch grimace was pinned up on the police bulletin board. At the *top.*

What? Me?

He stiffened, his head heavy, his throat dry. All went black and so very cold. Matthew collapsed. Smashed his head on a pushed-aside coffee table on the way down.

Out cold and suddenly absent from his body.

CHAPTER NINETEEN
TRADE DEAL

In a Cave, Somewhere in The Deep

SOMETHING WEIGHED HEAVILY across Matthew's chest and shoulders. His stomach rumbled as though he hadn't eaten for days, but he distinctly recalled standing in Arnie's sitting room mere seconds ago. Had a lot of time simply passed since then? A distinct *drip, drip, drip* echoed nearby. *Where am I?* If it weren't for a stream of greyish light that cut across his runners, he wouldn't have known he was horizontal. Strewn, flat out on a hardened floor. A dirt floor. Leaning his head, he made out a pile of rocks—a high pile of rocks—behind him and a pint-sized tunnel opening to his right. He rubbed the side of his head, exhaled, then rubbed and squeezed both eyes. A vague creature was coming toward him. He recognized the stroll, an actual spring in its step.

"Oh, eat my shorts. It's *you*." No sooner had those words come out of his mouth, a memory flashed instantly to a time before. A time when he knew this creature: the *goon* was one of the many choice words he used to describe him. An alien creep who interfered; messed with his head. Years ago. Kasartha was his name. Sarthie-boy. A nightmare kid who dragged him away from himself. Got him lost in his own skin.

"Long time, eh, Matty-boy?" Kasartha quipped with a chirp and an enormous grin. In his gnome-like form of a being, teeth too large for his oval, pale-green, boyish face, he stood not a lot taller than four feet head to toe. "Ya should'a greeted me better last night."

Matthew tensed his leg and hip muscles to pull himself up. He stood, finding himself a great deal taller compared to their last toe to toe encounter a good five, maybe six years earlier. "Whattaya want? I'm on to you." Though he hadn't employed it much as of late, Matthew's signature look of disgust was telling.

"My, my, Matty-boy, aren't you a handsome dude? You've grown. *So* tall now." Kasartha bit his fist and faked a pout. "I'm so proud of you. *So* proud." Bent with emotion, he lengthened his neck so he could have a direct face-on view of Matthew.

But Matthew just grinned. "Yeah, I've grown. But look at you, that stupid purple hat, those short, baggy pants. Same worn-out shoes, even! YOU haven't changed. YOU haven't grown any, have *y-o-u?* Same ol' wastoid you are."

Matthew oozed with confidence, pretending that quiver of angst—guilt, accusatory and hopelessness—meant nothing, as if swallowing a poisonous arrow would do no harm. *I'm to blame for Joppha being missing. And darn you Emerson, it's all because of you. We might never find him.* He squeezed his eyes shut and focused on the breath in his chest. It was heavy, and he pushed it down. So much came flooding back. Kasartha picking Matthew up from the schoolyard when Emerson's loyal bullies had left him for dead. Kasartha was his hero, his rescuer, his friend—or so he thought. Emerson was his number-one enemy back then. So much has changed. *Catch yourself, Matt, don't go back there, don't think like that.* He recalled how damaging his thoughts were back then and how far he'd come since. Flexing his muscles to stand tall with fists clenched, he demanded an answer from Kasartha. "And just *why* am I here this time?" Matthew cautioned himself, acknowledging his vulnerability.

"Matty-boy, you speak like we haven't been together for years. Sure, yes, not like this together," referring to this present meeting which happened to be taking place at Kasartha's cave in the dark ethereal universe, somewhere between Earth and the Kingdom. "But, hey…" Kasartha wound his way into Matthew's face again, "I'm your shadow. Where you go, I go. I don't think what you think. No." He pointed to himself proudly, "I put thoughts in your head, so you will think what *I* want you to think. Like it or not, Matty-boy, one fine day, you will have so many thoughts like me, you will become *just* like me."

"Nuh-uh. Not gonna happen. No dice."

"Sure as anythin'."

"Is that a threat?"

Kasartha defended himself. "Am I *so* bad? I am *not* so bad. What's so bad about me, Matty-boy? Tell me, what's not to like?"

Another memory dizzied Matthew's brain. An odd pair, he and Kasartha, traipsing through the cosmos like they were run-away aliens on some urgent mission. Only the stakes were real. His own identity. If it weren't for that long-jumping girl, he never would have realized those nuggets of truth he'd come to cherish and live by.

That long-jumping girl, Matthew mused as a light bulb lit inside him.

More images flashed back. *That girl.* Surrounded by guards. In a circle, her trapped in the middle, weapons pointed at her midriff, soldiers ready to attack at a given command. *That was her!* Throwing his head back against the stone wall, *duh,* then leaning against it so he wouldn't fall. *Now I know where I know her from! She came to me, out of nowhere, to help me then. She's come again. To help me find Jopphie. She said as much.* He smacked his forehead. "Amazing!" he said aloud, so astonished at the idea that this woman walked out of a dream and into his life. "My aunt; she said she was my *aunt!*" He had placed the familiarity of Pippi. She was the Pipiera from the vague, super-crazy experiences he'd had years ago. Matthew gave Kasartha a look as though he could confirm his suspicions. "You. You had her arrested!" he accused. "And now you've trapped me here! You're behind all this, aren't you!" Matthew swaggered up to Kasartha. "Where's Jopphie!"

Kasartha rubbed his chin. "You should have listened to me, Matty-boy."

"Not even."

"This is all on you, Matty-boy."

Matthew did his best to hide the choke. After all, he *did* feel responsible for Jopphie's disappearance.

"And," Kasartha sang, "you could have stopped all this. I…," pointing proudly to himself and switching to a scolding tone "…came to you. To tell you where your stupid little kid was. But, nooooo, you didn't listen. Me. Yes, it was me. *I* came to *help* you. And you basically ignored me!"

"Bogus," Matthew spewed. "When? Tell me when you came to help me find Jopphie."

"Last night, duh. And I recognized your little jumping girlfriend too. How'd you manage that…to get *her* into your life…your *physical* life?" Kasartha relished slithering his inspecting face directly at Matthew's. "Ya got connections I don't know about?"

Astonished, Matthew had to sit to allow all this to soak in. *Coincidence? That girl—my aunt—my dead aunt appears mysteriously and now is arrested. This goon-faced-crazy-dude traps me in some galaxy cave and leaves me for dead in Arnie's sitting room. And Jopphie is missing. No, not a coincidence. It's all connected. It's gotta be.* "I remember," he whimpered, including last night. He'd waved that visit away as a figment of a sick imagination.

Kasartha continued. He seemed so eager to share his brilliance…and his deceitful, powerful ways. "When you wouldn't listen, I *had* to do something, of course." He paced while Matthew sat still, listening, which was most pleasing to Kasartha. "Oh, the little dude would have been found. A young lad, traveling alone. He wouldn't have gotten far. Unless!"

"Unless what?" Matthew was afraid of the answer.

"Unless," Kasartha raised his finger in the air to demonstrate his brilliance, a great idea. "Unless he were traveling with an adult."

"You! You are 'the man' who was seen with Jopphie!"

Kasartha took a deep bow.

Matthew stood, hands in front and open, a show of an honest plea. "Where is he now?"

Kasartha crossed his arms and faced the opposite direction.

"Is he hurt?"

"No."

Matthew checked the terrain. The cave ran deep into the darkness, a path that could take him farther. "Is he here?"

No answer.

"IS HE HERE? DID YOU TAKE HIM?"

"No, chill out, would'ja? He's *not* here."

"What do you want from me? Take it, whatever it is. Just, please, let Jopphie get home to his parents safely."

Kasartha turned around and appeared completely relieved, as though a tremendous burden had been removed. His turn to plead, "Look at us, Matty, we are communicating, you and me." His hand gestures motioned as though there were an understanding between the two. "I've missed this. I miss you. Come back to me. Can we be friends again? That's all I want." Both hands pressed against his heart. He let out a gigantic sigh.

"And Jopphie?"

"The little guy will be set free. I promise. Besides, you do owe it to him. It was your fault, after all. It was in *your hands*—his care, right?"

Kasartha wanted to renew their relationship, and in return, Jopphie could go back to his parents. *I do owe him. Perhaps this should be my punishment*, Matthew thought. Despite the shudders at recalling his experience with this goon, he thought: *he's probably right*.

Matthew was desperate. Desperate to see Joppha home, safe with Arnie.

CHAPTER TWENTY

A STENCH CHANGES EVERYTHING

"WHAT THE HECK is that stink? *Gross!*" Matthew spat. He was sure he swallowed some of the wretched odor.

"Seriously? Think, Matty-boy. Think. Duh, sometimes…" Kasartha shook his head, then took a deep breath. Out the corner of his mouth, he added, "Play it cool, would'ja? My life is at stake."

"Dude, you're already dead. And seriously, what've *you* got to lose?" Matthew plugged his nose, "Gnarly!" The stench was overwhelming. "Oh crap, that's your uncle." *How could I have forgotten? What's next?* His brain in exhaustion overload, Matthew crouched, wishing he could simply disappear.

Kasartha shrugged off Matthew's ignorance and stepped, all puffy-chested, toward the ledge in front of his cavern. The sting in his nostrils and gag in his throat signaled that Kasartha's so-called uncle, the master of the cosmos—the Dragon himself, was about to approach.

Curled with his face—well, his nose and mouth in

particular—hidden as deeply as possible, Matthew did what Arnie would have suggested. He released a plea upward to the King. Surely, he could hear. Surely, he would help. *I certainly hope so,* he thought. Matt counted on his request being heard. *I really don't know how to get outta here.* He pled some more as sincerely as he could.

An incredibly clear command bubbled up, a wise voice arriving from deep within. *"Do not lie to yourself. I disapprove of you not."* Matthew's heart lifted as well as his head. He speculated on the source of the words. Shutting his eyes tight, he argued quietly. *I should be punished, right? Don't you think?* He challenged the voice and wished it would come back to clarify and put his mind at ease.

Matthew hurled. It had been urgent, and in the midst of it, another unpleasant odor floated about—peanut-y stomach contents. Wiping his chin and huddled inward, he heard their voices— Kasartha's and that so-called uncle of his—low and hushed. And nearby. He eavesdropped, keen to learn what a villainous space beast would even say.

Horrifying. The beast spoke clearly as though he were *just another man.* Not what Matthew anticipated. He had expected fire to blaze their surroundings. Instead, just simple words. Words that congratulated Kasartha with kudos, an attack well executed against Arnie.

"Paying attention, I like that, Sarthie-boy," Uncle groaned with delight. "You grabbed an opportunity and ran with it."

Kasartha bowed. "Just call me the king of opportunists!"

Matthew chortled when Kasartha's hopeful boast was met with a snort. *Okay, that was more dragon-like.*

"Err, just call me an opportunist. Never mind the *king-*thing." Kasartha walked back his pride meekly. Another snort, a powerful one that swept Kasartha off his feet. Once the goon shook himself off, he gestured a wave in return, "Aw, I was just lucky, Uncle. *J-u-s-t* lucky."

A command bolted from Uncle. "I *want* him. Stick to him, now that you're *in*."

"Yes, sir!" Kasartha sealed his understanding with a salute.

"Do not lose him. Like you did *him!*" Uncle was obviously referring to Kasartha's loosened relationship with Matthew. Kasartha had once boasted to his Uncle that he was *'in'* with Matthew, only to later lose that loyalty.

Matthew's stomach churned again. *Who does Kasartha have an in with? Might he be talking about Jopphie? Has to be. And if I will be a friend to Kasartha, he will release Jopphie, isn't that what the deal was?* He dared a full straight-on look. Only a portion of the space beast's head was visible now, his eyes—huge slits of yellow, the tip of his tail a long distance away. *Grody, he's one big sucker. Would Kasartha really betray his uncle, this king of all evil? All for a friendship with me?*

"And what are you doing with *him,* anyway?" Uncle snapped, nodding Matthew's way.

"Oh, uh, just gathering info. You know. Analysis and stuff."

Hatred and evil left Uncle's eyes. A fixation on Matthew seemed more delicious. "Having a bit of trouble, Matthew Mackenzie? Tsk, tsk, tsk. Earthly tours are overrated, don't you agree?"

Matthew stood tall. "All good," he announced boldly, wanting to add 'bugger off' but thankful he restrained himself.

"Let me give you some advice, lad. When your dear friend Arnie Decker demands that you get out of his life…*and he will,*" Uncle threatened, "pay attention! In fact, you'll do well to sever that relationship." The muscles in Uncle's face relaxed. "Then," he sighed, "all will be well."

Uncle turned his glare back to Kasartha, "He knows too much. Git 'im outta my sight. Outta my galaxies. Got it?"

"Yup, yup, got it, Uncle. Noooo problem. Outta yer space." Kasartha twitched nervously, hands behind his back, gulping his words as though they were too hard to chew.

Matthew stood still as a stone, as did Kasartha. The pair watched Uncle's nostrils slither down and out of sight. Moments later, once the odorous stench had cleared, Kasartha turned to Matthew.

"You heard him. Get up, I'm taking you home."

Matthew wiped his chin and slowly rose to his feet. "No. Take me to Joppha."

"No. Nope. No-way, hoe-say."

"Yes. Yup and yes-way, hoe-say." Matthew stepped over to Kasartha. "Listen, you little twerp, take me to Joppha. *Now!*"

Kasartha bought some time by scratching the back of his head. "You did just see my uncle, did you not?"

"So?"

"And you heard him? Did you not? Pretty sure he doesn't want you involved in this."

"I heard 'im."

"What part of *get him outta my space* did you not understand?"

Despite the awkward difference in the pair's height, they poked each other in the chest to make sure their own point was driven home with the other.

"He's *your* uncle. He ain't *my* uncle. What part of *that* don't *you* understand?"

Kasartha crossed his arms, turned, and pouted as a

three-year-old child might. "All you gotta do," Kasartha explained, "is be friends with me and not with Arnie. That's all. No biggie, right? It's not like the guy is your dad or anything."

"And Joppha?"

"Joppha will carry on. I'll…I'll even leave him alone. I promise."

"I'm on to you." Matthew didn't buy it. "Enough games. I'm taking charge. Let's go."

Kasartha churned and swirled like a tornado till he appeared as a dragon himself, twice Matthew's size, yet super-mini compared to Uncle. His tongue lashed fire enough to make Matthew jump around and back himself up against the inside wall of the cavern, eyes wide and mouth gaping.

Kasartha churned and swirled some more, transforming back to his regular, oval-faced, four-footer of what Matthew would call a goon. "Sorry, bud. Had to do it. I need you to listen! So, sit your butt down. Not there," as he pointed to the puddle of stomach contents by Matthew's feet.

Matthew sat a few feet over. Kasartha came and sat beside him. "Do ya do that often?" Matthew asked.

"Too exhausting. But I got ya! You, Matty-boy, are mister fraidy pants."

"No, I'm not."

"Yeah, you are."

"Get on with it."

"You see," Kasartha explained, "you could do me a huge favor."

Matthew's eye-rolling didn't require any further response.

"Hear me out, would ya? Just hear me out," Kasartha pled.

Matthew shrugged and shifted positions to give Kasartha

his back. He would listen, but he was not eager to learn what the guy had to say.

"I get why you're mad at me. Don't you think I know how important that *li'l Jopphie* is to you?"

"And…you care…because?" It was a sarcastic reply.

Kasartha slumped into a deep sigh. Taking a big breath, he opened his hands to show he wasn't hiding anything. "It's Arnie I'm after. He's my target assignment."

Turning quickly to face Kasartha, Matthew pounded out his questions. But most importantly, "Arnie? Why Arnie?"

"Uncle's directive."

"What do you want from him?"

"Dunno. We don't get to know. We just get 'em."

"He's never done anything to you! Leave him alone."

"'He's never done anything to you, leave him alone,'" Kasartha mocked back. "Yeah, right. You really don't get it. Look, all this is your fault. If you had kept listening to me, if you hadn't pushed me out, we'd still be friends, you and me. I'd still be on you, and you and that Arnie bloke would still be rivals." Kasartha switched into a sad little being. "You and I, we were so good together. Besides, Arnie's no fun. My life is miserable." His sobs muffled the rest.

Matthew had to get closer to hear, shocked by the closing comment of this little performance of his.

"Are you saying what I think you're saying?" Matthew asked. "If only I had listened to you, Joppha would be safe at home right now?"

Kasartha wiped his nose while he nodded.

Matthew stood and walked toward the cliff's edge. Releasing a silent chuckle, he rubbed the back of his neck. He'd been here before, at this very spot. A needle's edge poking into darkness, a deep blackness below and greyed-out, ominous mountain peaks towering above, each speckled with black holes. He remembered well everything now. It was all coming back in full detail. Countless others, just like Kasartha, lived in those black-hole openings, their own private, lonely caverns. All slaving for this space beast of a monstrous dragon they dutifully called Uncle. In a war against an unreachable King, they take orders to target particular beings on an Earth-journey. *What an existence.* Matthew shook his head. *Now THAT is sad.*

Staring into the blackness, he mumbled loud enough for Kasartha to hear, "You didn't get me, so you are after people I care about." He couldn't have seen Kasartha's shrug of uncertainty, and Matthew couldn't bear to check his response.

Remaining calm, he walked back to the still-sulking Kasartha. "So, what's your plan? Whattaya need from me? How do we get Joppha home safe…to his parents' home, in Havensight?" Matthew placed a great deal of emphasis on which home, to make things perfectly clear.

Kasartha jumped to his feet, renewed exuberance in his energy. "It's dangerous," he warned.

Matthew rolled his eyes.

"Hey, isn't this great? You *and* me. Working together. On a mission. Together!" Kasartha was jumping around, punching the air as though he were in training for a fun round of boxing.

Matthew rolled his eyes some more and placed one hand on a hip, teeth clenched with annoyance. "Just take me to Jopphie."

"Yeah, yeah, okay, boss. Let's go!"

CHAPTER TWENTY-ONE

HOPEFUL AND HELPLESS

In the Town of Havensight

ARNIE DECKER'S BODY wasn't used to adrenaline coursing through its veins, especially for hours at a time. His limbs were shaking and his chest was tight. A swish of blue uniforms, a ponytail flopping, voices chirping. And, 'Are you alright? Matty, wake up!'

Arnie was sure that voice belonged to Karo. *Cilia, I should tell Cilia.* He instructed himself a command. *Go get her.* After all, he was in command and on autopilot. *No, better sit down,* he warned himself. He landed in the comfy corner of the couch, a spot that was always reserved for him, the primary protector and head of this family. The cushions engulfed him with much-needed familiarity.

"Dad, where's Mama Cil?!" Karo yelped.

He squeezed the spasm that throbbed around his heart and held it tight. "In the bedroom. She needed…quiet. Hasn't slept," Arnie replied about his wife.

The blur of activity ensued. The invaders in his once-peaceful home—before his son had gone missing, that is—all crouched around the fallen boy, Matthew, following a disturbing head crack. Matthew lay crooked and non-responsive in Arnie's barely recognizable sitting room, thanks to tables and papers and walkie-talkies and flip charts and blue-suited men with heavy black shoes walking all over the newly installed and perfectly vacuumed wall-to-wall carpeting.

What he'd give to have his son, Jopphie, back with all his toy planes and army soldiers spread out over the entire width and length of the underlying hardwood floor, scratching it up really well with sudden, urgent maneuvers that he insisted were life-saving for an imaginary world he loved.

It was approaching twenty-four hours. Twenty-four hours since he had seen his son. That was when Matthew had picked him up to 'take him for a drive.' The household had been crazy yesterday, that dreaded morning which now felt like it belonged in another time zone, in another life, in another world, maybe even to another man. Anyone but him. Cilia had been busy with the twins; they were particularly fussy, both of them at the same time. Karo had gone to Marnie's home to spend time with her ailing grandmother. Joppha had been bored, but unlike most kids wanting attention, he was different. Rather than pester anyone, he would simply wander off. So, keeping the boy occupied had been a critical component of his and Cilia's daily lives. *Business at the church.* Arnie hung his head. *I left. I should've been here. I wasn't.*

Matthew had been offering for several days to take Joppha along to the bus terminal a good hour's drive away. He was picking up his high school girlfriend, Laura. It wasn't such an unusual request. Matthew and Joppha spent a great deal of time together. They were truly like siblings, more so even than Joppha and Karo, who were true siblings—partially, anyway. Cilia loved how Matthew had taken to their son, but clearly, she hadn't wanted Joppha to leave the community. She had warned that it didn't feel right. What if that car of theirs breaks down? What if Jopphie wanders off and gets lost in a crowd? What if, what if, what if? Anticipating potential pitfalls was something she was good and regular at. Arnie repeatedly told her she had a tendency to toss boulders into her own path, something she should be aware of. And stop.

Arnie rubbed his chin. Despite his wife's warnings and her rejection of Matthew's offer, he had blessed it. "Go ahead, explore a new world today, Jopphie! Have fun," he had said as the little guy scrambled into the back seat of Matthew's old Impala while Arnie headed off to his meeting, knowing that Cilia was inside, annoyed.

He noticed Karo, anxious to take action.

"Karo, stop!" Arnie called out as she sprinted down the hall to find Cilia. He was worried about his wife. She needs some rest; last night had been long. The twins were napping. "Let her sleep!"

Cil will get even more twisted up with emotions if she sees Matthew on the floor like that. She was angry with Matthew. She's angry with me. We've both betrayed her love and trust.

"Daddy, we *have* to tell her!"

"Yes, honey-bee, just not now. Let her rest. Come here," he coaxed her over to sit beside him. She did, although hesitantly. She snuggled into her dad and watched as Laura stroked Matthew's face while an officer held his wrist and checked his watch carefully.

"What's he doing?"

"Counting his breaths, or perhaps his heart rate."

Karo instantly got up. Arnie instantly pulled her back down. "Give them some space. He's gonna be okay," he assured her.

"We should call Mom."

"Just wait, honey-bee, we will."

The sirens of an ambulance were within earshot and getting louder.

Karo attempted to rise again. Arnie instantly pulled her back down. "But I should be out there, showing them where we live and, like, opening the door for them!"

"They've got this," he replied, nodding toward the officer crouched over Matthew's body. Arnie wished that ambulance were for him. How he would like to snuggle into a bed and pull a sheet fully over his head, forget about all this mess, even for just an hour; let others take care of him, of his family; rescue Joppha, wherever he was. *Some peace. Peace within. King, where is it? Why are you doing this?*

He had a good grip on Karo. She was itching to get into the middle of the action. He didn't need to watch her jittery legs to know she wanted to bolt again.

"You know, Daddy, that girl was arrested at Mom's. She's guilty, right? I just know she is. That's what *we* think, right?"

Arnie was silent. He didn't know the girl, had never heard of her until early this morning. There was talk of a strange woman arriving yesterday morning, that some man dropped her off by the farm north of town, and that she just happened to *stroll* into their lives. The police figured that the man, whoever he was—who nobody saw or could even confirm—might have then driven over to the bus depot. There was speculation about the possibility of this duo having something to do with a 'kidnapping'— a term that made Arnie wince every time it was used. It was a theory. And that theory included the possibility of Matthew having set the whole thing up, the entire plan outlined on a flip chart in Arnie's sitting room. Absurd. He wondered if Matthew had seen it, seen that he was a suspect. *Matthew? An evil mastermind taking a boy he already had practically full access to and enjoyed great love with? Makes no sense. I won't buy it.*

That was the possible theory of the hour: a potential scheme the detectives from two towns over were hashing out and speculating over while pacing Arnie's home for clues. It was one of several theories tossed around, up there with runaway and lost, runaway and hiding, a thief wanting that big purse of Laura's he was carrying and taking Joppha along with it, or even taken spontaneously by some needy, childless mother seizing a golden opportunity.

Arnie didn't know anything about this 'girl' his daughter was obsessed with. "Possibly. I don't know, honey-bee."

It was necessary to let go of his daughter so his head could fall into both hands. Of course, she bolted outside to meet the ambulance and would probably tell them what they should do once they arrived. He rubbed his face and held it. *Damn fools, they wouldn't check the buses last night, said there was no pos-sibility of Joppha getting on any of them. Had they only explored that option further, better, they'd have found him, and he'd be home or on his way home by now.* It was early that morning when a tipster had called the Havensight Police, noting they saw a boy with Joppha's description with a man in the middle of the night, walking away from a bus terminal—at the coast, no less.

Arnie watched the feet of two detectives as they shuffled

around Matthew, their voices instructing everyone to stay back and make room for the medical experts. His thoughts had grown sarcastic. *NOW, you're looking into the bus options? A little late.* Arnie wondered how a description of his son, Joppha, had been available at that station—a long, arduous journey away, given the plentiful stops on that route—for a tipster even to have seen it, all while the investigation had been confined to the area between his home and the local bus terminal.

He looked at the sprawled body on the floor. *Matthew, I bet it was you who got descriptions out.* "Thank you," he whispered.

Only, he's still out there. And dang it, how could you have lost him?!

CHAPTER TWENTY-TWO
TREK OR TWIST

Outside the Kingdom's Courtyard

THE TREK UP to the briefing room was as Megalos anticipated. He had done this journey a few times now, mostly since Pipiera came into his life. The journey sharpened him a little more each time he was called to the arduous task of this upward climb outside the protection of the Kingdom walls. And each time, he understood it all just that much more—just why the path was what it was. To travel not by sight but by trust. To avoid the temptation of self-reasoning and to remind him that although he cannot see the outcome nor what lies just ahead, he must rely on the King. To walk, like an Earth-journeyer is challenged to walk.

Trust and trust alone.

And so, he submitted. He leaned in and sank his energies into those ancient sandals of his, so they could take control of his steps. They would ensure that he didn't slip into a dark void, only he needed to keep focused on the present—not the step behind nor more than two steps ahead. Only the mere footing he was engaged in. If he could surrender to the sandals on his feet, his tension could release. It was a balance one had to practice. But once he got the rhythm right, he wondered why he had fought it. It was always a chuckle, always a lesson. Each time.

The trek up gave him plenty of time to reflect. He found himself shaking his head and grinning. *My dear Pipiera, you have certainly added some colorful drama to my life! What adventures are steeping now, I wonder?*

He was close to his destination, the place where the Authoritarians provided their briefings: what was happening and what would need to happen, sometimes even discussing options that could fit within the boundaries of the King's direction. Then, the attendees would all scatter and carry out their respective duties and tasks to keep the King's end goals in sharp focus. The Rebels always interfered. Plans always had to be adjusted. Sacrifices often had to be made, necessary for the good of eternity.

At last, his sandals slowed, halting in front of a thicket of greenery. He pulled open the ivy frame he had become so familiar with and used his own quadriceps to step inside. No matter how often he did it, that transfer of energy always brought some wooziness, particularly to his ankles. Inside the clearing, he shook his legs and grinned at the crowd already gathered. That journey, well, it humbled them all, no matter how big or strong one might be. All the attendees had that vulnerability in common.

James, the Authoritarian in charge, tipped his head and released a smile toward Megalos, then got back to scurrying about. He and Soogreese were lining up the Kingdom equipment. Bethany buzzed directly around Megalos's head while checking off something on her clipboard. Her pint-sized body and wings that hummingbirds were modeled after enabled her to breeze around quickly, studying faces, discerning emotions and scribbling down words practically before they slipped off anyone's tongue. Everything was on the table here in this space. All would be recorded for the Kingdom books and disclosed to the King himself.

Megalos tugged a handful of trousers up above the knees to loosen them so he could sit comfortably on the log, choosing a spot right beside Serena. She, herself, looked a bit frenzied—he knew the climb was challenging for her. Thankful she had made the trip, he nudged her affectionately with his shoulder, and she nudged back in return. They both loved Pipiera and appreciated the sacrifice she had offered up to take a stint on Earth simply to aid people they all cared about.

"Ya spilled some filling," he teased.

She smiled, "That was Pipiera. Besides, you like cherries, right? I'm sure it didn't go to waste." They both chuckled.

James cleared his throat, interrupting the thoughts of all. The meeting would begin. Megalos scanned those in attendance. When their eyes connected, his and Othis's, Othis succinctly squeezed both his shut, disproportioning his facial features briefly. Megalos couldn't help but chuckle; that was the big, burly warrior's way of an affectionate greeting. Normally, he held a mean and stern presence. Of course, he would; his job required it. As the leader of the Kingdom's armies, he spent a great deal of time battling in *The Deep,* warring with lurking enemies to block and hinder their spearing attacks on Earth-journeyers. It was constant. With each passing decade, the rebels became greater and greater masters of deceit.

The attacks caused a steady stream of requests to arrive from pleading Earth-journeyers, plumes of pungent aromas that would jet up like nasty smoke from deadly fires. Gad, the Lead Receiver, had a large team, breaking down the molecules and analyzing the properties and whatnots that made up each and every distinct aroma. In turn, a list would be conveyed to Othis, and in turn again, Othis would dispatch his many armies with distinct instructions—which rebels needed to be stopped, which Earth-journeyers needed to be shielded.

The war of The Deep, Megalos sighed. He was thankful for his own role, one where he processed and welcomed Arrivals upon the end of their journey. *It has discouraging moments too, but boy, wouldn't want Othis's job!* He gave a quick and silent thank you to the King that Gad and Othis were so efficient and effective at their roles and asked for their own hearts to be filled with peace. Particularly thankful that Matthew had lifted a few requests that reached Gad's team, he noted Matthew's growing habit of placing requests. *A good sign.* Megalos also thought of the acrid smells that simply didn't have the properties to rise high enough. Half-hearted requests never made it to Gad's team, though they certainly made for nasty odors and tip-offs to rebels throughout *The Deep*.

It was no surprise to see Gad, an energetic being with pumped-up, florescent-red runners and bright purple magnifying spectacles, standing beside Othis. As odd and opposite as they appeared from each other, their jobs joined them at the hip often enough.

James got right to it and laid out the facts, one at a time.

"First, it's no surprise. Rebel Kasartha is heavily involved," James announced dryly. Othis nodded an unenthusiastic 'yes,' indicating to all he was already aware.

"Second, Pipiera will be forced into a locked-away situation."

"What!" Megalos couldn't help it: his tongue lashed the question aloud. Bethany raised her eyebrows while jotting something down.

"All is good. We're on it; she'll call. We'll be ready," Gad assured.

Whew. Megalos knew his Pip's life was not in danger, as she was already a citizen of the Kingdom. But this little excursion, this mission she's on, could and will certainly impact her in other ways. The experience can be traumatic. *Oh, Pipiera, please forget all this business and just come home.* Megalos felt selfish, knowing that was simply what *he* thought, knowing there was much more to the situation, a much bigger picture, a longer end game, one that could benefit many. He reminded himself he was a protector, and sometimes a protector can protect too much.

James scanned the group, wanting to continue. It appeared that possibly something even more startling was next. *What else?* Megalos wondered. *Please, no more surprises.* Again, he was thankful that his own role didn't delve into the workings and involvement *during* anyone's Earth-journey. It was so… complicated.

"Joppha is on schedule to return. He'll be arriving shortly."

"What?!" Megalos jumped up abruptly, leaving Serena to grab onto the shaking log so she wouldn't roll off. He scanned for Aivy, who was absent from the meeting. Had she led him astray? *Pipiera has gone there under the premise of somehow preventing Jophiel's early return. This timing must be off! She's going to think she failed. Again.*

James responded with great calm, "Megs, that was always the plan. Don't be alarmed."

Dang, this Kingdom business, Megalos hoped Bethany didn't catch his thoughts.

CHAPTER TWENTY-THREE
SAVING JOPHIEL

At the Bog of Moorelingville

KASARTHA WAS TRUE to his word—this time. They had wasted no time as he and Matthew traveled quickly to where Joppha was imprisoned, tied to a dead cottonwood tree in the center of a bog: a swampy, eerie-looking place. They landed with a thick splash and a roll, head first.

Kasartha roiled in laughter. Matthew was not impressed.

"Why? Why would you bring him *here*?" Matthew was angry. Picking off plant litter and kicking away plastic debris, his heart sank. A forest of decomposing trees kept the sunlight out of the area. "Where is he?" Impatient, he demanded answers from Kasartha, who simply waved an instruction to follow.

They traipsed cautiously toward the center of the forest, stepping over logs, the murky waters getting deeper with each step.

"Why a swamp? Why would you keep a young boy in a swamp?" Matthew was right on Kasartha's tail, eager to get to Joppha.

Kasartha stopped to explain. "Oh, not just any swamp, Matty-boy. It's a tidal swamp. A *lunar* tidal swamp. For a guy who stargazes and—like—talks to the moon all the time, I thought you'd know more. Plus, I like to hang out here, especially at this time of year. It's, kinda, my *vacation spot.*"

Matthew pushed him down, then immediately picked him up by the elbow. "Keep going!"

"Tsk, tsk, you just do not appreciate me," Kasartha retorted, wiping down gobs of wet sludge from his torso.

The swampy waters, although continuing to get deeper, also got thinner, thankfully. Matthew hollered out, "Joppha. *Jo-ppha,*" as he scanned the full circumference. An owl hooted in the distance. Then, just yards away, a series of crows cawed and scattered suddenly. And there he was: young Joppha tied to a dead, black cottonwood tree, securely roped at his chest, water up to his hips, his wrists back and barely reaching around its circumference, his head hanging low.

Without even so much as a gasp, Matthew bolted toward Joppha, tripping on a log. Springing back up again, he dodged forward and landed face down in a thick pile of slimy plant debris. Angry, he continued, scrambling to reach Joppha. He could have reached him had his head not struck a hanging split tree branch. *Joppha!* was all Matthew could recall before a black darkness took his sight completely from him.

CHAPTER TWENTY-FOUR
SAVING MATTHEW

GRODY. WHERE AM I? Matthew's neck and shoulders ached, and his vision blurred. He was wet, soaked to the bone, his head resting on a greasy rock. Someone nearby with a calm, authoritative, yet somehow familiar voice called his name.

"Matthew."

He wiped the sludge away from his face. In a dip, merely a few feet away, a young boy's body was lodged against a tree. Given the awkwardly bent shape, he could tell the boy was tied to the dead trunk at a point below the water's surface. *Tidal swamp*, ran through his head. *Lunar. Joppha.* Matthew closed his eyes again, too weary to think. He felt his own body being lifted, securely, as if in the clasp of a super-large eagle.

Again, he blacked out. Until a siren could be heard in the distance, a siren that grew louder and louder. His vision restored, Matthew was startled to find himself hovering and moving fast above a road he recognized, claws securely hugging his waist.

"Hang on, just about there," Matthew heard.

The claws belonged to that familiar, assuring voice. Another déjà vu moment from years ago…*Jophiel!* Matthew recalled, and Jophiel snickered. He had temporarily escaped his little-boy body to bring Matthew to safety.

"Dude, we gotta stop meeting like this," Jophiel joked without missing a beat, his majestic wings soaring with such great ease.

An ambulance came into sight, it became obvious Jophiel was aiming for it. As they got closer and closer, Matthew recognized the car behind. Laura was driving Betsy with Karo in the passenger seat, and they too were entering the hospital lot. *Since when does she drive so fast?* He waved at them furiously, but neither looked up. Rather, they parked and simply ran in through the large double doors beneath the Emergency sign. Matthew laughed, "Hey, ladies! Uh, I'm up here. Just in case yer all lookin' for me!"

Jophiel laughed, "I can tell you're gonna be just fine, Mr. Matthew. You gotta promise me, though, stop listening to that Kasartha guy. You owe him nothing. Got it? Noth-ing. Zero. Zilch. You have all you need without him. You got a bright future. Besides, I need you to help me out, if you know what I mean."

Dazzled in awe and excitement, Matthew didn't really catch on to Jophiel's words. He even completely forgot where he had just been or even that a serious situation was taking place—Joppha's life was at risk! At the moment, he felt safe and excited, revelling the amazing, supernatural chase. They were about to land atop the ambulance. "Here we come," he screeched with elation. They crashed through the roof with ease and ghostly silence.

Uh, crowded, Matthew thought. How on earth would his friend Jophiel get inside with all these furiously busy, white-suited attendants? Matthew noticed in between them lay a greyish body on the stretcher and recognized it immediately. It was him.

Another déjà vu moment. Flashes of recollection. Jophiel had returned Matthew to his body once before. Matthew was sure of it.

"Oh no! No, I am *not* going back in." Matthew attempted to bolt.

Jophiel caught him by the scruff of his neck. "Yeah, you are, Matty. C'mon, it's not so bad. This time, you only banged your head. You're gonna be fine. Besides, I'm gonna need you…*are you catching my drift?*"

"You need *me?*"

"Yes, I will. No worries. When it's your time, it's your time." Jophiel laughed. "There's no escaping *that* date! But buddy, you have a high calling. And *now* is not *your* time."

Matthew nodded and looked sullenly at his body. "Yeah, yeah, okay." He swallowed hard and squeezed his eyes shut.

"Are you soaking this in?" Jophiel asked doubtfully. Matthew nodded as though he were.

And that was that. Matthew was sucked into his physical self, his open eyes darting back and forth randomly. While he tugged the oxygen mask, he heard his friend Jophiel. "You're gonna be just fine." He closed his eyes again. Shivering, he decided to leave the mask alone. *Okay. I'm gonna be okay.*

Then he swore a voice called out to him from somewhere far away, yet, inside his head. Again, the voice belonged to Jophiel. *"I'm gonna be okay, but Arnie's not. I need you to help him."*

CHAPTER TWENTY-FIVE
DEATH'S DOORSTOP

In the Town of Havensight

MARNIE GRIPPED THE inside passenger door handle tightly with both hands; it made the cab driver incredibly nervous. Feet tapping the floorboards, with gritted teeth, she clenched out a command, thinking she was quiet. "C'mon, c'mon, move it, let's go." She clearly wasn't happy with the slow-moving Mazda in front of them. "Ugh!" She waved both hands in the air. She definitely wasn't happy they had missed the yellow light. Red. They'll have to stop. Waste more time. Precious time, while her son Matthew lay in a hospital bed, out cold.

"Ma'am?" The cabbie knew her name. How could he not? It was a small town filled with small-town folk.

She eyed him carefully, knowing that he'd likely keep their conversation an arm's length away, be all professional and courteous-like, then tell everyone he knew what a crazy woman she was. The look in his eyes said it all.

Her gaze transferred outward toward the town clock. "Do *you* have children?" she asked the cabbie, knowing full well he didn't.

"No, Ma'am."

Then stop judging me, she thought to herself. *Three traffic lights in the whole darn town, and we have to hit each of them. Seriously! Is he doing this on purpose?* She yanked the door open. "I'll walk from here, it'll be faster," then slammed the door shut and marched several steps before halting abruptly. "Oh, shoot!" She realized she hadn't paid him, but by the time she turned around, he waved at her dismissively and drove off.

Marnie scolded herself. Again. Her behavior had been disgusting. She had been working so hard to stay calm and, no matter what, be polite, be assuring to others, be the mother she wanted to be, should be. But today, stress levels were exceedingly high, and her tolerance level was practically non-existent. Tears were gassy and stayed inside. Today was the day when she should let them condense and clamber on out, soak her face really well, but they were far too heavy to move, and so they remained, imprisoned in her chest. Her mother-in-law had died early this morning. A dear friend's young son is missing. And now, her son lay in a hospital bed unconscious. *Yesterday, at this time, I was making afternoon tea and all was well,* she mused. Relishing the 'yesterdays' of life was a habit of Marnie's.

The sky threatened rain for the second time that day. She could see the large H on the medical building behind the tall town center clock and began her stride. Even though she clipped a fast pace, she was certain the cabbie could have had her there by now if only she'd kept patient. A gust of cool air nuzzled into the gap of her neckline; she tightened her sweater. The news last night did warn of a spring storm, she recalled. *Why didn't I remember? I could've brought my coat. I could've brought Matty's coat, too. He'll need it.* The clouds looked like Cool Whip and were rolling in fast. *It's you, God, isn't it? You really don't like me, do you?* She ran across a road to beat some straggling cars and continued on. Hesitantly, she looked up. "Sorry."

It had been several years since she had talked to him—God, that is. She had thanked him over and over and over in the very building she was heading towards right now. Matthew had been unconscious then, too, for other reasons. She nearly lost him. Oh, just the thought of what that would have done to Marnie. And now, her Matty, there, again. Unconscious. "Are you trying to tell me something?" she asked of him—the God in heaven she'd heard so much of. *I'm sorry, I should have called,* she chuckled at the thought; how exactly does one *call?* What should she say, other than place him on alert that she might very well need him again? She nodded upward as if to say *hey, hello, let's start fresh again,* and scooted into the Emergency entrance of Havensight's one and only medical building.

She spotted Karo and felt immediate relief. Karo's eyes danced to a highly energetic tune, as did the hop out of her seat. It had caught the eyes of several slumbering slouchers in the waiting room. She ran straight to Marnie, eager to provide an update.

"Mom, don't worry. He's alright. In fact, he's gonna be discharged soon." Adding a whispered explanation as to her knowledge, "I eavesdropped."

"Whew," Marnie sighed and hugged her daughter.

"He just passed out, likely 'cause he didn't eat much, or you know, with all and everything today…"

Marnie continued to hold Karo close and tight, more for her own comfort than Karo's. Again, she wished she could release a few tears. But no, not yet; they're still blocked. Her daughter's words repeated in her head: *He's alright.* Once the embrace loosened, "Okay, so where is he? Take me to him."

"You got here quick, mom," Karo joked lightly, "considering we had your car. Boy, that Laura. When she wants to get somewhere fast! I didn't know old Betsy had it in her." This was Karo's way of letting her mom know Laura sped all the way over to the hospital. Karo had always enjoyed tattling; it was simply part of who she was.

More relaxed now, Marnie thought about her own anxiousness to arrive as soon as possible, and her frustration with the cabbie for moving too slowly. All she could do was chuckle and let out a casual, "That so?" *Thank heavens Matthew is okay.* That pleasant thought melted inside her. She quickly glanced back toward the glass double doors and the storm brewing outside. A 'thank you' escaped her lips.

Oddly enough, Karo led her mom past the row of curtained-off cubicles and straight toward a staircase, stating it was just one floor up. The look on Marnie's face was enough for Karo to stop halfway up and turn around. Her eyes wide, she leaned toward Marnie, "He was acting like a crazy man, Mom; they *had* to put 'im in his own room."

"I thought you said he was okay."

"Oh, he is," and she jumped up two more steps, loving the shock value of her message. Marnie just shrugged.

In the room, they found a single hospital bed, its back elevated for a sitting position and Matthew upon it, biting his bottom lip.

Hardly a crazy man, Marnie mused. She approached him

but only as far as the end of the bed, where she could soak him all in. She sat, gave his foot a squeeze and released an empathetic smile. Laura was at his side. It was obvious she wasn't going to move, not even for Matthew's mother.

"Heee scared meee!" Even when upset, Laura's words could be put to music, there was so much variation in her tone.

"Yes, he does that. Don't you, son?" Marnie's voice was steady and low. Seeing him for herself, her chest had fallen with relief. It was the best tease she could muster up.

Matthew hadn't returned Marnie's half-smirk with a grin; rather, he pursed his lips.

Karo directed an insistent command her brother's way. "Tell her."

Laura twisted her mouth and grabbed Matty's hand, not comfortable with the tension that was creeping into the room.

"Tell me what?" Marnie inquired curiously.

"You two don't believe me, so why should *she*?" Matthew blustered.

Oh no, not that crazy stuff like when he swore to me years ago that he goes off into the universe with other people when he blacks out. "You're speaking rudely to me," Marnie quietly scolded her son, and braced herself. Now she understood Karo's 'crazy man' remark.

"Matty, what's gotten into you?" Laura squealed.

Marnie smoothed out the thin blanket over his feet and took hold of his ankles. She squeezed them gently and spoke sternly, "Matthew, whatever it is, tell me." But her look was saying she didn't want to hear any of that green goon flying him around nonsense.

Karo stepped a little closer for fear of missing a word.

His bodily movements revealed his agitation. Pulling his legs away from his mother's grip, he sat up even taller, leaning as far back into the headrest as possible. His hospital gown sliding down his shoulder, he quickly grabbed it, then shook out his hair by shaking his head and giving it a scratch.

"Honey, are you alright? What happened? Tell me." *Please, Matty, I'm your mother, for goodness' sake.*

Rigid and serious, he requested one condition. "If I tell you, will you do something about it?"

Marnie caught the glances between Laura and Karo, and decided not to mind the girls. "Of course!" she announced. "Why wouldn't I?"

Matthew flopped back into a relaxed position but remained resigned to what he believed. "You won't. You won't listen to me."

"*I* will." A fresh voice had joined the conversation.

Charles had sauntered into the room proudly. He removed his flat twill cap with his free hand, the other leaning on his cane.

"Granddad!" Karo squealed and ran over, wrapping her arms around his waist with a tight squeeze.

How...? Marnie wondered, feeling bad now for leaving him at home, on his own. "Charles, how did you get here?"

"You think I can't dial a cabbie?"

It was a grumpy response, to which Marnie simply lowered her head. *I should have brought you along as you asked.*

Charles continued, "Give it to me, Matthew. I'll listen. What do you need me to do? I'll do anything." He was serious, though Marnie looked dismayed. Karo, still holding her granddad around his waist, shook her head back and forth. Needing to respond to Marnie's look, Charles explained, "I never listened to Frank. The least I can do is listen to my grandson." Turning to Matthew, "Out with it, boy."

Frank was Charles's son. The two had had a tumultuous relationship, one that never resolved before the day Frank's death took that opportunity away.

Matthew's eyes grew big and wild, encouraged by Charles's commitment. "It was just like a nightmare. But real! I know where Jopphie is, and we need to go and get him. Now! There isn't much time. I'm telling you, it's true. It was real."

His rant was met with three blank stares. None of which belonged to Charles.

"Okay then, grandson, where do I go to get him?"

Marnie frowned but remained silent, still feeling remorse for scolding Charles harshly when he insisted on coming along with her to see Matthew. *I really should have taken his emotional needs into consideration,* she thought. She dared not doubt him now. *Let this play out; it can't be real, anyway,* she convinced herself.

Matthew continued, thankful to have a single person willing to listen, someone who might actually do something. "In the middle of a forest, it was all boggy-like. I don't know where, but I could tell it must be on the coast, but I don't know why. The waters were rising…something to do with the moon. He's all tied up. Joppha's tied to a tree." Matthew's agitation grew fierce. He swung his legs over the side. "Get me outta here, Granddad; we have to go now!"

"Whoa, buddy," Marnie interrupted, "you are not going anywhere. You haven't been released. You've obviously hit your head; you are not ready to go. Not until the doctor says so." *Where is the doctor, anyway?* She wondered. *And what drug did he give to my son? He's acting crazy; not in his right mind!*

Matthew threw his hands in the air. "Told ya, you wouldn't listen," he snapped.

Karo shuffled over and patted her brother's shoulder. He immediately pushed her hands away.

"I need to find the doctor," Marnie announced dryly, then left the room. Her son is hallucinating; her father-in-law wants to play along; she has yet to get an outfit to the funeral home for her mother-in-law. *This can't be happening.*

Tapping her fingers on the counter's edge at the nurses' station, she could hear over the loudspeaker that the head nurse had paged Dr. Bonneville as she had requested. Marnie stared at the patient board. Seeing her son's surname posted brought reality to the moment. The sounds of regular beeping, phones ringing continuously, low voices in various discussions and the movement of white rubber soles moving back and forth behind her all lulled her into a series of yesterdays. Matthew on death's doorstep, and before that, Frank slipping through its doorway. Even though Dr. Bonneville had allowed Maggie to die at home, giving Marnie specific instructions on tiny prescription notepaper—as though tending to one dying was akin to ordering up some Tylenol—he was the last person she wanted to see. His presence alone brought back emotions and memories she wanted to forget. Death, death and near-death. But she needed him now. Again. What was wrong with her son? What will he say about all this nightmare nonsense? *I wonder where Dr. Alexien is these days. It sure would be nice to have her here with me now, and with Matthew too.* Dr. Alexien had been one of the attending physicians when Matthew nearly lost his life. She seemed to have come from nowhere and was such a comfort to Marnie, even counseled her a bit.

Marnie cupped her mouth and squeezed her chin. When she saw Charles heading toward the elevator, she ran after him.

"Charles!" she called. He had just pressed the elevator button. *Phew, got you.* "Now, Dad," as she often called him, "just where are you going? I can take you home with me. I just need to talk to the doctor…"

The elevator door opened. He secured his flat twill cap into place and stepped in.

The head nurse called to tell Marnie that Dr. Bonneville was available to see her now.

"I have to talk to the doctor. Wait. Wait in the lobby. I'll get you home safely. Together, we'll get everything ready for Maggie."

"You still don't think I can call a cabbie on my own?" He was calm, but the words were insulting.

"Dad, c'mon." The elevator door started to shut.

"I have something to do for my grandson." The doors shut.

What? Wait, where are you going? Marnie pressed the elevator button, but the carriage had already left.

"Mrs. Mackenzie," she was being called by an impatient nurse.

Argh, it's Mrs. Decker. Marnie had to make a split decision. She ran to Matthew's room and instructed Karo to take the stairs, get to the lobby quickly and find Granddad. "The two of you wait for me!" Then she hurried to the nurse's station to receive a report from Dr. Bonneville.

CHAPTER TWENTY-SIX
THE JAILED AND THE FREE

PIPIERA REGRETTED HER previous thought that her bedroom in Mrs. Damien's house was bleak, that it had felt like a prison cell of some sort. Because now she was sitting inside a real one. A county jail cell, some twenty minutes outside of town.

"*That* was luxury," she mumbled.

"You sayin' somethin' now?" A guard in the middle of the pod with three holding cells surrounding it sat at a table bolted to the floor, scribbling notes. He barely acknowledged her, despite his question.

"No. No," Pipiera responded from the smallest of the cells. *You know I could float to the ceiling, and you would totally freak out!* The inner temptation was strong, but she knew it wasn't a good option, one that was most definitely against the rules. But, oh, she chuckled at simply toying with the notion.

She had been handled roughly. She couldn't answer all the questions an interrogator threw at her. Who exactly was she? Why didn't she carry anything with her, anything at all?

No money, no identification, no keys, not even a comb? For all these questions she couldn't answer, she hung her head. *I skipped through all that stuff, I didn't think it was important.* She blamed herself for not being prepared. Alexien had warned her of such risks, of unpredictable situations, some might even feel like attacks. *Others will make absolutely no sense to you,* she had added. Pipiera had thought she was simply overanalyzing everything.

At least she was alone now—just one distracted guard and her, no one in the other two cells. A bolted-to-the-ceiling television blared. She had refused anything to eat or drink, even though she was so terribly hungry and thirsty. There was no way Pipiera wanted to use the toilet in her cell. It most certainly wasn't private. *If I take nothing in, nothing shall come out,* she concluded. She washed her face and hands and sat on the single hard bench, alternating between staring at the guard and the floor, no longer admiring the new, fancy, platform shoes given to her especially for this mission. They were fashionable, Serena had encouraged, but they have only gotten her into so much trouble. *Who'da thought dried mud was a crime here?*

Her face still wet, she wiped the moisture away. Some of it sweat, some of it tears.

Tears.

The last time she felt so trapped, there were tears. Recalling that time, her back straightened and hope enlightened. The ground underneath had shown her things then. *Careful,* she thought, reminding herself that here, in this place on Earth, she needed to guard her thoughts. They could imprison her far more than this jail cell ever could. She reminded herself that she was already free. She looked upward. "In due course, I'll be released from this *physical* prison. I know it. Thank you."

"You say somethin' again?" The guard asked, this time his face firmly fixed on hers.

"Uh, no, I was just thinking about stuff."

To her response, he let out a simple gruff and got back to his pages.

"What are you writing? I mean, surely, that can't be a report. At least not a report on me. There's not that much to write about." She snuck a laugh at the end.

He scratched the back of his head. "Nah, not a report. Just watch the tele. Keep yer mind busy on that."

"A poem? Are you writing a poem?"

The guard rolled his eyes and continued to ignore her.

"A song. That's it. There are never enough great songs. You are writing a song!"

This time a grin transformed his face. "Nah, not a song. Can't sing worth beans."

"Not anyone has *all* the talents. Not all songwriters can sing. And not all singers can write songs. You must know *that*."

Putting his pen down, he turned to face her. "My wife can sing. Like a bird. If I could write a song, it would be for her."

For a moment, Pipiera had connected with the man. They were actually exchanging smiles, though suddenly, he turned back and hunched toward his pages, clasping his pen. "It's *not* a song," he said.

Pipiera resigned herself to the bench and leaned against the concrete wall. The red second hand on the industrial wall clock with bold black numbers ticked like it was on a mission. A long, steady haul of a mission. *How long will I be here? What's next?* The notion of time transported her thoughts back to Jophiel, to the day she met him. He had told her that Earth-journeyers were obsessed with the concept of time. Instead of markers, they think measurements. Years, months, days, right down to minutes and seconds. She wondered what she was meant to accomplish in this phase, this time of being rejected, accused and imprisoned. *What if my being here right now is for a good purpose?* When she noticed the guard wiping his eyes, she decided perhaps it was.

"What's wrong? You okay?" She stepped up and wrapped her hands, one bar in each. He was clearly distraught about something. His wet, red eyes conveyed his dread, and his chest heaved with sobs. Pipiera wished she could get out of that cell simply to hold his hand so he could know she was present with him, as a comfort. He could trust her, she wouldn't run; rather, she would do what she could to feel his pain, lighten it, even, carry some of his burden. Whatever the reason for his tears, it clearly broke this man's heart.

Ignoring her offer of empathy, he sniffled, stood up and left the room, leaving Pipiera to feel somewhat useless on top of alone and struggling to not feel trapped. Discouraged, she returned to her bench, this time lying down, face toward the wall. She let her fingers trek along the edges of the glossy-painted, rectangular blocks. She shivered. A blanket would be nice. Now there's no one to even ask for one.

The guard slipped back into the center of the pod without her noticing until another one of his big wet sniffles gave him away. "My wife says journaling will help."

Pipiera looked over her shoulder toward him. He was talking directly to her this time.

"But it don't," he added.

She sat up and quietly spoke. "I'm listening."

He sniffled again. "Nothin' helps, nothin's gonna change."

"What's so important that you need to change it?" she asked sincerely.

He eyed her suspiciously. "You don't have kids, do ya? 'course you don't, you're too young." He shook his head and wiped his nose. She thought for sure he would clam up now, that he'd believe she couldn't possibly understand what he needed to release.

"You are right, I don't have any offspring. But, I know love. And I know heartache and I know…"

"Do ya know loss?" he interrupted abruptly, then returned to his seat. Threw his pen on the floor and wiped all his papers off the metal table.

Kids. Loss. I bet this man's child finished their Earth-journey before he could finish his. Like Matthew's nearly finished early a few short years ago. Like the possibility that Joppha could be forced to finish his early. Like I had to leave my earthly parents ever so early. Her thoughts trailed off, moving to the irony of the situation. He was the one imprisoned, burdened with heavy chains that kept his spirit low. She was free.

"I'm so sorry." Her words were so sincere, they seemed to have stabbed him, slow and gentle-like.

He nodded before curling into himself. Several moments of agonizing silence fell between them.

She had hit the nail on the head. *I must help him up, get him out of the mud pit; he's so stuck.* She wondered, though, was she breaking more rules or was he the reason she had been placed in this cell? *Let's go with 'no' and 'yes,'* she decided.

"You know, this time of life, this phase you are in, is an opportunity," she said cheerfully.

It took less than an instant for his face to redden. "An opportunity?!" he spat out.

Dial it back, she instructed herself. She let another moment of silence go by, waiting for the redness in his face to melt away. "What was his name?" she quietly asked.

"Marcus. How'd you know it was a boy? You gonna tell me you have some kind of superpowers now?"

Now he was being sarcastic. Though he remained where he was, seemingly interested in being emotionally connected to her. *He wants to talk about it.*

"It was just a hunch." And it truly was. Without thinking about it, Pipiera simply assumed it was a male child, and her assumption was right. *I wonder if I've met him, saw him arrive, even?* "Will you tell me about him?"

The man pulled his chair right close to her prison bars. Pipiera sat cross-legged on the other side. She wanted to ask for a blanket to sit on but now was not the time. This man, now inches away from her, was going to tell her a story. She would have to find comfort on the cold cement floor.

He talked for thirty minutes, stopping only to take deep breaths and wipe his face on the sleeve of his guard uniform. Pipiera had learned so much about Marcus: what fun they had on his last birthday, the playful battle over his name at birth, how he loved being called by his soccer coach to play goalie, the stitches on his knee when as a little fella he tripped and fell on a stone, how he and his dad played foot hockey under the supper table without his mama knowing. Pipiera had learned much, but nothing about how he passed.

The man grew silent, and his face turned into a greyish tone. He gulped and stood, then moved himself and his chair back to his metal table and picked up the pages strewn across the floor, along with the pen.

Pipiera was thankful for the break in conversation so she

could stand and shake the coldness out of her legs. They had grown stiff.

"Whattaya mean, *opportunity*?" He asked, obviously referring to her earlier comment. Pipiera didn't have a chance to respond. The front door to the office bolted open and, back in guard-form, he headed out of the cell pod to see who was entering.

He must be the only one working this place right now, she thought. Was this her chance to escape? She looked around. *No, can't see how to do that. But it'll happen. I just know it. I'll be out of here soon. I hope so, anyway.*

She could hear another man's voice jabbering away. *What, is that Charles?* It wasn't hard to listen in: the man's voice was rising steadily. "Oh my gosh, it *is* him, and he's demanding to see *his daughter*." Pipiera paced, realizing her error. "Oh, why did I ignore that rule?" she mumbled to herself. *I shouldn't have let Charles know my true identity. It was supposed to be our secret.*

Discouraged by her own loose tongue, she sat upon the bench and thought hard. She can't have Charles running around town claiming she was his daughter. But she sighed in joy, *even though I am.* When Charles came blustering into the pod and straight to her cell, she jumped up and felt her heart gladden with hope and thankfulness. She wrapped her hands around his, which were clenched against the bars. He loosened her grip so he could be the one grasping his hands around hers. Pipiera couldn't help it: her smile was ear to ear. "Thank you, *Dad*," she whispered.

"Now, Charles," the guard started, "I've known you my whole life. You ain't got a daughter." He paused and watched the two of them grin. "Do ya?"

"Before you were born," Charles responded without taking his face off Pipiera's. "You don't know her. She's special. Like an angel."

"Where's she from? Not around here. I know *that* much."

"She's not from here," Charles said.

Pipiera breathed relief. She might just get out of this okay.

"Let her out, Bruce!" Charles demanded.

Okay, so his name is Bruce. Huh, I didn't even ask him his name. Ugh, why is that a habit with me?

"We've got a boy to save." Charles was on a mission and didn't mince words. "Let her out."

"They kinda suspect she's got somethin' to do with that Decker boy missing. I can't just free her. You need to give me a reason."

"Ain't nobody asked *me* where she was. She's got an alibi. She was with me and my Maggie the whole time." Charles didn't flinch.

Removing his cap and pressing it to his chest, Bruce expressed his condolences. Then inquired, "You willin' to sign somethin' to say that?"

"Yes. Just get her outta here." Charles turned to steady a look in Bruce's eye. "Or another boy is gonna go. You and I both know what that does to a father."

Bruce reached in his left pocket for a set of keys and opened up Pipiera's cell. "I need ya to sign somethin' before you all go."

"No time, Bruce!" Charles grabbed Pipiera. It was amazing how fast he could move even with that limp and cane of his. "I'll sign whatever you want once we save that boy!"

Pipiera loosened herself from Charles and gently approached Bruce, touching his elbow. "No matter what, keep your faith," she implored. "No—matter—what. That's what counts. Promise you'll do that."

A honk in the parking lot stole Bruce's attention away. A cabbie had obviously been told to wait after dropping Charles off.

"Wait just a minute!" Bruce hollered after Charles. He reached into his other pants pocket and pulled out another set of keys. "I'll drive!"

Pipiera followed the two men to Bruce's police cruiser and jumped into the back seat. This time, not a prisoner. Rather, she was now part of the pair's rescue team on an earthly mission to save her Jophiel.

My King, you never cease to amaze me, she laughed.

CHAPTER TWENTY-SEVEN

NEED PROTECTION

CHARLES CONTINUED TO insist that Pipiera call him 'Dad.' She hesitated but admitted that it felt good. Really good. But what a guilty pleasure that was. By now, she had broken several rules. Revealing her identity and establishing a relationship to her earthly parents, well, Pipiera expected any moment she could be suddenly called home, back to her Kingdom. Reprimanded, even. She was no longer an influencer; no, she was now messing with the lives and events of people she loved. It was to be their journey, their events, their joys, and sufferings. Not hers. Sheepishly, she looked at Charles in the front seat of the car. He had turned fully and was steadily focused on her. "Okay. *Dad*," she smiled, agreeing to his request.

Bruce looked in his rearview mirror. "You two have a strange relationship," he commented.

Pipiera admired the peace that washed over Charles's face following Bruce's observation. He didn't even fuss too much when he finally churned his worn body back around to face forward in the front passenger seat and fastened his seat belt. Like ten—maybe even twenty—years had suddenly lifted from him.

She relished the moment, knowing there was much to discuss and no time to waste. The three of them were going to save the little boy Joppha version of her dear friend Jophiel — wherever he was. But for now, *this is what I missed. Thank you, King, this is precious,* she professed silently. Then added, *I pray it remains your desire that Joppha continue in his journey.*

"So. Just where are we going?" Bruce idled the cruiser as it faced the road, one foot on the brake. "Right or left?" he asked.

Time for business. Pipiera propped herself forward, "Tell me, Charles—er, *Dad,*" she blushed. "What exactly did Matthew say?"

Bruce eyed her, then Charles. The look on his face was saying he was suspicious of this so-called father-daughter relationship. Pipiera and Charles would have to ignore his suspicions, for now at least.

Charles wanted to use the exact phrases he had overheard. "Swamp, murky waters, dying trees, roped to a trunk. Swamp, did I already say that? In the middle of it, right smack in the middle of the swamp, he said. He was pretty freaked out by it, even said something about plastic garbage floatin' around and baby liz— no, alligator lizards. Swore he saw some."

Bruce interrupted to add in his advanced police knowledge, "Well, a boy with that kid's description has been spotted at the Moorelingville depot, you know that, right?" Then he rubbed his chin before stretching out both arms to grab the steering wheel. Applying a heavy foot and a right-turn squeal out of the county's law enforcement parking lot, they left it and its building completely abandoned.

"I take it you know where that is?" Charles spoke, slightly alarmed, "The swamp, I mean. Not Moorelingville. Even I know where Moorelingville is. On the coast, a good seven-hour drive from here, at least. And that's if we go direct, fast-like and no stopping."

Bruce Brogan took charge. The next few minutes left Pipiera and Charles both wondering what else Bruce knew. It had to be something; how else would he suddenly know where to go? They pulled into the short driveway of a modest bungalow on a quiet cul-de-sac. Bruce jumped out of the car and into the house.

"Think he lives here?" Pipiera asked.

"Likely. He knows something we don't."

"Look, Dad, you okay? I mean, it was just this morning that Maggie—Mom—transitioned."

Charles kept his stare on the door that seemed to have swallowed Bruce, saying nothing.

The patrol car's radio transmitted an all-officer alert, the facts all bulleted and very clear: "The Decker boy last seen at Moorelingville Bus Depot at one fifteen this morning, two possible eyewitnesses. One suspect at large. Description update: white male, approximately six foot, possibly taller, thin, dressed in suit and tie, wearing a quote, *droopy hat*, unquote, purple…"

Pipiera gasped! *Floppy purple hat, my gosh, Kasartha!* That hat was his signature. A longtime rebel to the Kingdom who she had faced before.

Charles looked at her sternly. "Don't tell me you know this bloke." She quietly nodded with both hands clasped to her mouth. "Better not tell Bruce you know him. He'll think you're in on it and lock you back up." She shook her head, agreeing to this.

The radio transmission continued, "The second suspect is in custody, a young woman known to the Mackenzie family. It is believed the two were working together. The Moorelingville enforcement team is on alert."

"Well, they don't know you broke free." Charles chuckled sarcastically, eyes gleaming. "Still ahead of them, we are!"

How could they keep Bruce from listening to radio calls, especially like that one? "We need Bruce on our side, Dad. The side that doesn't think I'm some kind of child thief."

Just then, the front door opened and out waddled Bruce, his arms packed to the brim with supplies and things. He could barely see for the load he was carrying.

"What's all that stuff?" Pipiera wondered aloud.

"Looks like camping equipment," Charles responded, attempting to inspect Bruce's load from where he sat.

Still holding on to the armful, Bruce opened his single-car garage door and, with his head, motioned for the other two to join him. Revealed inside the garage was a black Camaro with extra-wide tires. Bruce opened the trunk and dumped his load inside it.

"Oh, what a break. Looks like we're switching vehicles. We won't have to worry about the radio calls. Talk about lucky!" Charles glanced at Pipiera and queried her, "You arranged this, didn't you?" Pipiera denied having any such capabilities.

"If we need to get to the coast fast, we'll need this car," Bruce's eyes glistened with adventure. "This here car belonged to my Marcus. No one's touched it since…well, you know. But today's the day. We're going to save a boy, and we're going to use my son's car. He's coming with," Bruce announced with pride.

Pipiera knew little about which cars were fast, but she had a feeling she was about to learn; those tires looked like they would certainly make a difference. But first, she needed to give Bruce a hug. To think that he would unlock the jail cell, then suggest he take the lead by driving them, and now, use his son's car for this mission to save Jophiel because it'd be faster. To top it all off, he had honored the task at hand by deeming it *good*. Good enough to do in honor of Marcus.

"Ah, c'mon," Bruce said as she wrapped her arms around his waist. He wiped his eyes and insisted they check out the load squished and piled into the tiny trunk. "Ya see here, if we're going through the bog, we're gonna need some of this stuff." There were two sets of rubber boots, a couple of large rolled-up ponchos, headlamps, a hunter's knife, waterproof gloves, two walking sticks, a full package of J Cloths, binoculars, a set of walkie-talkies, a container of zinc cream, some serious bug spray and a box of Doo-Dads snack mix. "Me and my boy used to camp round there, the Marshlands of Moorelingville. 'cept we never went through the bog, especially not this time of year; too wet. The locals say it's the June moon that brings the tide in from the ocean, and along with it, all kinds of strange things. They say it's haunted. But I don't believe in that stuff. Still, some pretty weird things folks claim happen…every spring." Bruce had exchanged his law enforcement uniform for something more forest-themed. Looking to impress, he pushed aside the fishing vest to reveal a pistol tucked into and mostly concealed by a holster.

Ooooo boy, violence is not what I thought this would be about. Alarmed, Pipiera reached for Charles's hand, though he managed to clutch hers inside his own first. She wanted to melt. *How comforting.* What a special thing to have missed on an Earth tour, a reassuring hand squeeze. If this scenario hadn't presented itself, she never would have known its power. A gentle compression, so capable of removing a level of stress and replacing it with a warm, inner stabilizing feeling.

"Don't worry, little girl, this is for protection. Nothin' else. We have to be prepared for anything if you and I are marching into the midst of that bog."

Now, I'm a little girl? Hmmpf.

"What do you mean, you and her?" Charles seemed betrayed.

Bruce nodded toward Charles's cane. "Can't go in there like that, buddy. We'll leave you a walkie-talkie and you can be our watch. Just me and her are going in."

Charles chucked his cane into the bushes. "We'll see about that," he muttered and stomped, quite capably, to take his spot in Bruce's son's car.

Incredibly thankful Jophiel had been spotted and thankful for this apparent speedy transportation, Pipiera could only hope that maybe some kind of miraculous Plan B would emerge during the long trip ahead of them. Every minute will feel like an eternity. Before Bruce could shut the trunk, she snatched the Doo-Dads. Then she swiftly nabbed the discarded cane, squeezed into the back seat of the souped-up Z28 and breathed deeply. Her thoughts churned to the big issue: *Kasartha, he's behind this. Your pistol, dear Bruce, won't protect anyone.*

CHAPTER TWENTY-EIGHT

THE BELIEVING ENDS HERE

On Route, Havensight to Moorelingville

AT LAST, THE threesome pulled into a gas station to fill up and take a break. As soon as Bruce had entered the cashier booth, safely out of earshot, Pipiera leaned forward. "Dad, this Kasartha—the bloke as you call him, the one with the droopy purple hat—he's *like* me."

Charles looked concerned. "What in the dickens does that mean?"

"Like meee, only, the *other* side."

Her hinting hadn't cleared it up, according to the look on Charles's face.

"A rebel. You get it? The *other* side."

Charles looked horrified. "So, it's true? Two opposing forces? Huh, *no*." He rejected the very idea.

"Huh, *yes*." She wondered how she could get him to understand. *How can he possibly believe I am here right now, yet not believe there's…another kind of world out there?*

"Where exactly do you think I've come from, Dad? Where do you think I've been all these years?" Her questions were met with silence.

"Okay, then, believe this. Bruce's pistol is not going to help. You have to find a way to hold him back, don't let him enter that bog. I must go in alone! I know Kasartha; he's attacked…" She dropped off, believing she had said enough. Charles needn't know any more than what was necessary. He wouldn't believe her, anyway.

Charles sat up tall, a look of pride washing over his face: a sense of purpose for something greater than himself. He seemed resolute about a plan of his own, but Pipiera couldn't tell what that might entail. Had he promised Matthew something?

Bruce returned with three cellophane-wrapped egg salad sandwiches, three bags of chips and three bottles of Coca-Cola. "Everybody ready? Let's keep boogying!" he said. And off they went, skidding back onto the highway, tires screeching and Bruce releasing a "Hoo-ah!"

Pipiera silently called out to Jophiel. *Hang on, my dear friend, here we come.*

CHAPTER TWENTY-NINE
OL' FAITHFUL

In the Town of Havensight

MATTHEW COULDN'T REMEMBER everything. So much was still so vague, yet so much was crystal-clear. Joppha's life was in danger, and Matthew had been just feet away from rescuing him. Then he blacked out. *Did I fall? Is that what happened? How did I end up here—back in Havensight. Did I ever even leave?*

The chaos in his room at the hospital had stopped. Granddad, the only one who believed him, had left without him, but not before Matthew could whisper some instructions and share all the details. His mother, now frantic for whatever reason, was scurrying about and sent Karo on some mission. It was just Laura and him. She pulled up a chair closer to his bedside and sat down. He was pretty sure she must think he was crazy.

"I'm not making this up. I know where he is." Matthew wiped his wet nose with the back of his hand and breathed out a long stretch of wind. He could feel his heart pumping wildly. Agitated, he scratched behind his ears and down his neck. "I gotta get out of here." He was sure of that.

"Matty, relax. It's been a super-crazy day. Besides, if you don't chill out, I bet they'll stop your discharge. We'll get out of here, and we'll go home to your place. We'll figure all this out. You and me."

He snuffled and looked her way, "Laur, I really thought of all people, you'd believe me." He felt bad for the anger the tone of his voice must have conveyed, but this was no time for pleasantries. He could tell by the look on her face that he had stunned her. "I am not going home. I need to get back there. To Joppha."

She stood up and walked in circles in the small space beside his bed. "Okay, okay. So, what if I believe you? Let's say that nightmare you had after you passed out and hit your head—good and hard I might add—is, in fact, true. What's next, Matty? Just how exactly do we get him? What's your plan?"

So now you're challenging me? He looked the other way, preferring the flat stare of the brick wall. He felt a harsh squeeze on his toes. "Stop already!" He assumed it was Laura's attempt to shake him out of his stupid mood. *Well, it's not going to work.*

"Excuse me?" She responded with the same agitation he had just dished out.

Another voice chimed in, "Yeah, ex-*scuuu-uuuu*-se me." It was Kasartha. Sitting upon Matthew's bed, he had been the one applying pressure to Matthew's foot.

"What are you doing here?" Matthew quipped at Kasartha.

But it was Laura who responded. "Seriously?"

"Seriously?" Kasartha mocked with his annoying, cheerful voice. "Oh Matty, oh Matty, let's go h-o-me," he sang, this time imitating Laura. Kasartha rubbed Matthew's ankles as if it were some act of caring, then added, "Actually, bud, I think you need to come with me. We'll get back there—I promise. Together, you and I, we'll untie him, we'll let him go."

Matthew instinctively knew Laura couldn't see the green goon with the floppy purple hat on his bed. Regardless, his top priority was to get rid of him. *Then, after, I'll explain all this to her. Later, when all has calmed down,* he figured.

"Get lost!" Matthew instructed Kasartha, "I'm not going with you."

Laura stood up, tightened the wrap-around of her sweater, grabbed the purse she borrowed from her mom and moved briskly toward the door. As she paused for a last look, Matthew grabbed the moment to explain.

"I'm not talking to you," he said, realizing immediately that was not a good way to start the explanation. In fact, she took it the wrong way. For Laura, it was the end; she turned away and walked out.

"Look what you did!" Matthew blurted to Kasartha.

"Uh, not me, bud; she was just listening to you. Isn't that what you wanted? For her to listen to you? Looks like you got what you wanted if you ask me."

"I'm not asking you."

"Yeah, you are. C'mon, go ahead, ask me. Ask me to take you back. You want it. I know it. For the sake of goodness, how can you not? You don't want me to free your little buddy now?"

Since awakening, the only thing in Matthew's brain had been that image. Poor young Joppha tied to a trunk in a swamp, murky waters up to his chest, surrounded by eerie-looking trees with nothing but the sounds of crickets and crows and quick, slithering stirrings on the water's surface. He needed to get back there.

Matthew had an idea. He got out of bed as fast as he could, then pulled on his jeans and pullover.

"What gives?" Kasartha asked.

As he tied up his runners, Matthew instructed, "Together, we are going back there to get Joppha. But on my terms, *my* way. Not *yours!*"

"What, like we're taking your old Betsy of an auto? That's how we're doing this? It's, like, hours and hours to get there. Much quicker if it's my way, bud."

Matthew's thoughts swirled some more. *Direct, it's a six- or seven-hour drive, or maybe more. On a bus, that could be double that, at least. That means I was right. Joppha did get on that bus to the coast. He outsmarted all those security guys, and all of us! Did he plan this? Nah! No way. But where's that bog, exactly? How will I find it? Am I too late? But, I simply cannot do this Kasartha's way.*

"No. No more your way. My way. Come or don't." Matthew dared the threat, not convinced, himself, that it was a smart move. What Matthew knew for sure was that he didn't want to be under Kasartha's control and wanted no more blacking out. He was done with that, as long as he could help it. He wanted to rescue Joppha, but on his terms, not Kasartha's. Jophiel had warned him to stop listening to him, had he not? Matthew's brain contracted, confused as so many random recollections came to mind, none making sense, yet all calling for urgent action.

Leading the way out of the hospital room and followed

by his invisible visitor, Matthew dashed quickly to the Emergency Room lobby and looked around. No Mom nor Karo nor Granddad and, sadly, no Laura. *They all just left me, he thought. Perhaps I'm a bit crusty right now. Suppose I deserve it. It's better none of them are here, anyway. No time for distractions.* Kasartha was his only companion right now. "C'mon, my car's outside." Without his discharge papers or stopping to settle accounts, the two walked briskly over to Betsy. *Well, at least you're faithful.* It was a sarcastic thought, particularly as all Matthew had dreamed about recently was saving enough funds for a new automobile. Betsy needed to be retired.

But Kasartha stopped short of entering the car. "You go ahead, go to that gas station north of town. I'll meet you there. Need to do somethin' first."

Matthew eyed Kasartha and demanded, "Oh, no. You are coming with me. You know where Joppha is, and you are leading me straight to him."

"Yeah, but if we're gonna do this *your* way, the sloooow way, you're gonna need fuel. Right? I promise I'll meet you there."

Matthew hesitated. It would be tough, possibly even impossible, to find Joppha without the guy, but how could he make Kasartha stick around? It was a moot thought. Kasartha exited abruptly. Disappeared. Into thin air.

"Bogus!" Matthew yanked on the driver's door handle and gave Betsy a good kick. *Like I've got a choice.* He'd head to the gas station north of town. "You'd better be there," he mumbled through gritted teeth.

CHAPTER THIRTY
MEANWHILE...

TOO LATE. MARNIE returned to the nurse's station in good time, but Dr. Bonneville was already engaged in a deep conversation with a young couple. Marnie believed they had been visiting an elderly man in a room just down the hall from Matty's. She could tell the couple had the doctor locked into a conversation that could last a while. She couldn't risk missing him, so she found a post to lean against, out of the way of bustling nurses, patients and their visitors, and did her best to make sure others knew she was next in line for his attention.

The long hand on her watch ticked off one second at a time. She tapped it as though that would make the wait shorter. She wondered if Karo had caught Charles. *What a guy,* she thought and shook her head in slight amusement. Then a twang of sadness caught in her throat. *Maggie.* Marnie had grown so very fond of Frank's mother. And she loved how Charles simply adored his wife. A sadness fell over her, another moment when she missed Frank so very much, and she imagined how nice it would have been if he were here with her now, going through all these dilemmas together. She glanced at the twosome stealing the doctor's attention and thought how lucky they were to have each other.

A nurse pulled Dr. Bonneville away from the couple ever so gently to steer him toward another waiting visitor, a man. *Wait! I'm next!* Marnie stomped over to stand directly behind Dr. Bonneville. No one could butt in front of her this way! Dr. Bonneville seemed annoyed that Marnie had moved so close to him; perhaps he was concerned about the privacy of his conversation with this other fellow. Marnie didn't care. She had been waiting longer than the man he was chatting with now.

What if Karo didn't reach Charles in time? A terrible thought. *Might he be back at home now? I shouldn't have left him alone. Especially not today, of all days.* In a close-up view was the back of Dr. Bonneville's large round head, a single strand of hair bouncing up and down as he kept on chatting. *What do I really want from him?* Marnie challenged herself. *I want him to release my Matty and give me whatever instructions are needed, and then we can all get home. Quick. And all will be well—sort of—we go from there.*

He kept on chatting. She muffled a mischievous snicker. *Oh, the temptation to pull a precious hair out of his smelly head.*

At last, he turned around, not appearing too pleased to see her. "Mrs. Mackenzie, what can I do for you? Oh wait, it's Mrs. Decker now, isn't it? You just can't stay away, can you?" He crossed his arms over his super-exaggerated chest.

Marnie sensed the sarcasm in his voice. *I don't like you, either,* she admitted to herself.

"Just like your son," he added, presumably as a joke.

But that was no joke. Not that many years ago, Matthew had endured considerable trauma and had been in the care of Dr. Bonneville. On two occasions, Dr. Bonneville had actually given up, even declared Matthew deceased—prematurely, obviously.

The inconsiderate comments angered Marnie. "How can you joke about something like that? You just don't like me because I've been married twice," she spewed.

Dr. Bonneville opened his arms, surrendered his hands, and shrugged his shoulders. "And yet, you are here. Alone."

He irked her! Marnie hauled off and slapped the doctor across his face, attempting to rid him of that snarly and grotesque grin. "Discharge my son so we can get out of here, so *you* are out of our lives." Marnie had not expected this conversation nor this level of tension and release of anger. Her insides shook, and she wanted to cry. So many bystanders stood perfectly still around them, gawking with mouths open.

"Well," Dr. Bonneville cleared his throat, "Mrs. Decker, I have nothing further to say to you. Your son is an adult. He is the one I converse with. Should you require an update, speak directly to him." It just took one steely, hardnosed glance around for him to scatter the crowd of witnesses. Marnie stood alone. Very alone. Had she really just dismissed the only emergency doctor in Havensight, demanding he get out of their lives?

After finding a public restroom to wash her face and pull her emotions together, she shambled back to Matty's room. It surprised her to find it empty. A nurse had already stripped the bed of its sheets. Just as she thought she must have the wrong room, a glint of light caught something shiny on the floor underneath the chair where his jeans and shirt had lain.

A closer glance. It was a ring. A small, delicate, diamond ring. Karo had told her Matty had bought a ring for Laura. Could this be it? She held it in her hand. Was she losing him? It felt too soon for this. She wondered about her own purpose in life. Obviously, being a mother—well, that job seems to be cut in half now, now that Matty's a so-called *adult*. And Karo, she spends more time at Arnie's than at home with her. And with Maggie gone now, it's just Charles. *Oh, boy, Charles, where are you?* Marnie moved quickly toward the stairs. With any luck, Charles and Karo would be in the lobby waiting for her, just as she had instructed. And with even more luck, Matthew and Laura would be there, too. Then they could all go home together. She still had a family, didn't she?

On the way to the stairwell, another nurse called out after Marnie, "Mrs. Decker?"

Marnie turned and responded with a calm and mature, "Yes?"

"Here," the nurse gave her a crisp, white business card. "This doctor from out of town dropped it off. She gave specific instructions to give it to you directly. She's here today for some meeting and wants to connect with you."

Marnie nodded again and took possession of the card. She could hardly believe her luck. The gold lettering read DOCTOR ALEXIEN, along with a local telephone number. *What a coincidence!* Marnie gasped with a grain of much-needed relief.

CHAPTER THIRTY-ONE

THE SKY IS FALLING

KASARTHA SAT ON a large boulder strategically placed to beautify the entrance, his feet kicking back and forth against the brass lettering that spelled out HAVENSIGHT MEDICAL CENTER. No one passing through the swishing doors stopped to give him even so much as a glance. And why would they? He remained unseen. Covert, deceptive, and disguised as nothing, but mostly feeling sorry for himself. Invisible to even Matthew now.

Kasartha watched Matthew back Betsy out of the parking spot. She spurted angrily as he steered her toward the main road. A lightning pang of remorse and loneliness struck inside Kasartha's chest. He rested his head in both hands until a series of sharp and angry barks interrupted his self-pity. He waved a large, lean dog away, employing a hideous snarl and a minacious fist. It took both owners of the menacing pooch to soothe and quiet it down, providing assurances it was barking at nothing but air. Kasartha mocked the scene. *If only they could see me, they're the ones who'd need to be stroked.* Imagining the thought made him snicker.

He hated how emotions still held such power and wished things could have been different. But they cannot. And Matthew was central to this cause.

Some three hundred years earlier, Kasartha had walked the Earth. A cruel man he was. *It wasn't all my fault,* he encouraged himself. His own life had been full of violent attacks. He had grown up with it, learned to love the hard, darkened world. In fact, he was responsible for taking the life of his own son, a vulnerable boy of thirteen. Cold-blooded. An angry killing. And as if that weren't bad enough, he didn't regret it. He had moved on. Another town, a new wife, and another child—all ways to prove that the last words from his dead boy's lips, a curse, could never come true. "You and all your kin, I curse them *all.*" Those words haunted Kasartha even to this day, recalling his own promise in return, "I'm gonna make sure you don't have any kin."

Kasartha shook his head to clear it. He couldn't describe the mysteries beyond his own earthly death, only that now, in this existence, his loyalty was dedicated to Uncle. He had made that commitment long ago. *Like it or not, here I am.* He wasn't even sure when, exactly, he had made that choice, only that his conviction was recorded. His soul-stone handed in. No getting it back.

At first, Kasartha showed great promise to do Uncle's work. It was simple, Kasartha had thought, charged with the task of collecting his own descendants for Uncle. How hard could that be? Hanging around obsessively while they carried out their Earth-journeys, attacking with seedlings of emotions that would eventually lead them so far astray that they wouldn't be able to find their way back, lest they needed *his* help?

Uncle was growing weary of Kasartha, no longer hopeful of what, or who, he was capable of delivering. *He doesn't believe I can do it. What's worse, I fear he doesn't believe I want to do it.* Kasartha scratched his forehead and wiped an eye. Matthew reminded him of himself, of what he could have been if things had been so different all those years ago. Enraged with jealousy, Kasartha was obsessed with delivering up Matthew. Just had to. *Problem is, Matthew simply doesn't have enough interest to follow me. He thinks I'm gonna follow him, huh? That's not how this works, Matty-boy.*

A sudden drop in temperature abruptly followed a downward thrust of wind. Passersby stopped mid-step, clutching their stomachs and covering their mouths. Some bent over, others gagged, while a couple of folks looked up with startled appearances, questioning a screeching sound as it grew in intensity. Those bent over seemed to struggle: should they cover their ears or hold their breath? Kasartha feared, but not like those around him did. They would be frightened of the immediate and mysterious stench and the deafening shrill. Where could all that be coming from? And what was it, a metal-on-metal grinding like an earthquake in the sky?

Kasartha knew exactly what it meant, who it was, and where it was. Uncle. He was coming. Kasartha just knew he was coming for him. *No sense escaping. He knows where I am.* Kasartha shook. *Might this be it? Time for doom. He's gonna send me to work the elevator shaft, deep below. I'm useless. My deliver-ups don't stick.*

People scrambled for cover. Under bushes, between parked cars, into the building—though that was a fiasco as curious people inside the building were running out at the same time to have a look-see. The revolving doors jammed; panicked voices rose. "Like *your* world is falling apart. Silly fools," he snickered. Even so, Kasartha wished he could trade places with one of them, any one of them. But he couldn't. He sat and waited, knowing Uncle's face would soon appear in the sky—completely invisible to these terror-stricken earthlings racing around to nowhere safe. *I'm washed up,* he moaned. *This is it. His wrath is pretty much here.*

Anxious, Kasartha watched as blackened clouds wisped away and suddenly revealed shades of peaceful blues. It was confusing to the masses: the noise pollution had stopped, though the stench sure hadn't. Then it appeared, a sight for Kasartha's eyes only. The beginnings of Uncle's face, starting with his nostrils, tall and dark inside. They reminded Kasartha of the many cave openings he and his colleagues call home. Then his eyes appeared, large and—surprisingly—wide and bright. *Well, that's a good sign,* Kasartha mused. When Uncle was angry and preparing to charge and accuse, his eyes would inevitably be deep red and yellow and in slit-like form. *Maybe, just maybe, I'm gonna get off. One more chance?*

Now several dogs could be heard, even on neighboring streets. Continuous, annoying barks ferociously aimed at a clear sky, owners kneeling to hold them tight, asking their four-legged friends to tell them what they see. Kasartha glanced around at the chaos one more time. *Boy, would it be something if you could see Uncle. Hah! If only you knew of his imposing, behemoth existence, of what he wants of you.* Kasartha lowered his head. *Of what he expects of me.*

"Sarthie-Boy," Uncle spoke in a casual tone as if they were two friends who bumped into each other in a coffee shop.

Looking up and afraid he'd start to blabber, Kasartha gave a simple, "Uh, what's up, Uncle?"

The rest of Uncle's long nose and chin sharpened into view. Kasartha could see that Uncle held his lips tight. *A little too casual. I shouldn't have said that.* He approached again, got straight to the point. "You've come because I've failed. I know."

"Good. Then *I* don't have to tell you what a failure you are," Uncle replied.

Kasartha choked and shook his head slightly. He wanted to argue, but what was the point?

"Make him follow you again." The tone was clearly a demand. A nonnegotiable demand.

"How?" Although needing advice, Kasartha was thrilled to have Matthew back at the top of his target list.

"Step it up."

'Step it up'? I'm good at my targeting job. I can inspire all kinds of good stuff: anger, especially. I'm the king at accusing—making them feel responsible when they're not! Whisperin' to them they're not worthy of anythin', tellin' 'em they're u-u-ugly. Whattaya mean, 'step it up'? Kasartha bit his lips and obediently bowed before responding, "Yes, Uncle. What exactly are your wishes?"

"Oh, stop it, Sarthie-Boy."

Kasartha hopped off the boulder and stood up tall. He attempted again, only this time with some honest pleading; perhaps Uncle would be less annoyed. "How? I…well, I'm not sure what you mean…what you want me to do, exactly? Matthew's a tough nut to crack these days. But give me more time. I'm sure I can do it, make him follow me again."

"Matthew? I told you, forget Matthew. For now."

Dang. "But why? I swear, just give me more chances. I know I can…"

"I said, forget Matthew. For now," Uncle boomed impatiently. "Something more delicious has come up."

Kasartha raised his eyebrows. *Something more delicious than Matthew? And he's asking me?* Well, if that wasn't the boost of confidence he needed. *Perfect!* He cleared his throat and happily puffed out his chest. "Intriguing. Intriguing, indeed." He paced as though deep in strategic planning. He raised his finger. "I know. You want me to target Karo." He mimicked Karo skipping rope and chewing bubble gum. "Great idea, boss! That'll distract Matthew. It'll twist 'im all up with emotions he never knew he had!" Kasartha moved on to mimic a fierce twisting by removing the hat from his head and mangling it up. Then he threw his hat on the ground and stomped on it over and over, all to display that he possessed the capabilities required to carry out this plan. "Matthew will be so distraught…and, of course," Kasartha puffed out his chest again, "I, *me,* fully at your service…will be right there to pick 'im up and shake 'im up. He'll follow me then! Great plan, Uncle." He bowed.

Uncle rolled his eyes, causing more eerie and unexplainable screeches across the sky. This time, there wasn't a single bystander who hadn't taken refuge. Most were crouched together, still shaking. Two gentlemen had made a run for the pay phone, one in the booth, the other guarding it. *Who in the heck are they gonna call?* Kasartha mused.

"No, you nincompoop. Seriously, Sarthie-boy, I don't know why I haven't tossed you down the shaft yet." His eyes narrowed into slits.

Deflated, Kasartha scratched his neck nervously and waited for more instruction.

Uncle arched his neck forward as if that were necessary for Kasartha to hear. That was clearly not the case. Uncle's voice couldn't be any clearer. His eyes grew devilish red. "It's battle time, Sarthie-boy. You ready?"

"Me?" Kasartha was a targeting agent. He had been a bystander and witnessed a few battles but never participated in one himself. Never had he been an opponent. "Uh, who would I be battling?" He hoped Uncle couldn't pick up the apprehension in his shaky voice. "Just wondering." He forced a chuckle.

"Jophiel."

"Jophiel!?" There was no hiding Kasartha's gulp; his brain swelled from the swallow, just a little, enough to make him dizzy but not collapse. *This is not a targeting job. This is revenge. Uncle's revenge.* He was being asked to do Uncle's bidding. "You want me to *battle Jo-phi-el?*"

Targeting the mind of little harmless Joppha and leading him on was one thing, but going tête-à-tête with the spirit within the boy, Jophiel—the legendary escort with all the might of his Kingdom—*whilst* in his all-powerful spirit form? That was clearly another. *The self-destruction would be mine!*

Uncle simply nodded. "Block him. Keep him from re-entering his sinews. This is your big chance, Sarthie-boy. Prove to me *your* loyalty." Then he disappeared, evaporating without a trace. The squealing echoes ceased.

Bystanders slowly took steps with vigilant eyes still facing skyward, noses cautiously being released from pinched fingers and cupped hands. Whatever had been rattling their ear-drums was gone. Whatever had been forcing their throats to gag evaporated. Had they all imagined it? Kasartha could tell most were confused and eager to move on as if nothing were wrong, as if perhaps it had just been the wind. Crestfallen, he sat back upon the large rock.

He'd have to forget about meeting Matthew at the gas station and get to the bog quickly, before Jophiel takes the dive back into his Earth-journey, into the vehicle of that little boy, Joppha. No doubt he'll hang close. That's where I'll find him.

Kasartha took a deep breath. Growled at a dog with persistent, angry eyes. Then disappeared. He had another job to do. Not one he was looking forward to.

Well, this ain't gonna win me any favors with Matty-Boy.

CHAPTER THIRTY-TWO
REUNITED

On Route, Havensight to Moorelingville

AS THEY PULLED away from fueling up, Pipiera leaned back, wanting to relax yet needing to take inventory. Thankful that Charles and Bruce were catching up from days gone by, she could take some quiet moments to think. *What a mess. What on Earth am I to do next? How can I even help? Oh, Serena, what have you talked me into? And Alexien, you didn't help much, either.*

Eyes closed, one hand wrapped around a sandwich, the other on a bottle of pop, her mind worked hard to sort things out. Regretting some emotions, she wished she could start over with Marnie. It was unsettling to Pipiera that their relationship had been founded upon mistrust. *I need to fix that.* She thought of Matthew and being arrested in front of him. *That couldn't have been reassuring. Especially when he was just starting to believe in me, trust me. I need to fix that relationship, too.* One by one, she counted off the other people she had met so far: Emerson, Mrs. Damien, Karo, Laura. *None of them trust me, none of them.*

A stench of sulfur drifted her way from the front seat. Bruce and Charles were chomping into their egg salad sandwiches. Her stomach rumbled: it was hungry, yet the motion was more like a warning, as if a reminder to 'heed what you eat.'

A sudden and fierce breeze intruded her thoughts. Panicked, she interrupted Bruce and Charles with a plea to crank up the windows. But it was too late, massive white flurries entered and swirled ferociously. Something jabbed her elbow, a movement that ended with cola spilling over her shoes and all over the floorboard. The flurry became recognizable. It was Jophiel!

He immediately placed a finger on her lips to shush anything she could say.

His presence, his smile, that wonderful aroma of the Kingdom courtyard! One deep, satisfied gasp made by Pipiera caught the attention of Charles, who turned quickly to see if she was alright.

"You okay?" Charles asked. He was obviously unaware of Jophiel's massive presence in the seat beside her, a presence so enormous it bent and twisted and partially folded up. A big, white and gold fluffy mess with blinking eyes and crinkled wings!

Uncomfortable as Jophiel appeared, his big grin shone from one earlobe to the other. Pressing his finger against his pursed lips meant she needed to avoid making any fuss about his presence. Only she could see him, anyway, so that would be easy enough, wouldn't it?

"Yes, I'm good. Just thinking about poor little Joppha,"

she responded quickly. Affirming that neither Bruce nor Charles had any notion of Jophiel being in the back seat of the car, she happily snuck a sideways glance to focus on the grin of her dear friend, the very spirit of the little boy, Joppha, who they were all on a mission to rescue. A silly grin took over her own face as she watched her friend twist and churn till he found a comfortable position.

Jophiel sighed, "A racing car, really? *This* is your rescue vehicle?" He poked her in the ribs, subtly reminding her she couldn't converse back. She crossed her arms abruptly simply to tease him back but knew her wide, excited eyes would give her away. She was so very pumped and excited to see him.

Before Jophiel had taken a fall to Earth to assume his own Earth-journey, he had asked her in a letter to watch out for him. And she had agreed. *Here we are, my friend, just as I promised. But what a disadvantage, you can talk, but I can't!* She hoped he could somehow read her thoughts.

"Well, well, a fool has anchored your tongue?" he teased.

She laughed silently and shook her head, thinking at the same time just how soothingly his voice resonated, head to toe and inside out. Seeing him again made her realize just how much she missed him.

"Surely, fools are thought wise if they keep silent," he jabbed her again, then brought to a resolution his joking around. "But you are no fool, Pipiera. I applaud what you are doing. Thank you. Sincerely." His grin turned serious and suddenly matched the intensity of his eyes.

She did her best to return his gaze and couldn't help but wonder, *does your presence here now mean young Joppha's Earth-journey is complete? Was it not the reason I came, to stop this, somehow?*

He seemed to have known what she was thinking and reached out to stroke her cheek. "I am not the one you need to be focused on. I've got this. You, my dear, are here to inspire Matthew. You need to focus on *him*."

With a cocked head and her mouth all twisted up, she wondered how she could convey to Jophiel that she had gained little ground on that front.

Again, he instinctively knew. "You're focusing on me, aren't you?"

It was obvious she was. What else would she be doing in the back seat of this vehicle speeding away to find young Joppha? And when they find him, they will rescue him and return him safely to his parents. *Then Matthew will be better, won't he?* She thought. Pipiera felt water welling in her eyes. *I'm failing, aren't I? What am I to do?* She shrugged and stared at the egg filling that was beginning to slop out between the two slices of white bread.

"You gonna eat that?"

She shrugged again.

He whispered in her left ear, "Don't."

She fumbled with the edges of the cellophane, waiting for more direction from her friend.

"Hey, cheer up!" Jophiel seemed surprised that Pipiera appeared so despondent. He watched her wipe her nose with the back of her hand. "I'm guessing the last day or so hasn't been easy on you."

She shook her head, gulped, and peeped out a little, "No." Fortunately, her squeak hadn't caught the attention of either Bruce or Charles. They were too busy chatting away, still comparing notes about their sons.

Jophiel squirmed and wiggled his back end to become

more settled into the tight back space. "Good thing it's a long drive; we've got lots to cover," he informed her. He picked up his legs one at a time and let his knees dangle over the front seat on either side of the driver. An unsuspecting Bruce hadn't a hint of the intrusion and continued chatting away, happy to have Charles's full attention.

Pipiera burst out laughing, stirring Charles's curiosity. "What's up? What's so funny back there?"

"Oh goodness, nothing, Dad. I was just thinking about the funny things little Joppha says and does."

Charles chuckled and agreed, "Matty always said so, too. Said he had quite the character."

"Has," Pipiera corrected, "*has* quite the character." She glanced at her big friend sitting next to her, knowing he was completely invisible to the pair in the front seat. She winked and gave him a warm, radiant smile.

"How d'ya know 'im?" Bruce watched her face intently from his rearview mirror. "If you just got to town and you haven't bin in awhile, how d'ya know 'im?"

It was a good question.

Jophiel's arms crossed, and the look on his face was stern. He was obviously wondering how she was going to manage Bruce's question, or so she thought.

"Dad?" Jophiel asked, astonished. *"You've revealed your identity?"*

Ooooo boy, Pipiera thought. *Busted.* She felt Bruce's glare in that tiny mirror, but it was nothing compared to the heated, questioning gaze coming from Jophiel's eyes. She swallowed and knew she had to answer Bruce's question first. Whatever she said, well, it would just be another lie. Pipiera scratched the back of her head and felt her chest tighten. *Oh, I've messed this whole thing up,* she thought. She leaned back and closed her eyes. *Think.*

"Uh, guys, I'm going to expel the contents of my stomach again!" she cried.

Charles turned quickly and reached as best he could to grab her hand. "You alright?" The color had drained from her face. "Quick, pull over, Bruce," he instructed.

When the car stopped, an anxious Pipiera encouraged Charles to open the only passenger-side door and lean forward to allow her to wriggle out from behind his seat and scrambled onto the side of the road. She jumped a wide trench that ran alongside the highway, separating it from a farmer's field. It was an overgrown field of lavender, woody and extraordinarily high, with little color at all. She sat cross-legged and stared at the unruly growth. A horrible sadness overcame her. She was homesick. Homesick for her Kingdom.

Charles did his best to scramble out of the car himself, but as the vehicle was low to the ground and he needed his cane to lift himself, he gave up after three attempts. He couldn't have crossed that trench, anyway. So he called out to her.

She could hear her dad's voice. It was a little more shaky than usual. "Penney. Penney. You alright, dear?"

She nodded in silence and gave him a backward wave, keeping her gaze on the conflicted land. That is, till Jophiel's presence suddenly blocked her view. His awkward movements and groaning as he worked toward mirroring her cross-legged position made her giggle somewhat. The two sat in silence for a moment. Pipiera knew well that both Bruce and Charles would be watching, seeing only her. Waiting. Waiting for her to make a move. Be sick or something. Or say something. *But what?* She could only hope this distraction would make Bruce forget about his question. Though now he'd be even more curious, wondering why Charles called her Penney, not Pippi. Letting her head fall, *this is getting so complicated,* she thought.

Jophiel lifted her chin. "A vague familiarity—yes. A revelation—no, that was not meant to be. But…" He checked to make sure her eyes were truly connecting with his. "That is now in the past. We must deal with the present."

He was referring to the escaped secret—her relation to Charles—Pipiera knew that. "What should I do next?" she begged. "How do I fix this?"

"Well, I think first, you're going to have to heave or something. They're expecting it."

She laughed. "Okay. And after that?"

"Moving forward, you need to be careful what you eat."

She instinctively knew he wasn't referring to food for her physical body. He was referring to what thoughts she was allowing herself to digest and be satisfied with. If she were going to deliver foods of encouragement and inspiration, she would have to remain healthy.

"Now, heave." He smiled and pointed toward the ditch. "Then, I'll walk you through your next steps."

CHAPTER THIRTY-THREE

THE BURDEN

PIPIERA WAS SURE the drive to Moorelingville was simply never going to end, though she was thankful for the continuous hum of the rumbling motor. It provided a solacing backdrop for replaying in her mind all the things Jophiel had explained to her before he made his exit from her presence. How will she see him again, she had asked. In little Joppha? And would he recognize her then? Jophiel wouldn't answer; he only insisted that it was critical to return to the bog, to stay close to little Joppha's mortality. She had giggled at the thought and even asked him how he managed to squeeze his enormous set of wings into that tiny body. Jophiel had admitted he was enjoying the break and would wait till the very last instant to reengage. They both laughed at the wonderful curiosity of Joppha's mind and his insistence on a better, more welcoming place that had to be out there somewhere. Jophiel had also thanked Pipiera, at which she blushed and realized how much she treasured this opportunity.

Still, I can hardly wait till we will all be together in the

Kingdom! None of this stuff down here to be concerned with. No more battling. That'll happen soon enough, she encouraged herself.

It was just Bruce and Charles and her now. They accepted her explanation that the aroma of the egg sandwiches had turned her stomach; she wasn't used to that sulfur smell. Bruce dutifully ate her sandwich and she, his potato chips. They let her rest quietly in the back seat as they drove through countrysides, passing fields of various crops, evergreen forests, and several small towns. Deep breaths and stares out the window helped to skirt the awkwardness of Bruce's many glances through the rearview mirror he adjusted to keep her in his sight.

She settled eventually and reflected on Jophiel's words. "Truths are learned firsthand," he had said, "and it's not what happens to them, it's how they respond." He was referring to all Earth-journeyers, but in specific, he noted that Matthew was about to have another, much-needed 'growth spurt.' After Jophiel explained the various paths that lay before poor Matthew, Pipiera had argued that it wasn't a spurt he needed but rather more of an eruption. Right now, although on a path upward, he was about to face sheer rock. To put it mildly, a steep learning curve. *How would he overcome the steepness? Can he even rise to the top? That must be—no, that is—why I'm here. At least I've got that completely straight now,* she thought. Her aunties had tricked her. Pipiera wondered who put them up to it. *It wouldn't have been Papah Megs. But maybe Bookie, or most likely, Aivy! No matter, they had good reason.* She was sure of that.

Kasartha had been a longtime study of the Authoritarians, apparently. It hadn't really absorbed into Pipiera just how dangerous he was and just how much of a fixation he had on Matthew. She was thankful for Jophiel's warning and reminders, though discouraged he couldn't, or wouldn't, answer her questions as to what would happen when they arrived in Moorelingville. Locating Joppha was *still* on the table and she *still* needed to 'do her thing,' whatever that was.

Charles muffled a cough, catching her attention. "You okay up there?" she asked, knowing that today's tolls had to start showing on him soon. He must be exhausted.

He nodded, "A little wiped, gotta admit. And you?" She responded with a similar reply.

Just a couple more hours away from Moorelingville. First priority was Joppha. Then Matthew. Her eyes gently closed. *Still, I need to come up with a plan.* She couldn't help but think she was at least one step behind Kasartha.

CHAPTER THIRTY-FOUR

THE BATTLE

At the Bog of Moorelingville

IT DIDN'T TAKE long for Kasartha to arrive at the bog; in fact, it was instantaneous. He mused at Matthew's insistence on taking old Betsy, preferring the long route over his ways, and right when the life of his so-called little buddy was at stake. *What a guy. What a time to get all moral-like.*

Just as Kasartha had counted on, Jophiel was indeed hanging out close to little Joppha's mortal torso, right where Kasartha had left it, tucked inside a shallow cave of rocks up a hill, protected from the swamp waters.

Uncle said, block him.

For a short while, Kasartha spied from a distance, completely amused. The huge essence of energy was whistling, of all things. Carrying on with his feet in a frolic, wings at ease, body grooving, arms happily waving about.

Kasartha spat with disgust.

Jophiel's fancy footwork abruptly transformed to a firmly

planted stance, legs wide apart, his body rigid and no longer bouncing. Kasartha watched as Jophiel raised his face directly to a tiny slice of blue-grey sky. A steady flow of air lunged upward from his lips, a fierce, drawn-out whistle. He hit a high note and, with no strain, simply held it as if it were a sharp-bladed sword in warning position, ready to slash.

Does he sense I'm here?

Thunder followed a lightning bolt, and a deep blackness fell.

Catching his own jaw, Kasartha watched in awe as Jophiel's wingspan unfolded with a disciplined slowness as if they were tall theatrical curtains pulling open one final time. A ripple shivered its way up Kasartha's spine. *Yup, he knows I'm here. And something is over.* He could sense it. He just hoped it wasn't his own existence.

Gulping and staying silent, Kasartha scanned the environment. No one was in this space other than Jophiel and him. No lost or brave hikers, no Joppha rescuers, no battling soldiers from that Kingdom army, no other of Uncle's nephews attempting to wiggle in on his brave charge, and no stench. Uncle was not watching.

The two were alone. *Just you and me,* Kasartha breathed out quietly.

Though scattered, heavy water drops fell from high tree branches and were swallowed by the sludge underneath. Jophiel's war whistle was more like a howl now. A murder of crows overhead ruffled their feathers while another large lot darted to adjoining treetops. Not a single 'caw,' though. Kasartha felt their sharpened stares. *They're expecting a battle. Did Jophiel summon them? Or did Uncle give them a heads-up?*

Kasartha chose to remain a safe distance away. Just watch.

The incoming darkness to the thicket comforted his nerves and provided a sense of safety, something he needed to frame his mind, to bring an onslaught of courage to its forefront. To fill his cerebrum with *one thought only*: block Jophiel. *Do not* allow him to rejoin Joppha's torso. This would not be an easy task.

Fueling himself with pride, he convinced himself he could succeed in a battle with the all-powerful Jophiel. *So what if he's got the backing of his Kingdom in those wings of his? I've got Uncle's blessing.* At least he hoped he did, anyway.

A vibration from that enduring whistle of Jophiel's oscillated toward Kasartha, visible even to an earthling's eye. That was all it took for Kasartha to second-guess the probabilities of a successful block. The ripple penetrated Kasartha, warning of Jophiel's confidence in his swordsmanship. The whistle itself transitioned to a long and graceful blade, carefully crafted. The thin edge glistened with an ability to slice even the tiniest of quarks—or Kasartha, whichever dared to get into its path.

Jophiel grabbed the sword he had just breathed into life, both hands gripping it tight and high. Without turning around to face his opponent, he opened the conversation. "You approach me from behind? You are a bigger fool than I gave credit. State what you want."

Your moment to act, Kasartha conversed with himself. If he had his druthers, real courage, he'd run away, forget all this, and go back to a peaceful existence where targeting was his only purpose. But facing Jophiel would be less of a threat than facing Uncle if he took the scaredy-cat option. He deliberated his move. *Shall I take a run into him from behind? Hmmm, full speed. If I collide at the back of his knees, he's sure to fall. But what then?* His first move would be a critical one.

"Go back to your Kingdom," Kasartha replied with a commanding voice, surprising even himself.

Be real. How long could I hold him down? Not long. This blocking business makes no sense. Why would Uncle expect I could battle Jophiel? I'm a mind attacker. My targets are Earth-formed. I could handle Jophiel when he was in Joppha's form, when he had no recollection of his true identity.

But not like this.

With sword high and ready to swoop, Jophiel turned toward the tree Kasartha hid behind. It's not as though he even needed a weapon. Jophiel was nearly four times the size of Kasartha at least. And those wings! The muscles across the span were thick and solid.

What was Uncle thinking? Unless... Kasartha surmised. Unless Uncle wanted him destroyed. And what better way than to have him battle physically with Jophiel? *Or, just maybe, he means for me to use my superior skills? Yeah, face it, I've mastered targeting minds over the generations.*

He studied Jophiel for a long moment, attempting to discern.

Is Uncle questioning my value again? If I don't prove myself to be a dedicated rebel, convicted in my belief totally to him.... oh, I can't bear to think what will happen to me.

Kasartha tightened his belt as if to squeeze the fear out. *I shall prevail!* He focused on belligerence, striving for a mind like Uncle's, the pupils of his eyes narrowing to slits. "Go back, I say. And I repeat it." Again, he surprised himself, the echo of his booming command creating energy ripples of their own. His shirt buttons popped as his chest swelled in size.

The two held gazes in a stare-down.

Finally, Jophiel made the next move. Dropping his arms,

his sword shimmied into a thousand teeny lights and fell to the ground, dissolving completely. "Kasartha. You know who I am. Right?"

Kasartha kept up his bully stance, and a fine one it was, if he said so himself.

"You do recall it was me—*me*—who not only saved you, but kinda stuck up for you? Remember that? C'mon, you gotta!"

Jophiel was speaking about an incident years earlier when Kasartha managed to get himself into the Kingdom's court-yard, all with Jophiel's impromptu help, all inside a complete whirlwind of chaos.

A relaxed hand on his hip, Jophiel sighed and explained. "Let me picture it up for you: stuck in the mud, underneath Matthew, on my side of the riverbank. Ringing any bells now?"

Kasartha remembered it well. How could he not? "I deceived you," he responded, firmly outlining each word as an offense.

A slight chuckle gave another hint of Jophiel's transformed mood. "Nuh-huh, no, you didn't. Come on, give it up."

"The only thing I'll give up is your head on a platter."

"Seriously?"

Your attempts to soften me aren't working. Kasartha encouraged himself with this thought.

Jophiel continued. "Okay, okay. I give you that. Deceit. But it was Matthew you deceived. I was simply a witness. So there. Happy? Are we done here?"

Kasartha released a rumbling *grrrr* in his throat and squeezed his fists to tighten up his forearms. *You don't take me seriously, either. I'll show you.* Leaning forward, he took a charging leap at his oversized celestial foe.

But the next thing Kasartha felt was not his own shove into his opponent's knees but rather a brick-stopping pressure forcing his nose to one side. His feet churned like some wild, super-powered roller disk, only stuck on the spot and sinking deep. Slimy, sloppy, polluted mud slowed him down. He was up to his knees in it, and because of it, his faltered attack ceased.

Jophiel released the palm of his hand from Kasartha's face and took a step back. One step was all it took to miss the swinging arms of the rebellious troublemaker who was stuck in the mud really well. Jophiel chuckled heartily, "Hey, little buddy, we've been friends for a while now. Isn't that what you said to me on the bus?"

Exhausted, Kasartha stopped swinging like a madman. Instead, he'd maneuvered Jophiel's hand so he could clamp a finger in his teeth, good and hard.

"Oeowhhh! Guessing that was a short-term friendship." Jophiel yanked his hand back and pressed the aching finger into his own chest. It would heal there in an instant. "What do you want with Joppha, anyway? He's just a kid! Not even related to Matthew."

Kasartha was in no position to argue any longer. Knee deep in thick sludge, his feet couldn't move. "Get me up," he demanded, assuming a position of authority. But in the presence of the mighty Jophiel, Kasartha could feel a drain opening, his energy swirling and slipping down and away like dirty wash water. He was vulnerable and, admittedly, completely helpless. "I beg of you," he added.

Jophiel crossed his arms. The sheer size of his abs, particularly from Kasartha's position, would have been enough to scatter ten dozen Kasarthas.

Kasartha took stock of the scenario. *Uncle's wrath is still bigger. There'd be no escaping it. Not for me, anyway. Not now, anyhow.* He swallowed and waited. Would Jophiel pull him up out of the mud? Let him go? He was reminded of Miss Penney, Pipiera, picking up fledgling stones at the River of Times and tossing them into the crystal stream. "Isn't that the kind of thing your kind likes to do? Save guys like me?"

"Not until you tell me. Why are you leading Joppha away? To here, of all places!" Then Jophiel clutched Kasartha by the scruff of his neck, yanked him out of the mud and held him high, so the two could be face to face. "Or might your *uncle* be carrying out revenge on *me*?"

Revenge was illegal. Kasartha knew he could target and target and target, work hard to disrupt the lives of Earth-journeyers, but he had no authority whatsoever to play out the act of revenge. Only Uncle could do that, and as far as Kasartha knew, revenge was an act agreed upon with the Kingdom in advance. All was fair in the end, they'd say. But Kasartha wasn't sure who, exactly, was keeping score nor how or certainly when that 'end' might be. If he, himself, was caught in some matter of acting out revenge? That would, without question, be cause for the worst of all eternal punishment.

Me? Blocking him? That's exactly what Jophiel suspects. Revenge. And I'm the one who'll go to prison for it. Kasartha felt woozy, rattled by the thought, plus hanging in midair by the scruff of his neck didn't help. He'd been cornered. By Uncle. *I'm living in a nightmare.*

Jophiel tossed Kasartha with so much ease that there was hardly a move of his muscles. Kasartha landed on his butt, displacing several quarts of sludge. The back of his head banged against a tree trunk, scattering hundreds of oversized earwigs.

"I'd say your so-called leader, Mr. Uncle, is tossing you out with the trash."

"Even trash ends in a superior place," Kasartha grumbled, pulling several strands of hair that were caught on the bark of the tree. He then grinned hugely at the night-loving creatures crawling over his shoulders before flicking each off. If only he could quit these assignments, hide and never be found. Not be called upon by Uncle ever again.

What will happen if I refuse to carry out Uncle's bidding? What's worse, what will happen when he sees I've failed? Again.

It would have been better if Kasartha had been exterminated in battle. If so, he could have been a hero. But he knew Jophiel wouldn't offer that solution; he wasn't the type. Whatever his reasons, Jophiel would leave Kasartha to suffer his own consequences. Rather, Uncle's consequences.

CHAPTER THIRTY-FIVE
ESCAPEES RUN IN THE FAMILY

In the Town of Havensight

BETSY WAS REFRESHED, a full fuel tank and radiator all topped up. No Kasartha to be seen. Anywhere. Matthew huffed and paced, stopping only to kick the curb, causing a Texaco sidewalk sign to cackle and wobble. "Where is he?" Catching a disapproving eye from the gas station attendant pumping for some spiffed-up teen in a Ford truck, Matthew couldn't care if they overheard. He paced some more and mocked Kasartha's words, "I promise, I'll meet you there, yeah, yeah, yeah." *Why do I believe him? Why do I listen to him? Why do I even give him my attention?*

Matthew really thought he had grown out of all that, such sudden bursts of rage. Truth was, it was still a struggle. He'd been doing so well, practicing restraint and self-control. For years he harbored a deep resentment that his dad left him—went and died. Since then, he'd learned the consequences of unresolved anger. Removing the scarred covering took courage. A lot of courage. Changing the message took time. A lot of time. No longer does he tell himself over and over that his dad abandoned him. Rather, now, his message is different, a truth he knows to be solid. *Dad, you love me, and our separation is temporary, you didn't choose to leave.* Matthew confided once to Emerson that acknowledging and getting rid of those hard feelings he had comfortably bonded himself to was like booting out a sword-wielding enemy from his heart.

Taking a deep breath, he acknowledged today's anger, anger that his little buddy was missing while in his charge. *Of course I'm angry*, he thought to himself, *okay, okay, it's natural, just don't let it eat me up and take control of the narrative*, he cautioned. With another self-soothing inhale, he grabbed hold of a fond memory: he and his dad and mom all cuddled on his sleeping blanket in their yard, in the thick of night, ogling the stars. That memory was his rock, like a get-out-of-jail-free card. He kept it safe in the back pocket of his mind and pulled it out whenever needed. *We'll get you Joppha, I promise. We'll get you back to your family.*

With a nod to the gas station attendant, a young man he recognized from his high school years, he gestured an apology. Another deep breath. He cast his attention on the rural countryside, and a niggling reminder of that Dr. Alexien came to mind. He chuckled, *her toolbox. You'd be happy to know I use it, Dr. A!*

Dr. Alexien had helped Matthew years ago by encouraging him to employ a variety of tactics—tools, so to speak, to aid him through moments like this. He had mocked her then, but through the years, he learned first-hand their value, especially her deck of 'why cards.'

"So," Matthew said aloud. "Why? Why is all this craziness

happening? Why is Joppha in danger? Why did I lose him? Why is it my fault, or is it? Why can't I seem to get a grip? Why is this Kasartha guy back on the scene, and why, why am I listening to him? And why am I so angry?" He knew he couldn't get all the answers, but he envisioned all the 'why cards' in a chaotic mess on the ground. Could he pick up at least one as a start to organizing his thoughts? Wiping his cheeks with the back of his hand, he admitted the card most familiar was the 'why am I angry?' one.

Death.

The answer came loud and clear, he didn't like death. "Grammie," he whispered. Already it felt like an eon ago, but it was just that very morning. Her kind face and warm touch. Eyes that needled right through. "You left. I need you. Joppha. Oh, Grammie, what if Joppha's dead?" Matthew fell to his knees and burst into a full sob. It *was* a possibility. Pinpricks were puncturing his theory that all was going to be okay. "And you call me some kind of protector?" A dark invader was on his doorstep and knocking—tap, tap, tap—threatening to feed a message, one that would take him back to that hollow abandonment with a surge of fierce resentment. He noticed the gas station attendant and the swanky teen both looking his way. *Dang,* he realized he had been making a scene.

"Uh, could I use your phone?" Matthew squeaked out.

The attendant pointed to the pay phone at the side of the building while the other kept a nosy watch on Matthew's movements.

Matthew cleared his voice and raised himself slowly to a tall, confident height. "'course. Thanks." Jingling some change in his pocket, he headed over. He had already come up with a plan. His dime returned a dial tone. He circled round the numbers. *Good, it's ringing.*

"Yeah, hello."

"Emerson!"

"Matt? Where are you? Do you know how upset Laura is? She called here all cryin' and stuff, says she never wants to…"

Matthew interrupted his friend and urgently tapped his fingers on the side of the phone. "I'll fill you in later. Is your dad still coming today?"

Matthew couldn't help but notice the spiffy Ford truck-driving teen's gaze. Even when the guy spat his gum onto the pavement, his eyes stayed glued. *Who dresses up like that on a Saturday?* Matthew mused.

"My dad?" Emerson could be heard in the receiver. "Uh, yeah, he's flyin' in, says he wants to take me to lunch. Huh! Like I wanna have lunch with *him*. I don't know why he doesn't just…"

Matthew impatiently shifted his weight and looked up and down the street. Still no Kasartha. He knew what he should be doing right now was patching that mess up with Laura, not to mention encouraging his friend to, at last, once and for all, let go of the decade-old angst toward his dad. But Emerson always insisted he couldn't, on account of he figured that would disappoint his mom. Matthew had to interrupt Emerson's excited yammering once again.

"Emerson! Bud, I need you to *listen!*"

The attendant had quietly stepped closer and fidgeted with a nearby tire pump. It struck Matthew he just wanted to eavesdrop.

"Huh? What's wrong? Where are you?" Emerson asked.

The conversation had gone full circle. *Let's try this again,* Matthew exhaled.

"Your dad. I need his plane."

"What? Are ya crazy, dude? What's goin' on? My dad's plane? What on Earth for? Like you know how to pilot! Seriously…"

Again, Matthew interrupted, "Need *him,* too; he can drive, er, I mean fly. I need to get to the bog, the bog on the coast. That's where Joppha is; no time to drive."

That's where Joppha is. Matthew wanted to close his eyes and wish this all away. Did he really just hear himself say that? Is Joppha really so many hours away? *Little dude, I wish you were here. Here with me. Safe. I. Am. So. Sorry.*

"The bog? What'tha! How'd he get there? Oh, wait, no! Bud, you were right; he got on one of those buses! He musta hid himself real good." Emerson was getting excited.

"Dunno. But I know he's there."

"How?'

"How what?"

"How d'ya know he's there? Was there a witness or something?"

"Yeah, yeah, don't matter. I just need to get there really fast. Will your dad fly me there?"

"Oh my gosh, what timing! A cabbie's pullin' up the drive. It's gotta be him. I won't ask; I'll tell him! And bud, I'm comin' too. Meet us at the airstrip."

Matthew hung up the receiver but found two men standing in his way, the attendant and that spiffy Ford truck-driving teen.

"You got somethin' to do with that boy taken from town?"

Mister Spiffy growled, the attendant beside him holding up a tire wrench.

"What? No!" With the threat of violence promising nothing good, it was a saving grace that Matthew could run. He sprinted as fast as he could, jumped the gas pump curb, scrambled into old Betsy, and off he went, leaving nothing but gravel and dust flying behind.

Phew, Matthew thought, though he couldn't help but notice the sight in his rearview mirror: the attendant writing down Betsy's license plate.

"That's gonna track them to Mom, but I can't worry about that right now!" He headed straight for the regional air club, where he counted on Emerson's dad, a man he'd never met, to get him to the coast as fast as possible.

CHAPTER THIRTY-SIX
THIS MUST END

In the Outer Courtyard of the Kingdom

"MY PIP IS in jail, and Jophiel's coming home."

Megalos brooded and slouched, running his thick fingers against the smooth edge of his ornate bench, the only piece of furniture in his Tower Room, all while Aivy leaned against the wall by the window, sneaking a peek outside its circular frame every now and again. And when she did, Megalos snatched a glance her way. He wanted more sympathy and wasn't getting it.

His voice still throaty, he laid it out, "And you knew all this. You knew Jophiel was coming home for certain, didn't you? And with such timing that Pip had no chance whatsoever to even think she could make a difference. You set her up." He tried not to sound accusatory or even angry. Though admittedly, it was tough to hide. When it came to his own family and those close to his family, he couldn't think straight and struggled to put it all into a right perspective. The Kingdom's perspective.

Aivy frowned at him while her finger swirled around, making a whirlwind motion.

He was embarrassed she had to flash that eyebrow 'V' his way and her subtle message came through loud and clear: *instrumental growth comes from chaos.* Still, he needed her to understand. "It's because of me." *Darn, I didn't want that to sound like a sulk, but I'm guessing it did. Now I'm in for a lecture, just like the ones I give to others.* Just the thought made him chuckle and surprisingly, even to himself, helped his mood somewhat.

But there was no lecture. Aivy sighed deeply. "You're being saucy."

He nodded. She was right.

"I get it, Megs. You think it's because of that curse you made on the day you separated and arrived. Here." Aivy continued to summarize his consequences, "The King forgave you, remember?" She eyed him with even more sharpness than the 'V' brow moments earlier.

"Yeah, but…"

"Yeah, but nothing. Your earthly father," she moved to squeeze into a spot on the bench beside him, "…your earthly father, Kasartha, seems to be the one who is *now* cursed. But that is not *your* doing, Megs. You know that!"

"Yeah, but…"

"Yeah, but nothing! That beast of a dragon…" Her core shimmied on the bench, despising even to give air space to the name of that thief. "He's the one causing harm. That's *who* he is!" She lifted her shoulders and raised open hands, making it clear that neither she nor Megalos could control the beast. Softening her tone to remind him of something he already knew, "That's *what* he does."

"Yeah, but…"

"Yeah, but nothing!" A lull hung. Energy drained from her face. She wasn't getting through. "So. What are you concerned about? Really concerned about? Let's talk this over."

His lips pursed as his head sunk into his broad hands, hands that were meant to protect. *I can not tell her. Ironic.*

Surrendering to his mood, she returned to the window and consumed the awe. A glorious horizon. Swells of waves drifting forward, full of chatty flowers and kind, often humorous escorts, bringing Arrivals safely inward through the vast outer courtyard to the gate's entrance. Incredulous excitement, pure joy.

Time to get serious. Body stiff and straight, she turned to Megalos and summed things up. "Joppha is coming home. C'mon, Megs, you gotta be happy about that. You said yourself you missed the, and I quote you, 'big guy.' It's his scheduled return; he signed up for that."

Megalos's head continued to lay heavy as a rock in the crutch of sweating palms.

"And Pipiera, your dear Pip, Megalos, she's going to be fine. You know that. Yes, she's going through some challenges right now…and things aren't going…er…as she'd anticipated. But that's your Pip!" Aivy laughed out loud. Pipiera never did like to follow rules, nor did she consider consequences too much. But that never mattered. "She's dearly loved and has nothing but good seed in her heart. Need I remind you she's a Kingdom citizen? She is going to be just fine, Megs."

Still no reaction, though he did blink a few times.

"Now, let's talk about Matthew." She crossed her arms and tapped her right foot.

Her impatience caught his attention. "The boy's gonna be

fine. I know the whole he's-on-his-journey thing. I get that." He muttered.

She moved closer, kneeling in front of her sad friend. "So, what is it?"

His stomach muscles tightened to protect a knot inside. *I can not tell her. I mustn't tell anyone.*

A horrified squeal came from Aivy as she sprang to her feet, "Haaaaah!"

Had she read him? Did she figure it out?

"Kasartha? No! Please tell me, Megs, you are not feeling concerned about *him?*" She paced the small room, seven steps in one direction, then back and forth again.

His back muscles strengthened and stiffened, suddenly defensive. "He *was* my Earth father."

"He cursed you! Said he'd ensure you'd never have a family. Or did you forget that?"

"I cursed him first! Besides, I forgave him. Remember that?"

The floorboards creaked as though anxiety itself replaced the golden threads that tied them together.

"*You* have been forgiven, too. Remember?"

"You already said that. But…" Megalos puffed with annoyance.

"But what?" Aivy pleaded. After a pause, she continued, attempting to reassure her friend. "It was his choice. He didn't want to know the King. C'mon, Megs, you know how this works." Quieting her voice, "It's because you work *outside* the Kingdom walls… the capability of remembering affliction. The suffering, the torment that comes with your job. Mine, too." She touched his cheek and whispered a reminder, "We agreed to this when we accepted our roles."

He rubbed his chin and nodded. "Still, I cursed him first. I wish things could have been different." The humiliation. The beatings. His earthly pa had struck him with a cast-iron pot and buried him under a pile of rocks like a farm dog. He, himself, a premature arrival.

"Yesterday is yesterday," Aivy said matter-of-factly.

"And the present is the present," his tone becoming argumentative.

"I do not like where this is going, Megalos," she scolded while backing up a stride.

"Does *he* know Joppha is scheduled to come home?" His question was cutting, his tone demanding.

"Who?"

"The beast. Does he know?"

"What, the Dragon? Doubt it, pretty sure not. How could he?"

Megalos stood, his turn to pace. His next gesture was something not unfamiliar, but rather common: his infamous face rub. Aivy held her breath, likely wondering what in the name of the *kingdom* he was thinking?

"Okay," he said cheerfully.

Cheerful? She narrowed her eyes, not believing his sudden mood change. "Uh, 'okay' *what?*"

He felt the sting of her stare but did what he could to dismiss it. "You're right. As usual, Aivy." Surrendering his hands to the air, "What on *Earth* should I be concerned about?"

Her glare hadn't softened. He approached her cautiously and gently cupped from the top of her head to her dimpled chin in his protective hands. "Seriously, Aivy, you are right. Everything is going to be okay."

He felt her query searching his eyes before she finally allowed a sigh to escape. Then she wrapped her arms around his waist as far as they could go. "Megs, you are so dear. You carry such burdens on your shoulders. This job can be weighty. Just hope your Matthew boy will one day be able to fill your shoes!" She lectured about separation rules and scolded him one last time over the need to be cautious with empathetic emotions for that Kasartha, regardless of prior relations. At that, she left, finally appearing to be confident that all was well with Megalos.

But it wasn't. And neither Matthew nor Jophiel nor even Pipiera was the one Megalos was festering about, not this time. He couldn't do much about their situations. And he was well aware of the risks associated with emotions surrounding one's separation, but he'd had enough. He had to stop this nonsense once and for all. Absentmindedly, he measured his gait—three steps one way, three steps back—until he conceived an actionable plan, though he dared not speak of it aloud. *I'll make a deal with him, this duplicitous, so-called Uncle. I'll let him think I can provide the Kingdom's permission to end Joppha's journey early. In return, he'll owe me. I'll demand that Kasartha must stop targeting my line, the family he so desperately wants to be his.*

Megalos stopped to gaze out his window. He would deceive the great deceiver. *There could be no harm done, only good—right?* By now, he had practically rubbed a layer off his chin. *Joppha's arriving soon, anyway; that's what Aivy just said. And this way, Kasartha can catch a break. Such cruelty. Forcefully tasked to harm your own family line.*

Loud chatter from below drifted into his window; a very excited new Arrival was shouting happily. A happier bubble traveled its way up inside Megalos's hefty chest, bringing to mind his friend. "Yeah, it'll sure be nice to have our Jophiel back," he whispered, imagining the moment briefly before returning to the daunting thought of meeting the Dragon face to face and wondering what, if anything, could go wrong with his plan.

What if that beast refuses? Say he, that master of deceit, catches on to me…catches me in a misrepresentation of the Kingdom? He'd have caught me in the act of deceit. I shall hear his ridiculous roar of laughter; it'll shake the heavens.

The thought of failing burdened Megalos. Returning to his bench, he sulked at the consequences. *That beast will have a legal right to harm. If I fail, it will cost a descendant dearly.*

He hadn't cried for decades, so the sobs of entrapment felt unusual to Megalos. *Perhaps it's time I retire, get inside those Kingdom walls, where I will no longer feel this turmoil, no more tears.* A breeze swirled into the window, bringing along with it more buoyant shouts, sunny-ing up his mood until he slapped both knees harshly. "Oh, snap up!" he scolded himself. He had known the cost, that cost of knowing, when he signed up for this job. Safe inside the Kingdom, citizens weren't subjected to the fears of the Dragon's work. And most of the time, Earth-journeyers were completely blind to all the constant warring. Squeezing his knees till they hurt, he resigned to gratitude. *Othis and Aivy, James and Gad, and all the other Authoritarians, they live in this state of knowing, knowing what battles are brewing, which journeyers are struggling, whose stone is at stake, cast in a whirlwind or stuck in the mud. And the King, my gosh, my King, he sees all, he knows the end game. Just how does he do it? I should be proud to be on this team.* Megalos stood. "I *am* proud to be on this team!"

The decision to give up one's stone was always, always,

between the King and the Journeyer. Megalos would take comfort in that. Angst churned over the potential consequence of failing: another premature arrival, possibly, or increased attacks on an existing or even a future descendant; worse, all the consequences combined. Megalos was desperate to end this targeting business to this family, his line, the line he cherished the most and promised to protect, the reason he became Head Gatekeeper. To stay abreast of their battles and be the first to welcome them home. Nodding approval of the plan to himself, next would be its execution. *It'll be worth it. One might suffer more, all so that others could suffer less.*

His sigh was the deepest he'd ever had. *My dearest Aivy, I couldn't possibly share my plan with you.*

CHAPTER THIRTY-SEVEN
A STORM INSIDE THE COCKPIT

On Route, Havensight to Moorelingville

A TRIANGLE OF TENSION manifested inside the cockpit of Mr. Damien's newly purchased Cessna 152 single engine plane. Emerson's insistence that his dad *must* take them to Moorelingville and allow Matthew passage in the baggage compartment behind the seats didn't do much to help the already lacking and severely strained father-son relationship. But Matthew pushed their dither and agitation about regulations and whatnots aside. He had other, more important, things to worry about: Joppha's safety, maybe even his life. And *that* was worrisome.

Matthew caught sight of a nervous glance around from Mr. Damien just as he squeezed onto the tiny bench. *This wasn't how I pictured my first time flying,* he thought. Curious, he poked his head to check out the front—instruments and dials and gadgets stretching across the dash. *No, don't tell me Emerson's got some controls!* He swallowed the emerging second thoughts.

"Tell me again," Emerson's dad asked gruffly once he completed what Matthew figured was a quick pre-flight inspection and had started the engine, "why you two think it's *your* job to be saving some kid and not leaving this business to the police? Like, what special powers might you have?" It was a brief taxi to a short runway. A weather report followed by clearance from the airstrip's traffic control interrupted, and Emerson's dad responded clearly, "Good to go."

Relieved to finally get going, Matthew pushed through the sinking sensation as the plane accelerated and left the runway, angled upward. The hum was loud and constant, and for a moment he was sure they were sinking. Holding himself tightly across his chest, he was careful to ensure his tucked-up knees wouldn't knock against Mr. Damien's seat. *Wouldn't want to disrupt the pilot.*

"How much does he weigh again?" Emerson's dad inquired of Emerson, nodding toward the one he was sure was the instigator of this whole rescue scheme. Matthew.

Now that's a question ya should've asked me before I got in this thing, was what Matthew wanted to say, just as he felt Emerson's sharp slap to a knee. *Seriously?* "'bout one-thirty," Emerson answered. One thing he and Emerson had in common was a tall and lean build, though Matthew was surely weightier than Emerson claimed.

Emerson remained tight-lipped and Matthew hugged himself even tighter while the grumpy pilot exchanged several communications over the radio. "It's bumpy, approaching two-five-hundred."

The plane continued to climb, and eventually, the ride settled into a smooth, comforting hum. "Cruising at eight thousand," Emerson's dad reported to that steady radio voice, which was much kinder than the one in the pilot's seat.

A pleasant thought crossed Matthew's mind, then a huge grin across his face. He let go of himself to admire the view. *Who needs you, Kasartha? Look, I'm flying without you.* The bubble-like windshield surrounding the trio made it easy to see for miles in all directions. A vision from his past flashed— flying through the cosmos, hanging onto Kasartha's ankles. An experience he could share with no one. *Hmmm, maybe I could tell that Pippi girl? If anyone would believe me, she should.*

"So, son. Have you given it any more thought?" Mr. Damien's voice was oddly encouraging toward Emerson. Matthew wondered what that was about. "It's an excellent position, and it's yours. But I need you sooner than later. As soon as possible, actually."

What? Matthew wondered. *A job? Emerson's never said anything about this. Is he thinking of leaving Havensight? Leaving me?*

Emerson stiffened up and returned with a bullied tone, as though he were disgusted, "Not. Now. Da-a-ad."

Mr. Damien ran his own company upstate somewhere. Matthew knew that and also knew he was remarried and had a couple more children. Kids Emerson didn't like, or at least, *chose* not to like. Mr. Damien had left Emerson's home when Emerson was just a kid, and after that, wasn't available much. Throughout high school, Emerson had the reputation of a bully because, well, he *was* a bully, and Matthew knew that firsthand. Years later, Emerson admitted the error of his ways: he truly had thought bulldozing others was critical—you know, to be man-like. Paying people to do stuff and pushing others around, he had been trying to simulate his dad. Emerson and Matthew had bonded over the struggles of growing up without a dad. For Matthew, it was as though a key unlocked a steel door, enabling a steaming blackness to escape, taking with it enemies he'd been harboring and protecting. It had been that Dr. Alexien's dare to invite Emerson for a game of catch; he had thought she was nuts. She had played his pride; he couldn't refuse the dare. Matthew also had Arnie Decker to thank for being a sideline father figure, and he supposed whatever he learned from Arnie, he shared with Emerson, kind of like a domino effect.

But there had never been talk of Emerson taking up a job with his dad.

An even deeper sadness hit Matthew. *Everything's falling apart. I can't lose Emerson, too, not on top of everything else. Will that dark, haunted cloud come back?* He wondered if that was possible or if he had blown it off well and good, gotten right out from under it.

The airplane stalled, and the wing on one side drooped downward. "Whoa, crap!" Frightened, Matthew felt his body slide to the right.

"Calm down, calm down." Mr. Damien adjusted some controls and maneuvered the small plane to a level position. Matthew wondered if he had carried out the stall on purpose because he didn't like the way Emerson avoided his question.

I'm gonna kiss the ground when we land. Matthew was having second thoughts about this mode of transportation. *Focus,* he told himself, *just get there, get Jopphie and get home, walk if we have to.*

Mr. Damien wasn't finished and would not be chided by his own son. He made fun of Emerson's going-nowhere future in small-town nothingville, living in his controlling mother's armpits for the rest of his life. The air in the cockpit thickened with lingering emotions of anger, bitterness and a desire for revenge, all the things that had created a bully out of Emerson, all the things he and Matthew had bonded over and worked through together these past several years. The decibels of sound rose and once again, the plane climbed steadily. More altitude, more noise, more tension. Another stall.

Matthew couldn't be sure if the sinking feelings in his gut were because a bully was in control of their flight or for witnessing his friend at the hand of his abuser. He looked downward out the window and got even dizzier. Looking into the clear blue sky above them provided slight reassurance. He thought of his own dad and smiled. *I know you're up there. I love you. I still miss you. Tell me, if you can, what should I do?* But, there was no whisper in return. And the plane continued to climb sharply.

"Okay, okay!" Emerson yelled. "I'll take that stupid job. Just stop, already."

"What?" Mr. Damien laughed, "You think I'm climbing to scare you? Ha, you really do need some sharpening up, son. Don't you worry; I'll teach ya what life is all about." The plane leveled, its engine quieting down considerably. Suddenly, too quiet. Emerson didn't say a word for the rest of the flight and wouldn't look Matthew's way.

CHAPTER THIRTY-EIGHT

THE RESCUER

At the Bog of Moorelingville

MATTHEW'S MIND RACED furiously, even faster than his feet. Glad to get out of that plane, he bolted away from the landing platform, straight toward the coastline. He raced along the water's edge, not wanting to listen to any more of Emerson's explanations, and let the roar of the waves block it all out. *He's leaving, so no sense hearing him out.* Emerson followed, keeping up with Matthew as best he could, pleading for some kind of empathy, some type of friendly reassurance.

"He's gonna make her move! My mom. He can't wait to tell her I'm moving out, so no more payments. No more house. What's she gonna do, Matt? What was I supposed to do? Let 'im crash us to bits?" Stopping to catch his breath, he hollered one more time, "Ma-a-tt!"

Emerson needed consoling. Matthew knew that much but now was not the time. "Gotta get Joppha, deal with yer own problems!" He yelled back. *He's leaving me, right when I need him most, my best friend. Some friend.* Winds of abandonment were chilling. If he kept running, he could avoid them. *Jopphie! Focus, get Jopphie!*

When Emerson realized Matthew wasn't about to slow down, he turned back toward the airstrip, toward his dad, and that new future that cornered him. And with a nasty storm approaching quickly, his dad's preference was to get back to Havensight asap.

Matthew sensed his friend was no longer behind him. With a swipe of his hand, he wiped the unwanted sniffles away, angry this whole Emerson and his dad business had interfered with his Joppha rescue mission. He would direct the anger to an even greater determination, resulting in longer, faster and stronger steps.

The large, grey and angry waves mirrored the sky, and Matthew ran hard until his anger dissipated into a sappy sorrow. Arriving at a bushy opening, he took the narrow, boarded path that led to a public parking lot. Matthew found it empty but for a single car, one he couldn't help but notice: a sleek, souped-up black Camaro sitting in front of a graffitied Moorelingville Bog Parking sign. Closed due to flooding, he was sure it said.

Flooding. This is the place! Amazing. Just like that nightmare, all was familiar, and all lay before him in reality. No time for wondering how that all happened, or even how he happened to find this place…the place he felt sure Joppha had been taken and tied to a tree. Had he not fainted at Arnie's, would he have *known* to come here? Had Emerson's dad, a pilot with his own plane, not just arrived in town, how else would he have gotten here so fast? He wiped an annoying sniffle and cut across the lot toward the bog's access point, giving no mind to the occupants in the car. *Likely some dude and his girlfriend,* he figured. He stalled at the entrance. A brief memory captured his focus. One of Jopphie's sayings came to mind, the kind he and Emerson jokingly referred to as just another JS'er. *Where's the gatekeeper?* Joppha often said gatekeepers either protect you or they imprison you. *Well, Jopphie, if you're imprisoned in there somewhere, I'll find you!*

Three paths. The one on the left appeared drier than the others, though a washed-out painted map showed it took its passengers on the outskirts, a safe passage around the bog. The path on the far right was nothing but mud and would lead him right back to the shore, toward a beach area, ideal in the summer months, he supposed. The path in the middle led directly to the center of the bog. Matthew could see it was overtaken with ankle-to-knee-deep waters in sections, dark and polluted, assuredly brimming with life—creepy, slithering, scrounger types. A mosquito cloud blocked the entrance just beyond the first set of trees. *That* was the path he needed to take, and he knew it. *Daunting and imprisoning.*

The brewing storm was settling itself, thick darkness falling. A bolt of lightning struck, showing off its power, clapping thunder confirming the close proximity.

Matthew pushed down the swells coming forth inside his chest as though they themselves were born of the ocean. *No coincidence,* he thought. *I must be in the right place.*

"I'm here," Matthew whispered. "And I didn't listen to Kasartha, like you said. I got here on my own." At least Matthew had that to edify himself. Saving revelations of that nightmare took shape—that oversized guy with enormous eagle wings, Jophiel, had carried him out of this very bog.

And you were firm with your instruction: Do. Not. Listen. To. Kasartha. Matthew gulped. A lunar tidal swamp, Kasartha had called this place. Mysterious. Haunted. Strange things were known to happen here.

He hesitated—a lightbulb moment. "Jophiel was you, Joppha! *You are him!*" He wondered if anyone else knew this. Arnie? Or would Arnie believe it if he didn't know?

Water seeped into his runners and countless midges buzzed around his head, all causing him to realize he had not prepared for any kind of swamp rescue. Still, he had to enter, even if he was uncertain what he would find. And afraid. Will he find Joppha tied to that cottonwood tree? Or might he see a ghost of the boy? Might that big dude, Jophiel, be there, waiting to return Matthew to a medical bed somewhere? Was he really Joppha? What would that even mean if he were? He swallowed hard. *Haunted,* he pushed down again as Kasartha's warnings bubbled up.

Sucking in a deep breath through wide nostrils, "I'm going in," he resolved, sneezing out tiny gnats with a blow. Matthew ducked his head forward, tunneled his way through slush and waved his way through the mosquito cloud. He had entered the dark forest. Trudging several more steps, his arms were out wide to feel the way through trunks of trees, some brittle, some slimy. All with an eerie lust for the living yet hanging onto a mother called death. Still spring, budding growth hadn't overgrown yet, and Matthew wondered, *does anything green even grow in here? Ugh.* He shivered and affirmed quietly that he was a fresh, open-air kinda guy. This was not his scene.

"Jopphie," he hollered aloud, cupping his hands to his mouth, hoping the sound waves could reach deep into the bog, closer to where Joppha was last seen. "Jopphie.

Joooppheeee." An owl screeched, and Matthew's ears perked. He remembered an owl from the nightmare. *Yes! I'm on the right path.* "I'm coming, Jopphie, I'm coming!" he yelled aloud with purpose. His voice silenced the owl and caused some crows atop the trees to rustle. A howling wind and pounding rain could be heard, but not a drop fell inside the bog. The waterlogged ground beneath his feet was quite enough clamminess, he thought, thankful for the lack of falling drops on his unprotected head.

Stroking back a mop of hair, he instructed himself to step cautiously. The muddy Earth sloped downward toward a pool. It appeared shallow enough: three steps, he figured, would get him through. His jumping skills won't help him here; it was far too slippery. A firm step and two frogs jumped aside. Step two, this one with a splash, scattered horizontal flying things, bugs he had never seen before. A cautious step three, and he skidded and grabbed a low-hanging branch in time to catch his balance and swing himself to the other side. He made it, though soaked from the knees down. Something slithered across his runners. He quickly moved deeper into the woods, avoiding gnarly roots. The thought of Joppha enduring and suffering in this place added to his fierce determination: keep going. No one should be entrapped in a dark desolation like this.

Matthew continued to follow the hoot of the owl, choosing to believe the creature, though hidden from his view, was guiding him, leading him to where Joppha was. Or, alternatively, trapping him, like Joppha.

When he reached a clearing and slapped a three-inch mosquito on the back of his neck, he struggled with doubt. *I don't recall this.* Perhaps he wasn't on the right track. In his nightmare, there had been no wide opening where the sky lay bare above. Appreciating a glimmer of evening light, and still no falling raindrops though the sound of a nasty storm carried on, he searched the grey outlines. *There it is!* The top of a single cottonwood tree, mature and majestic, farther into the woods on the other side of the clearing. "Joppha! I'm coming!" he called out meekly, suddenly falling prey to an overwhelming exhaustion. Wanting to sprint, instead he collapsed to the ground. He forced himself to get up. His legs felt like cement, and he succumbed to their heavy weight. He fought to get on his knees, but an odd, invisible pressure held him down.

"Don't worry, Uncle Matty, I'm fine."

Matthew swore he heard Joppha's voice behind a pile of rocks. *I'm losing it,* he thought. He dared a slow, stretching turn of his waist toward the voice. And there he was. Joppha. Only in a ghostly form. A transparent version of his little six-year-old body. Jeans full of muck up past his waist, one runner missing. Hair tussled, forehead grimed, vest torn up, the end of a rolled-up magazine tucked snuggly inside his shirt. Wholly alive. An enormous, genuine smile across his face, dancing eyes sending darts straight through Matthew.

Tightened throat muscles prevented Matthew from any kind of intelligible speech.

Joppha kneeled and planted his face right up to his uncle's, and he simply grinned. Joppha kissed Matthew. Brief but purposeful.

Huge, salty teardrops fell. Matthew's.

Joppha stood, turned, and without a whisper of a sound, walked away, back into the bog.

Trapped inside a feeble incoherency, Matthew could do nothing but stare at the spot where his little friend had disappeared and hold down the sobs with the might of his heart.

CHAPTER THIRTY-NINE
DISAPPEARING INTO THE STORM

"OOOOO, SO *THAT'S* a muscle spasm." Pipiera arched and stretched, relieved to have arrived, finally, and escaped the confinement of that back seat. Cramped, bumpy and unpleasantly loud at times. She peered around the public parking lot while ferociously rubbing her back and then shaking her head sadly to see so much graffiti on the signage. The Moorelingville Bog was a conservation reserve protected and managed by the community and boasted a playground for nature lovers. But not during seasons of flooding, which coincidently happened to be right now. The Bog was closed to all, hikers, photographers and bird watchers included.

A gangly young man flapping his arms around his head was entering the center path; the image caught her breath. "Could that…be *Matthew*?" Looking around, she saw that no other cars were in the lot. "How'd he get here?" Was her mind playing tricks? She needed to find out and bolted toward the entrance, only to have her body shaken by the pull of Bruce's arm. He had grabbed her and pulled her back.

"Oh, no, you don't, little missy! Nuh-uh. We need to go in *prepared*. You'll be eaten alive—that is if you don't end up in the sludge. We move together, you and me." He eyed her closely and patted a leather holster on his right side, "Along with my little friend," he added. "This time of year, plenty of strange goings-on in there, those woods." He pointed toward the super-large full moon that hauntingly taunted its presence behind some incoming storm clouds and away from the setting sun. "But don't you worry none," he said, grinning and grabbing the handle of the pistol at his side. "I'm trained to use this." He let her go and began sorting the gear stored in the trunk.

"But," she pointed toward the path, "I think I just saw Matthew."

"What?" Charles chimed in, "My grandson? No, can't be. I left him at the hospital. He can't possibly be *here*." He studied his daughter for a moment; a young, energetic woman who had miraculously just waltzed into his life, in the flesh, alive, after dying some fifty-five years earlier. "Or, could he?" Anything's possible, he must have thought.

Bruce went on and on about the dangers of going into that boggy and blackened forest without proper protection. As he chatted about strange stories of terrible past happenings in there, Pipiera's certainty grew, and she debated in silence. *That had to be Matthew. He didn't have any protective gear on. I'm going in,* she decided. *Besides, I think mosquito clouds, slithering snakes and deep muddy crevices are the least of our worries.*

And… if there is a ghost in there—a rebel—your weapon of steel, dear Bruce, won't do a thing!

The sky lit up with a flash just as it roared and dropped a thick blanket of blackness.

Pipiera bolted again, a successful getaway this time. Bruce hollered after her, "And they've never found the murderer; people've disappeared in there, never to be heard from again!"

Now that, I believe, could be true! She sprinted even faster.

CHAPTER FORTY
THE FALL

*D*ANG. BRUCE WAS right, at least about the flashlight. Pipiera could've used one right about now. The changing pace of the blood in her veins upon entering the path was not from coldness; rather, the absence of knowing what lay ahead readied her body for flight. No light, and no solid ground, a gruesome, mucky formula underneath her feet. She sensed all the belly-crawling life below her and above, in the bark of the trees. Apologizing in advance to Serena, she justified her actions. *I'm about to break the rules. No one can see me, anyway!* Lifting herself gracefully, she hovered high enough to maneuver around the treetops to find and follow Matthew.

She hadn't noticed that Bruce, all geared up, had nearly caught up to her just as she rose effortlessly above the treeline.

A lightning rod flashed, reverberating flicks of brightness, warning her to stand still, at least until the turbulent rumble had settled. An unknown force, a rushing spiral of sorts, whizzed past her right foot. Then another fury sped right past her ear. Unnatural pops from below, followed by bellows of accusations. Bruce.

"I knew there was somethin' strange about you! Real off-like." He aimed, getting ready for a third shot.

No time to explain. Pipiera fled, diving downward into the thick of the bog so Bruce wouldn't have a clear line of sight. *Seriously? He thinks I'm dangerous, ha!* She stayed mid-height and slinked through the bog, crossing through limbs, one tree at a time. No sense pretending she was just as human as he was—not now, anyway. Bruce knew the bog better than her. She needed him to find the center where Charles had repeated what Matthew told him in the hospital. That was where Joppha was tied to a cottonwood tree; that was where Matthew was heading. She faulted herself for not waiting. Now, Bruce was hunting her instead of looking for Joppha. She could imagine Serena's scolding, *I told you, never break the rules!*

She moved as quickly as she could, squirrel-like, running on the limb of one tree, jumping across to the next, moving deeper and deeper until she reached a canopy of trees where little light could come through even on the brightest of days, hiding her entirely from view. She felt safe from Bruce. How she would explain herself to him, she'd have to sort out later. Through cracks and cackles, another flicker of lightning revealed an open space that lay ahead beyond the thicket. She moved quietly toward it, not wanting to disturb a fat snake wrapped around a low-hanging, lateral bough below her.

At last, she reached a clearing. Pipiera looked carefully around before entering. No Bruce. She hoped neither would there be that Kasartha rummaging around. A whimper-ing caught her attention, and she spied its source. Matthew beside a shallow pile of rocks, a human ball hugging himself. Rocking.

An army of crows waiting for something to devour cast their anger on Pipiera's presence. "Go on, get out of here!" she commanded, their noise causing Matthew to look up in time to see Pipiera float down toward him. What a vision that must have been.

Well, the jig is up now, Pipiera thought, releasing a nervous chuckle. *Time for truth, I guess. I hope he can handle it.* Her feet landed gently on the ground right beside him, her eyes never leaving his, which were now wider and rounder than the evening's moon.

Neither spoke for what seemed an endless pause. Her lips were tight, that is until a large sigh managed to escape. "I'm guessing I owe you an explanation," she said. "But first, we need to take cover. Bruce is out there. He has a gun."

Matthew blinked. "Is Joppha dead?" That being the first and only concern in his mind, Pipiera's warning went ignored. "Never mind, don't answer that. I *know* he is."

Pipiera was taken aback by his directness. *Does he think I had something to do with Joppha's situation?* "I…I don't know, Matthew. Jophiel, your Joppha, is my dear friend. I came to help him."

"Well, you're not doing a good job," Matthew snapped.

His attitude truly annoyed Pipiera. "Seriously? Why are you so bully-like with me?" She laid it out there. It was a fair question, she figured. It must have gotten to him. He retreated back into a ball.

"Don't you even want to know who I am?" Pipiera asked, curious as to his nonchalant acceptance of her. "Like, you've got to have questions! Aren't you even curious? Most people would be freaked out."

Matthew continued to rock. "I remember you," he mumbled. Then added, "I'm not afraid of you. Or any *Bruce*, for that matter."

She sat beside him. "I'm your dad's sister," she whispered. "Did you figure that part out?"

That caught Matthew's attention. "Dad didn't have a sister." He thought for a moment, trying to pull at recollections, "Or, did he?"

"Yeah, he did." She wished he'd remember more details. *This is getting tiring.*

"So, after you die, you get…superpowers? Get to spy on your family and float around?" He was being sarcastic.

"It's not like that."

"You're just like Kasartha."

"Uh, no, I'm not! Have you not even figured *that* out by now?"

Long pause.

Matthew took the bait. "So, my grandparents, they…they are your parents, too?"

She nodded. *Yup, bingo, now you got it.*

He blinked several times. "They never talked about my dad. Did… did they love him?"

Oh, again, I wasn't expecting this. "We don't have time for this right now, Matthew." But he seemed so despondent. Pipiera looked around. No Bruce, thankfully. He must have taken another path or gotten lost. Though she doubted that.

"Of course, they did. In their own way, Matthew," her voice consoling. She dug a hole with the heel of her right shoe. "Sometimes, emotions get in the way of things, especially past, hurting ones. Ones that block our thinking and stop us from opening our eyes to what's right in front of us." *Now, get up, we gotta move.*

He sniffled and changed the topic, "So, why did he have to die?"

"Your dad?"

"No!" His angry, expectant glare caused her to step back. "Joppha. You must know. There must be a reason," he challenged.

She didn't know the reason, other than perhaps it was his due expiry, or perhaps Kasartha had caused something. Perhaps Matthew was wrong, and Joppha was still on his Earth-journey, somewhere, and they just hadn't found him yet. *I hope he's wrong.* Though admittedly, she felt that same feeling. Jophiel had indeed completed his Earth-journey, her instincts informed her. She saw Matthew's limp, distraught body, his pale face, the lostness in his eyes. She wondered, "How do you know? How can you be so…so sure?"

Matthew's hand trembled as he pointed to the spot where Joppha had stood. "He was right there. He…he…he *kissed* me, said he was fine."

Oh. With that explanation, Pipiera knew it for certain, Jophiel's great separation had happened. At first a stab of sadness consumed her, but then, she couldn't help it. A gleeful, "Oh my!" escaped. Yes, of course, she had come to help him. But yes, of course, she was tickled they could be together again. Never fear separation of their friendship again, ever! That was exciting. She checked Matthew. Had he caught any glimpse of joy from her? His head was lodged between his knees, his back trembling from the sobs.

The wash of failure overcame Pipiera. "Matthew, I'm here

for you." She needed to console him. *What words would be best?* she wondered.

"It's all my fault! My fault!" He screeched so loud that the crows cawed in return, some circling as though prey might soon be served.

"No, Matthew. No, that's nonsense, don't employ those thoughts, those words," Pipiera begged. Wrestling in the bushes bordering the clearing alerted caution. Was it Bruce? *Ugh, why don't I have a flashlight? I should have at least brought some light.* She didn't like this environment, a somber grey mood laying heavily around them. She held her breath, hoping it was an animal of some sort checking out their voices, curious—even annoyed—over their presence. *King, watch over us,* she pled.

An argumentative Matthew stood. "Yes, it is," referring to his fault. "I did it. I killed Joppha, and you can't do anything about it. It's done!"

"Matthew, stop this!" Pipiera's heart pounded, her head feeling hot with frustration. *He mustn't believe that. This is Kasartha's doing, planting such ridiculous accusations.*

But he continued his rant, "Kasartha was right. I am to blame."

"Matthew, he would have died anyway." If Jophiel's tour expired, then he was never meant to journey past the tender Earth age of six. She knew that better than most. But of course, Matthew wouldn't. He couldn't.

A click, metal on metal, coming from the bush.

Uh, that's no animal.

Bruce stepped into the clearing, his loud presence hollering victory. "I knew it. They always say it's the people close to ya you can't trust. You and 'im. Workin' together, eh? Friends of Joppha, friends of Arnie. Yeah, right. What you two did to that kid, to his family…I'll make sure you get yers."

"No, no, Bruce, you've got this all wrong!" Pipiera's dart toward Bruce was met with a gun blasted upward into the grey sky. She stopped abruptly; he had her full attention.

Then he took aim directly at Pipiera. "Ya fooled my buddy, Charles; you ain't foolin' me. Step back." She did. His accusing aim moved straight to Matthew. "You killed him, didn't you? Ya just said it."

"Yes. I did." Matthew, on his feet now, held both hands up in the air, surrendering his guilt.

"No, Matthew, no!" Pipiera gritted her teeth, wanting desperately to take charge of this…misunderstanding. "Bruce, *listen* to me. Matthew did no such thing. He's saying that because he *feels* responsible. He. Did. Not. Harm. Joppha. You must believe me!" Pipiera knew Bruce harbored anger and deep hurt from the loss of his own son, and this situation likely raised it all back up to the surface. Unhealed trauma. No one to blame. She pursed her lips and wondered just how she could possibly make a difference and wondered whether, in fact, her own presence on this little mission had made things worse. *Now what do I do?*

More rustling in the bushes.

Another click, metal on metal. Bruce focused his aim steady on Matthew.

"No!" Pipiera jumped in front of Matthew.

An adrenaline-filled Charles clambered out of the bushes, pushing Bruce aside.

The gun blasted.

Matthew fell.

CHAPTER FORTY-ONE
THE PLAN

In the Outer Courtyard of the Kingdom

ALONE, MEGALOS CHURNED Aivy's words over and over. 'Your earthly father, Kasartha, seems to be the one who is now cursed. But that is not your doing,' she had said. "Yeah, my dear Aivy, maybe that wasn't my doing, but I intend to get that curse settled. Once and for all. I must. For the sake of all descendants."

He was about to go on an excursion, only this time, Megalos wouldn't take the path to greater heights where over-arching understandings exist, where discussions that take the beginning of time to the end of time into consideration. No, this time, he would travel downwards to The Deep, with a single task in sharp focus, like an arrow. Past the lower levels of the Kingdom, trespassing spatial voids, and cutting through the ice fields. His destination: the River of Times. That was *the* dividing line. Where the crystal waters from the Kingdom fell from great heights and mixed with the weighty dark waters pushed up from below. An ever-flowing river that carried the stones of life, each stone representing an Earth-journeyer until it was picked up and delivered to one side or the other.

At the River's footbridge was where Megalos would go to summon and wait. He would sit and mindfully will a dare for the Dragon to come. Personally. Megalos was planning a tête-à-tête with the beast of the cosmos, the leader of the rebels, the most deceitful one of all who ever existed.

He had not sought the King's blessing for his secret plan. "I must fix this myself. I caused the birth of this curse." The King had long forgiven Megalos for the curse, though the Dragon will lord it over Kasartha for the rest of Kasartha's days, forcing him to attack an entire line of descendants, the line taken from Kasartha and gifted to Megalos. Punishment. Eternal punishment. Determined, Megalos would stop this. *I'm not much of a protector if I cannot save my descendants from this harm,* he rationalized his plot.

His mission was a simple one. Megalos would work a trade with the Dragon: the premature separation of Jophiel in return for relieving Kasartha from this business of attacking the line of descendants. Simple, maybe, but it caused his throat to tighten just the same. Megalos was counting on Aivy being correct—that the Dragon was not aware Jophiel was already scheduled to arrive. So, in fact, Megalos will be giving nothing away, rather something that was already planned. He justified the plan to himself: *in theory, I normally don't know the arrival schedule in advance, so then, in theory, I am negotiating in good faith.* He rubbed his chin and closed his eyes tight. *And since I am giving away a premature separation, one already planned and sanctioned by the Kingdom, I don't need authority.*

A man of action, not a man of 'in theory' kind of stuff, he prayed this would work.

He slipped into the travel tunnel, ensuring no one spotted his exit.

229

CHAPTER FORTY-TWO
THE DEAL

At the River of Times

MEGALOS WAS RIGHT. He knew if he planted his feet firmly in the soil on the Kingdom's shore of the River of Times, beside the footbridge, and remained silent with his best bully stance, the Dragon would appear personally. Rebel loyalists would scurry and stare and snarl, but most of all, they'd excitedly await the confrontation that would surely happen. The Dragon had a particular interest in Megalos as Head Gatekeeper of the Kingdom, but even more so, as a *personal* enemy. After all, it was Megalos who had jilted him out of an entire line of descendants, a line he was fighting hard to win back, one at a time.

Megalos was thankful Othis's army had taken little notice of his presence. Likely presuming it was a fully sanctioned visit, they went about their usual business of battling with rebels atop and along the Kingdom's side of the flowing waters. Surely, the Head Gatekeeper of the Kingdom wouldn't be there if it weren't for a Kingdom-purposed visit.

Making deals to allow a premature arrival in return for a handful of Earth-journeyers to be left in peace was a common negotiation. One man's suffering to prevent the attacks on several others was a well-adopted strategy used as situations necessitated, according to the Authoritarians. A way to win small battles in the grand war.

The beastly Dragon did indeed arrive, showing only his head and tiny shoulders as usual and attracting many onlookers, all preferring to keep their distance regardless of which side they fought for. All battling had paused, Othis's soldiers and Uncle's minions standing still. Occasional blinking occurred, the stench burning every nostril for miles.

Uncle laughed at Megalos's offer. "Jophiel? Oh, my Megalos Dimietris, aren't *you* the sly one?" he groaned with a sickening delight to his tone.

Megalos had to remind himself of the words he had shared with Pipiera many times: *the smallest in the Kingdom is greater than the most deceitful of all.* And that included this space beast who ruled and romped as he pleased in The Deep. Megalos was not the smallest in the Kingdom by any means but butted up against this beast whose followers call him Uncle; the sheer size difference could challenge even his belief.

The middle of three fingers on the Dragon's right hand pointed directly to a water swirl in the river, a fast, deep and dark whirl with a glowing light at its core. "Look, my friend, our infamous Jophiel is already trapped." Uncle chortled even more, his shoulders shaking from a belly laugh. Then with eyes narrowing and his neck stretching across the waters, "He's *already* returning, Dimietris. And you *know* it."

Anticipating the charge, Megalos remained calm and firm, laying out the scenario, claiming Jophiel's light was bright, and he was sure to overcome this storm, even with the boundary of a young boy's mortality. His negotiation continued.

Uncle said nothing.

"It's time to stop," Megalos persisted.

If there were ever a chance for the King to allow Kasartha to become a Kingdom Citizen, it would be at the complete discretion of the King himself; Megalos knew that. He also knew such a move to be rare, so he'd have to let go of any such notion, there was nothing he could do about that. Though, it *was* feasible to request Kasartha be relieved from the Dragon's charge of attacking his line of descendants. That would be the tactic for this negotiation. A win-win: most certainly a win for his current and future descendants, and presumably, considered a win for Kasartha. Thus, marking the end, once and for all, to this ridiculous curse.

"As to harm; he has cast sufficient," Megalos summarized, referring to Kasartha's actions.

"*I* decide what harm is enough!" Uncle snapped, spittle slithering down his neck and dishing out even more stink.

Not allowing him the satisfaction of a gag, Megalos crossed his arms over his puffed chest.

"Okay, Megalos Dimietris. How about this?" Uncle's words slithered. "Your little replacement boy comes home early, and I shall cease *all* attacks on your measly line. All the more time for *personal* training for the glory boy. Sounds acceptable to *me*."

Strong was the desire to shut his eyes ever so tight and wish this whole mess away. *What am I doing?* Megalos challenged himself. Uncle was referring to Matthew. The Dragon would accept a stoppage to the line of attacks if a premature separation could be arranged for Matthew. Megalos chewed about the incredible turmoil. *I don't want my line to suffer anymore. This rebel business has to stop. It MUST stop! Surely, Matthew would learn to understand this. Would he forgive me? Would the King forgive me?* Megalos wallowed in regret but dared not show it.

"No. Not Matthew Mackenzie." The words escaped his tongue. Firm and finite.

Uncle turned his back and began to slip away.

Desperate to put an end to this curse, "Wait!" Megalos cried.

CHAPTER FORTY-THREE
THE RISE

At the Bog of Moorelingville

TWO KINGDOM EAGLE couriers landed, so incredibly graceful, so incredibly casual. *So amazing. And what succinct timing!* Pipiera mused. *Like they were on standby, waiting for this.*

"Oh. Bit of a gathering, is it?" One teased, his voice like a balm reminding Pipiera of Kingdom ways. Forgetting the earthly situation at hand, she breathed a sigh of relief.

"What happened here?" Another voice chimed in. This one she recognized as Jophiel's. But...a lesser age?

Pipiera swirled around immediately, and there he was. Little Joppha, a young Jophiel. A young, small, boy-like Jophiel. No towering height, no powerful wingspan; in fact, no wings at all. Just a boy.

"Jo – Jophiel?" Pipiera squeaked.

"'tis I." He grinned and came closer to give her one of his famous and familiar jabs.

She danced excitedly around him in circles.

"Hey, you're making me dizzy," he laughed.

"Look at you, just look at you! You are a Kingdom Citizen… well, you're gonna be! You did it! I am so excited," she cried, still neglecting the earthly scene at hand, a trauma of sorts.

"Thank you, Pip, for watching over me. I always had this… this feeling you were. But…" he glanced toward Matthew and leaned in closer to Pipiera. "Uh, why's he…with us?"

Matthew stood casually, scratching the back of his neck while his physical body lay crumpled on the ground.

"I was pretty sure he wasn't part of the plan," Jophiel confided. "Did something go wrong?"

The three of them, Pipiera, Jophiel and Matthew, watched as Bruce and Charles crept close to the body on the ground, one arguing, the other wailing.

"Seriously?" Matthew asked in an oddly calm manner. "This is how it all ends? You knew this?"

Pipiera shook her head in horror, "No! No, I promise I didn't know!" Her voice caught Bruce's and Charles's attention.

The eagle couriers moved in, interrupting their little chat. They had a job to do. They latched on each side of young Jophiel and started to launch.

"Hey, wait! Aren't you forgetting something?" Her use of authority stopped them in midair, and they swiftly landed once again. "Him!" She pointed at Matthew. "And me, of course. I'm thinking my mission must be finished, wouldn't it be?" The latter question was posed to no one; rather, it spilled out aloud on its own.

Both eagles shrugged, one pulling a tiny piece of paper from his pocket then shoving it back in. "Just one. Joppha Decker, six-year-old boy." They started to rise again.

"No!" Pipiera demanded, "You have another. You are sure to get another command." She smoothed out her jumper with both hands. "Now, spare us the formalities, Matthew and I will go with you. I shall accompany you to deliver both boys to the Kingdom gate, together."

Looking at each other, the two eagles hesitated.

"Look," Pipiera's voice grew stronger, her back taller. "*I am the Head Gatekeeper's assistant.*"

One cocked his head. *No, you are not*, was surely what he was thinking, she figured. Her shoulders slumped, "Okay, c'mon, you guys, you know me. *Pipiera?* I used to hang out in the courtyard all the time. *Remember?*"

"Ah yes, the *gate girl*," one said affectionately, the other nodding approval and offering up a friendly smile.

"*Ple-e-a-se!*" she whined.

The pair shrugged, then nodded for all to get ready. The two eagle couriers would deliver up Joppha Decker, Matthew Mackenzie and Pipiera, the gate girl, to the Kingdom Courtyard, where the boys would meet the Head Gatekeeper, Megalos Dimietris, and Pipiera could explain the extra parcel. *Surely, they must be expecting him,* she thought.

As they rose, Pipiera scanned the dark scene below her, the blackened bog. With the moon still offering some evening glow, she spotted two figures. One, with a gun hanging limply at his side, standing over Matthew's earthly shell, the other looking up, stunned, directly at her as she continued to rise up, up and away.

"Oh, dear. *Dad.* Oh my, you can *see* me! I got carried away. You must know I had a mission to do. I'm *so* sorry; I've left you again…but I promise, I'll watch over you!"

CHAPTER FORTY-FOUR

THE NEWS

In the Town of Havensight

"HE MADE SUCH a joke out of it, of *me*, being married twice. Of *Matthew*, regaining consciousness. He had the nerve to joke about both those things!" Marnie allowed the crushing drips of her escapade earlier that day to fall directly into the receiver. Maybe she could regain some self-esteem. She had called Doctor Alexien. "You were there, all those years ago, at Matty's bedside, too. Imagine that. Joking about a…a miracle. Can you believe him?" The vision of Dr. Bonneville's face and his harsh words were still seared on her brain.

"I was, indeed, there, Marnie. And a miracle is no joke." Dr. Alexien didn't seem alarmed even a little by all that Marnie complained about.

"And to top it all off, he didn't even ask about Maggie!" Marnie cupped her free hand, circling the receiver as if to ensure that no one could hear but Dr. Alexien. "I hauled off and slapped him." She wasn't proud of that, but getting it off her chest to someone she could trust was helpful.

"You what? Oh my, Marnie!" That had caught Dr. Alexien's attention. She couldn't help breaking into a laugh. "Oh my, no wonder he canceled our meeting this afternoon. Say, Marnie, I'm free. Want to get together? It sure sounds like you could use a friend right now."

Marnie hemmed and hawed. So much was simply out of place, so much she needed to take care of, so much about which she had no clue what to do next. "Yes, sure, I would really love that," Marnie replied. "But you'll have to come here. I don't know where Charles is. I have to presume he and Karo are together, and they'll be home anytime now. They'll need me here. And Matthew? Well, I thought he'd be here by now, too. He's been discharged, at least I'm pretty sure he was. Who am I but just the mother to know these things?" she chuckled sarcastically. "I'm guessing he went to Laura's parents' place in town. So, please, Dr. Alexien, come here if you would." Marnie still had several calls yet to make for Maggie's funeral. The day was overwhelming indeed, a trusted friend could be just what she needed right now.

Perfect timing. The doorbell was an interruption, a welcomed distraction. Marnie had just laid out three of her mother-in-law's favorite outfits on Matthew's lower bunk. All Sunday bests. A long-sleeved, pink-collared dress, perfect for a sunny but still cool spring day. A turquoise jacket and skirt with matching hat, perfect for a summer wedding. And the third option, a puffy, mellow-yellow blouse with big red posies and a navy skirt. Marnie was checking out the shoe options and bumped her head in the closet when the bell rang.

"Oh, that was fast!" The warmth from hugging Dr. Alexien stirred Marnie into a deep sobbing: a release of sadness, the fear of losing control, and anxiety from so many responsibilities, none of which she felt she was managing well at all. It felt so good to let it go, even if it were for mere seconds in a row, enough to drown in a caring embrace.

"Should we go inside, Marnie?"

"Oh, of course." Time ran out for Marnie to feel embarrassed over her burst of crying when a black town car pulled up to the curb, and a sharply dressed man in a black suit abruptly stepped out. Seeing her on the porch, the man called to her, providing the reason for the visit.

"Mrs. Mackenzie? I'm here for Mrs. Maggie Mackenzie's outfit."

Up the front steps he skipped and held his hand out to shake hers, "I am truly sorry for your loss, Marnie. May I call you Marnie? I'm Roy Fellows, by the way, at your service." His enormous business smile showed off a set of bright whites.

"Ah, of course, yes, just a moment. Could you wait here?" Turning to Dr. Alexien, "Could you help me for a moment?" Marnie pulled her in by the elbow and led Dr. Alexien up the stairs to Matthew's room. Pointing to the three outfits, "Which one? Help me pick. I couldn't make a decision if my life depended on it today."

Dr. Alexien chose the turquoise outfit. "Got a blouse to go with this?"

Marnie sorted through the jammed closet, "Only about seven, all white!" She laughed. "Here's one with silver around the collar."

They both eyed a pair of silver flats. "Perfect!" Dr. Alexien exclaimed and helped Marnie package up the outfit for this gentleman waiting on her front steps. "You'll need some stockings, too," she added.

Marnie caught a wave of reality. This was it. Maggie was really gone. She had grown to love this woman, Frank's mother. "Oh, why couldn't I have had her in my life earlier?"

Dr. Alexien sat herself down beside Marnie. "You had the blessing of taking care of her. She had the blessing of getting to know you. She saw what a loving, caring woman you are and discovered just how much you loved her son. That must have given her peace, Marnie. That was a wonderful gift." Pause. "And, sometimes, we just need to be thankful for what blessings we have been given."

Marnie resigned with a sigh and agreed. She took the outfit to the man on her front step and reminded him of her own legal name. Mrs. Decker, not Mrs. Mackenzie.

The women rested at the kitchen table, teapot steeping. Once the brew was poured, Dr. Alexien opened up *all* the cans of conversations they needed to have, one at a time. Worms all over, so to speak.

Hours were filled with words, questions, concerns, tears, worries and laughs till so much time had passed that Marnie jumped out of her chair. No one in her household was home! Just where was everyone? "Goodness!" she cried. "I must make some calls. Charles must be lost!" Brushing her forehead, she reached for the phone, and it rang just as she was about to grab it. Startled by the ring, she expressed a hopeful explanation, "Oh, maybe that's him. He might have gone to the hardware store; he loves to peruse those shelves. Or perhaps he and Karo went for a long walk …or for lunch somewhere? Surely, he's okay."

Another loud ring startled her, and she realized her hesitation to answer. *What if it's bad news? Hasn't there been enough for one day?*

"Shall I answer?" Dr. Alexien asked, recognizing Marnie's fear. She knew more tough news would be coming Marnie's way. That was the reason she managed to plant herself in Marnie's kitchen, ready to support whatever was coming next.

"Hello?" Marnie responded eagerly.

"Mrs. Mackenzie?"

Marnie rolled her eyes. "No, but Mrs. Decker is here," she snapped.

"Oh, right, of course, I remember now. Mrs. Decker. Marnie, right?"

"Yes, who is this? Do you have Charles?"

"Detective Johnstone, Ma'am. Charles Mackenzie, a man, looks to be in his eighties perhaps. Are you looking for him as well?"

As well? Who else should I be looking for? She thought for a moment. "Karo, my daughter, is she with him? Is she with Charles?"

"No Ma'am. But…" The Detective didn't get a chance to explain.

"Oh, no. Matthew. Is *he* with you?" She placed her free hand on her hip and narrowed her eyes. "Are they both at the station?"

Dr. Alexien rose and crept over to where Marnie stood, ready to catch her should she fall.

"No, Ma'am. Both your son, Matthew Mackenzie, and I'm guessing it's his granddad, Charles Mackenzie?"

"Yes," Marnie responded, remaining stone still and quiet for the rest of the message that would come next.

"Well, Ma'am, Matthew's been shot, and Charles was a witness. A firsthand eyewitness, but on account of his heart racing, he and Matthew are both on their way to the Moorelingville Health Center."

"SHOT? …Moorelingville?"

Dr. Alexien embraced Marnie. Holding her up, she encouraged Marnie to request more information. Instead, as Dr. Alexien had anticipated, Marnie fell backward. Holding her securely, Dr. Alexien dragged her into the living room. Maggie's hospital bed, stripped of its sheets, was the perfect spot. She coaxed a shocked Marnie to lie down and told her to close her eyes for a few moments. "I'll stay with you; I'm not going anywhere." Then Dr. Alexien plopped herself in a comfy side chair and slouched with great relief. She picked up the receiver of the extension phone beside the chair and advised the detective that Mrs. Decker would be on her way to Moorelingville shortly and thanked him kindly for the call.

Now, Dr. Alexien would simply just wait for more instruction from the Authoritarians.

CHAPTER FORTY-FIVE

THE ARRIVALS

In the Outer Courtyard of the Kingdom

"MEGS, THEY'RE COMING, they're here!" Roly hooted, calling his superior; that man who trained him, that man he looked up to, that man who'd hidden himself away in that watchtower of his even as Arrivals came one after the other and never came to help. Megalos had locked himself away, grieving madly and brooding badly. As soon as Roly witnessed two of their trusted eagle couriers dropping off three figures at the horizon, recognizing one of them to be Megalos's Pipiera, he just knew this *had* to be part, or even all, of the reason for Megalos's unusual behavior.

"Megs!" This time Roly's voice expressed serious annoyance.

Roly's yelp was signal enough, and Megalos absorbed its meaning loud and clear. He knew when he looked out his window, he would see a premature Arrival from his own line.

Matthew. He reassured himself; he had to do it, stop all this Kasartha attacking business. But no matter the reasoning, the justification, the in-theory crap, he scolded himself, *this doesn't feel right. Oh, what have I done? Who am I to make such a deal? An unsanctioned one, at that. I don't deserve to keep my role here anymore. I should just retire, and let the boy take over right away. I should've just let that beast walk away.*

Megalos heard Roly call impatiently for the third time. *I'll need to train Matthew to talk to Roly about that tone. 'course, he's short on his Earthly training, so good chance he won't be getting to be my replacement any more.* He wondered, *would it simply be passed to Roly? That's not so bad. And Matthew is safe.* He reassured himself that all was good. *At least, won't it be?* He worked on convincing himself.

Then he heard Aivy's voice. "Megalos Dimietris. You get down here right now!"

That was *not* a command he could ignore.

The ornate bench creaked as he stood. Hesitating, he avoided the window and went straight to the circular stairs, descending slowly, one at a time. He would soon meet a fate, he figured; one he dreaded. One he deserved. He had no right to negotiate with the Dragon, not without the King's blessing. *But someone had to stop this curse.* Again, he justified his actions to himself.

Megalos stepped into the Courtyard as though it might be his last time doing so in the prestigious position he held. *Some Head Gatekeeper*, he whimpered. *I've brought so much harm.* He squeezed his chin; *I can only hope the good I've done over the last 300 years makes up for my actions today.*

The breeze felt and smelled wonderful. *Lavender. Pipiera's favorite. And so fitting; here she comes.* He was excited to see her but ashamed. *What will she think when she discovers that the reason she's bringing Matthew home prematurely is because of me?*

He stood still, needing to register it all, watching those riding a wave from the horizon toward the beloved gate he protected so.

Pipiera. My dear, beloved and courageous granddaughter. Of whom I am so proud.

Jophiel, a young boy. At last, ready to become a Kingdom Citizen, no longer an Escort.

Matthew. A premature arrival. How will I explain?

Their eagle couriers scurrying off, the threesome arrived with big grins and faced their greeters, Roly, Megalos and Aivy.

Megalos noticed Aivy had dropped the crossed arms she had held in place for him moments ago so she could pull little Jophiel in for a big hug. "I'm so proud of you! This is such joy, an exciting day indeed. You, my dear friend, today is the day! You shall become a Kingdom Citizen."

Megalos remained silent. He would let Aivy and Roly take the lead. He would answer as and when and if required. That would be the best way to get through this awkward scene. Pipiera was catching on to his odd mood; she cocked her head and watched his face intently. *She knows something's wrong; she just doesn't know what yet.*

Aivy smiled at the other boy. "Matthew, it's good to see you, but," she chuckled, "you are not due to arrive just yet." Her questioning eyes moved to line up with the surprised look in Pipiera's.

Pipiera jumped in, of course, feeling the need to explain. "He was shot. In the bog, just now. It made sense to deliver him up since the eagles were there for Jophiel."

Aivy smiled calmly and asked Matthew, "What might be going through your mind right now?"

Is this some kind of test? Surely, this is the home he is to be delivered to! Surely, he'll pass his scans. Megalos's thoughts were silent but frantic. He debated internally; was there a possible outcome he had not anticipated?

"Ah, totally cool!" Matthew's arms were spread out as wide as they could reach. "Look at this place. Gotta love it." He paused and gave Megalos a sly grin. "I know you, I'm sure of it. We've met, right? I've been here before, I know it!"

Megalos did not like the way Aivy pursed her lips; it was an unnatural smile.

Matthew continued on with an excited rant as he placed his arm around Pipiera, "And this here little gal is my aunt. Do you believe that? Cra-a-zy, ain't it!"

Pipiera's head dropped. That was clearly not information she should have shared with Matthew, not until he had become a Kingdom Citizen. "Sorry," she whispered quietly, obviously feeling some heat from Aivy's glare.

"What? No!" Matthew had just caught the eyes of his grandmother, who was chatting away with onlookers at a nearby picnic table. He bolted, as did she, and they met halfway, greeting each other with incredibly joyous hugs.

Aivy took the opportunity to speak to Pipiera and Megalos while Roly attended yet another Arrival. Megalos noticed Aivy didn't seem concerned should Jophiel overhear what she had to say. Likely, he figured, because of Jophiel's history, his previous role as an escort for the Kingdom. "Pip," she said, "Matthew is not on the arrivals schedule. What have you done?"

Oh goodness, she shouldn't be blamed! Megalos jumped in.

"It's my fault. *I'm* to blame. But surely, Matthew's loyalty is… is to the King, our Kingdom. Has to be!"

Aivy held up a hand to stop the direction of the conversation. She may not have been much taller than the six-year-old version of Jophiel, but her ways were just as commanding as the umpteen-foot, fully wing-spanned version. "That is not what I am questioning. This is not about loyalty. This is about fate. It is *not* his time. He should not have separated."

"But he did," Pipiera persisted. "I saw it for myself."

"You acted too quickly." Aivy was annoyed and abrupt.

Matthew bounced back into earshot and requested, "Can I see my Dad now? I need to." His grandmother joined him by his side, linking arms. "We both need to see him," they chimed. Matthew was bouncing with excitement, and so were Maggie's eyes.

"I wasn't expecting my grandson," Maggie calmly announced, giving him a big squeeze. "Pipiera, you must go back and be with Marnie. I've grown so fond of her, and, oh my, she's going to need someone to lean on. Especially *now.*" It was a fierce directive.

Pipiera did her best to swallow a big wad of disappointment. *Mother,* she whispered, but her mother was engrossed with Matthew's presence. It horrified Megalos to watch Pip's face. Pretty sure she wasn't expecting *that* to be their first conversation upon meeting again. *Never should I have interfered with the King's order of things. This, too, is my doing. If only I could undo my actions.*

Aivy was shaking her head and for good reason. Arrivals and Citizens cannot make such demands; only the Authoritarians and only when sanctioned by the King.

"Matthew, you must go back." Aivy was firm. The fun was over.

"Huh? Why?" Matthew clearly wanted to stay.

"But, but, Aivy, there's nothing to go back to. He was shot. I saw it for myself." Pipiera was concerned, though her voice was crackling.

"Yes," Aivy responded. "But not fatally." She squinted and clinched a thumb and finger together, adding, "Just a good grazing, actually."

Pipiera's face went pale. "Oh, my."

Megalos held his breath.

"He's going back, and you are, too, both with a charge."

Matthew gulped, "What does that mean? Doesn't sound good, a *charge*."

"Listen up," Aivy instructed. "One. Your mother. She needs you. Build up her loyalty. Two. Emerson. He needs you. It's a matter of eternal life. Three, most important of all. Arnie. Feed him for the rest of his days. He'll need the words, the same words he's been feeding you. Got it?"

Matthew dared not do anything but nod. Aivy turned to Pipiera, who stood ready to listen.

"You are going to prison. Bruce Brogan's prison. Let him catch you. Then, *you* release *him*. After he's free, straight back here. Got it?"

Oooo boy, that could be years, long Earth years, Megalos thought. *An already grief-stricken father—when that Bruce Brogan learns he just shot another man's son, how will she set him free?* He mourned silently. *I might not see her for decades.* "But…," Megalos began to blurt a resistance. He didn't get far, Aivy shushed him.

Pipiera choked out, "Yes, Ma'am."

"Don't call me ma'am." At that, Aivy turned to smile at the irresistible new Jophiel. A gentle motion with her finger meant, *just a moment, I'll be right with you.* Then she escaped through the gate and into the Kingdom, all while muttering to Megalos that she would deal with *him* later.

CHAPTER FORTY-SIX
BACK AGAIN

In the Outer Courtyard of the Kingdom

IT DIDN'T TAKE much more than a gentle nudge for Pipiera to lure Matthew away from the tension rising at the gate. *I need to talk to him in private,* she thought. The pair backed away. "Let's walk," she coaxed.

Withdrawing from the commotion would do her good. That whole scene was not how the long-awaited meeting with her mother was supposed to be. She hid the nervous energy welling up inside as best she could. *Focus,* she encouraged herself, *fix this business with Matthew first. That's the least you can do.* Like being pushed overboard unwillingly and told to swim, Pipiera would learn firsthand how to build resilience in the wake of great disappointment.

"I'm going back? I can't stay?" Matthew seemed appalled. "Why? Did I do something wrong?"

Pipiera responded, hoping he would understand and forgive her. "No! No, Matthew. I'm sorry, it's all my fault. I just…just assumed you had separated for good. I thought that gunshot…well, I thought, frankly, that your Earth tour was over, put it that way."

"So it's not? Just like that, I get bounced around again?"

"Please forgive me. I've been trying to help you," she lowered her head. "It's really complicated to understand. Even for me."

He could see she was despondent, skittish even. The shaking in her hands gave it away. He scanned the horizon. "Incredible," he breathed the word softly. Returning his focus to Pipiera, he softly whispered back, "Really complicated," and nodded as though he understood. "You were just trying to help me. I see that now."

She wondered if what he saw were the levels of harsh disappointment in herself and others. *Did my mother just reject me?* She wanted to run and cry. Instead, she encouraged Matthew. That was her job.

"I didn't do a very good job. But you, *you*, Matthew, I applaud you. You were trying to get to Jophiel. And you made the effort, *without* Kasartha. You found another way."

"Yeah, but it didn't matter much, did it?" He glanced back at a happy Jophiel play-fighting with Megalos, the scene lightening his mood. "Ah, he's okay. Look at him over there; he's so awful darn happy."

Pipiera sighed and leaned in to make a confession, "These missions, they are so confusing. I think I know what I'm supposed to do, but then all clarity disappears. Like a crazy, wild storm surge appears, and that sense of fear, the unknowing, just takes over!"

"Like trying to jump that river! Do you remember?" Matthew spoke of a time years ago, when on her first mission,

Pipiera had convinced Matthew to take a leaping jump over the River of Times to save his life.

She gasped, "*You* remember that?"

"Clear as a bell. You know," he looked around, "it's all so clear here. Everything makes sense. Everything is…*perfect*." He studied her again. "So, exactly how many of these so-called missions have you been on?"

"Well, just two."

His roaring laugh surprised her, but not as much as his arm tightly squeezing her waist.

"My Auntie, the mission worker," he teased. "And both of those involved me, didn't they!"

"Yup, they sure did." She watched Matthew's face grow serious. *Just when did you grow up?* she thought to herself, *and I'm not just thinking about your height.* "Hey, do you remember when I came out of your closet with Jophiel?"

He nodded fondly with a huge grin. "I sure do." Matthew grew serious again. "I get it now. How fortunate I am, I realize that too. Well, if I must go back, then I will go back," he said with purpose. "I will do all those things that she said. What was her name?"

"Aivy."

"Aivy. Yes, I will do all those things Aivy instructed. I must do what I'm called to do. And what an honor, I mean, *what* an honor! Whatever I do will be with this place, this Kingdom, in mind."

Pipiera admired this boy, this man. "I am so proud of you, Matthew."

"And, as I understand it, sounds like you are about to go on Mission Number Three?" His eyebrows raised, "We shall both have a purpose."

Her mouth twisted. "Yeah, but you won't remember all of this. Well, spits and spats, I suppose."

"You'll help me, though, right? Set me straight. Remind me, teach me, tell me when I'm off track?"

"I'll do my best. I promise you that. But it sounds like I'll be in a prison of some sort. That jail cell. My influence might be limited. Especially with that Bruce Brogan!"

"And I, dear Auntie, will come visit you. Heck, I'll even bake you a cake and bury a file in it." That made him chuckle, even though Pipiera didn't get the joke.

The two faced each other, and with firm stances and mindsets, they shook hands.

"Hey," Matthew said. "You owe me. How about that *long-jumping date?*"

"You *do* remember everything!" She giggled. That had been a promise she made on her first mission, to call Matthew sometime, and they'd go jumping together. "Never too late to make good on a promise!" She ran ahead. He followed. They jumped the Arrival waves straight out to the horizon before riding one back, where they would regroup with Aivy, and where the eagle couriers would be ready to escort them to Earth.

CHAPTER FORTY-SEVEN
GROWING UP FAST

I T WAS CLEARLY not a *usual* process, and not just *any* Arrival. It was *Jophiel.* And Megalos was tickled to receive him. *After all these centuries, my friend, this is your moment,* he reflected. A sigh of satisfaction was called for, but laying flat on his stomach, the boy on his back, there could be none of that.

"I gotcha now!" Young Jophiel squealed. Sitting atop Megalos and yanking his left leg, proud as punch. The pair were laughing so hard that no one really had the other. Megalos reached up and around, trying his mightiest to grab hold of those little stocky arms wrestling his ankle, but Jophiel was just too tricky to pin down.

Megalos hadn't laughed so much for such a long time. And he sure needed the relief this provided. Despite everything, it was indeed a day of celebration. Lovable, dependable, loyal Jophiel was home. He would focus on that, the joy of the moment.

"Always knew not to get on your bad side," Megalos cheered.

Jophiel halted as though Megalos had said something wrong. "My dream, my dream has come true," said a conquering Jophiel. If he were the type to do so, he would have pinched himself. Instead, Jophiel lay atop Megalos and gave him a big bear hug. He'd watched Megalos give big bear hugs to Arrivals for decades and decades. Now, he could finally give one himself, though his arms barely reached.

"Aw, come on." Megalos hadn't felt such tearful waterworks since Pipiera's arrival.

Jophiel jumped up and stood beside Megalos, who was still sprawled out flat on the ground. "You've been like a mentor to me, Megs. I admire you. Your steadfastness, the work you do for the Kingdom, you just keep going. It's gotta be tough, knowing all you know, seeing all you see. And worst of all, *feeling* it. It's like you're still there, battling through the dark fog of emotions."

Jophiel may have arrived in a six-year-old form, but his wisdom was far greater. He had been a Kingdom Escort for hundreds of years, ensuring the safe travel of Kingdom Citizens for brief visits to Earth. He knew all too well the price the Authoritarians paid to intervene in the lives of Earth-journeyers, the same as the likes of Megalos who worked *outside* the Kingdom walls. They couldn't escape the darkness surrounding the Earth, the Dragon's own arena, as those inside could. It was painful to witness, but their fierce courage protected the futures of many.

But an Escort was not a Citizen.

Jophiel had dreamed of one day becoming a Kingdom Citizen himself. To do that, one must take the fall, become an

Earth-journeyer, and accomplish an assigned purpose. More often than less, the paths were many, the choices deceiving.

He wiped his cheeks. Wet. Jophiel had never felt tears on his face before. "Let's get the show on the road, as they say. Start the processing."

"Aivy wants to be present. She'll be back shortly. Let's… let us head over there, and we'll catch up a bit till she gets back." Before heading over to the picnic table area, Megalos confided, "She's a little upset with me." Releasing a sigh, "And rightfully so."

Aivy returned with a couple of towels and caught up to them. "Looks like you both need some growing up to do." The tease in her voice provided some instant relief to Megalos. *Might she no longer be angry with me? I can hope.*

"Why the towels?" Megalos asked. Aivy always seemed to have prepared and ready in hand whatever anyone needed, at the exact time it was needed. That's when he realized that both he and Jophiel were covered in mud—with sparkling gleams of purples and wonderfully scented like fresh vineyard grapes were at their peak time for harvest.

"Yes!" Jophiel gave a fist bump, "Always wanted to do that!"

Their tears had mixed with the soil of the courtyard as the two had been wrestling. Tiny flowers already grew from the batter made by their thoughts and the ground they stood upon, a purple jelly extract that covered their limbs.

As the pair joked and wiped themselves down, Aivy asked Jophiel, "What age?" Megalos knew she was giving Jophiel an option of the approximate age he would like to be once he entered the Kingdom, once he'd be crowned a *Citizen*. Jophiel was far too wise and experienced to remain a six-year-old.

Megalos guessed he'd go for mid-twenties. *Nice she's giving him the option,* he thought. They didn't always.

Aivy appeared to get a little emotional herself. *Is that a tear? Aivy? Never have I witnessed such,* Megalos mused in surprise and wonder. He blinked as her face twisted up and she brought her hand to her mouth. She grabbed little Jophiel and hugged him ferociously. In return, Jophiel tucked his head under her chin.

"Welcome." She could barely get the word out.

Releasing him, fixing her hair, then placing her arm around his little shoulders, the same shoulders she once could never reach unless she employed a ladder, she pointed toward Matthew and Pipiera. They had been jumping together in the lavender patch. "Watch this," she said.

The three witnessed Matthew and Pipiera, who stood face to face in the distance, making a firm handshake, appearing to agree on something.

"They're making a pact." Tears now streamed down Aivy's cheeks. "Matthew's going to get through the next phase of his journey, after all." Her exhale revealed a long-awaited concern she must have been holding in tight. "Thank you, Jophiel," she whispered.

Jophiel grinned. "Ye-aah. We did it." His response to her was quiet and reflective.

Then, not able to contain themselves, Aivy and Jophiel slapped their hands together in victory and carried out a happy dance, all while Megalos stood by, wide-eyed. "What? You two *planned* this? Like *all* of it?"

Four eagle couriers arrived, two for Matthew, two for Pipiera. "They must go back now. He, to a medical bed. Her, to hide in that bog." Pausing for a moment, Aivy added, "You should have trusted the King, Megs."

It was then Megalos realized, Jophiel's Earth-tour had a purpose—more like a scheme—a sanctioned one at that—to stop the attacks. *How generous of him to have such a goal for me and my family. And …I blew it!*

At that, Aivy reentered the Kingdom, leaving Megalos to carry on with the official processing of Jophiel. The entire time, Megalos's thoughts circulated wildly, *so she does know what I did. The King must know, too. Now what? One day Matthew'll learn I used his future to negotiate. What will happen to Pipiera? What will Matthew have to endure now? And all the future descendants? Oh, I let myself get lost, I blundered.* He shivered at the thought of the beast. Did that Dragon get the last laugh? *I don't do well around him.*

Processing completed, Jophiel placed his hands on Megalos's. "It's going to be alright. You wait. You always told me that, Megs. We must trust." It was quite the sight, a young little boy consoling the oversized Head Gatekeeper.

Megalos kneeled and wrapped his arms around his dear friend. *If you only knew what I did.* Rather than trusting the King, he had attempted an unsanctioned negotiation with the Dragon himself to stop the attacks. Megalos quietly wondered just how severe the consequences to others would be. Right now, nothing felt right and good as it should, and he didn't feel worthy of Jophiel's embrace.

CHAPTER FORTY-EIGHT
CAN'T WIN

At the Bog of Moorelingville

KASARTHA RUBBED AND twisted his own hands, gritted his teeth, and even attempted to pull each thumb right off. "Dang you," his fist pounded, slicing wildly through the bog's dark, thick air. *All too easy. Can't be right.*

They were moving fast, and all he could do was watch. Kingdom couriers arrived and, in no time at all, lifted *all three* of them in their clutches. "The kid, the gate girl *and* Matthew! They got Matthew, too. Go figure. No one ever tells me anything. How can I be sure I did my job?"

Jophiel hadn't fought him at all. He just waited, toying with Kasartha like he was killing time. Almost like his time was up naturally, and he knew it.

Kasartha wracked his brain and paced. *I didn't block him. Did he play me? What will Uncle say? How do I play this?*

There was no one to run to, no helpline, no life buoy, no

mentor. No hope. No sense in self-harm; he'd only have to live with whatever additional pain he'd add. Kasartha trembled at the swing of his options—either Uncle deceived him and intended for him to be annihilated by the great Jophiel on purpose, or Uncle actually thought he could successfully block the powerhouse. *Did Uncle deceive me? Or do I dare deceive Uncle? Tell him I was successful.* "This is living hell!" his lungs ached as they blasted the words into the sky.

A rush of wind, black and fierce, circled high above, making a screeching sound, the same sound that gave the bog its haunted reputation.

A shadow covered the glow of the moon. Uncle's figure took up the entire sky as one stubby arm reached into the bog, and one finger claw hooked into Kasartha's suspenders. Away Kasartha went, in a flash, no longer on the planet and far, far away from the trauma that had just been dished out deliciously, not only to unsuspecting Earth-journeyers but also to those pesky Kingdom interveners.

CHAPTER FORTY-NINE
A DEBT PAID

In the Town of Havensight

ARNIE DELIBERATED, BUT not for long. He would call in a favor. Havensight's Detective Johnstone had said many times he owed Arnie. Being an associate pastor at his church brought Arnie into the darker side of some community families, one being Detective Johnstone's. In particular, the troubled life of his son. Well, it was time for payback. It irked Arnie to remind him, but it was necessary. All hands were desperately needed on deck. His young son was missing.

"Ah, come on, that's out of our district," the Detective said, pushing his black-rimmed glasses up, back into place. It might have been Arnie's crossed arms that convinced him to drive Arnie out to Moorelingville, but likely it was the broken vessels in Arnie's eyes. Stress-filled and all red.

Arnie wasn't about to leave this matter with yet another community police force and simply sit still, miles away. He called Laura, Matthew's friend, to come and stay with Cilia, Karo and the twins. If he were to follow this lead, he'd be gone for several hours, if not a full day. With the King's grace, no longer.

"Make sure they eat," was his command as the Havensight detective and Arnie scurried off before his family or any other could try to stop them. It was a single tipster who called in, claiming to have seen a boy with a description matching Joppha at a bus depot on the coast, and Arnie knew, instinctively, it was his son the tipster saw.

Only when Arnie felt comfortable that his driver was heading in the right direction and at his utmost speed did a wave of exhaustion hit hard. He passed out cold and gained hours of much-needed, solid sleep. When he awakened in a stupor, he rubbed his forehead and squeezed that back neck muscle, the one that felt like rock. Shocked at the deep darkness of night, panic set back in, a feeling as though he had been kicked in the stomach, betrayed his son. How could he have possibly dozed off for so long?

"Why did you let me sleep?" he asked the detective angrily and then quickly flipped his tone to inquire if there were any updates. There were not. Feeling unwell, Arnie resigned to accepting the hum of the motor as the only available action to take for the moment, though it only added a painfully slow and steady thread of anxiety. There wasn't much else he could do until they arrived at the Moorelingville Bus Depot. He prayed there would be some clue or another tip by the time they got there.

"Well, there *was* something," Detective Johnstone hesitated. "But it wasn't about your locating your son. It was about that woman."

Arnie sat up. He had indeed been curious about this mysterious young woman everyone was in a huff about. Arnie was not as quick to pass judgment as many others in the community. Holding her under suspicion at the county jail seemed preposterous to him, her claim that she was a friend of Matthew Mackenzie being her only crime.

Now on alert, he wanted more information. "What about her?"

The detective scratched his chin. "Turns out she's quite a trickster."

"Trickster? You mean like a fraud or something? Does she know something about my Joppha?" Arnie was getting anxious. *Calm, calm, stay calm,* he warned himself. A heart attack right now would do no one any good.

"Well, she's obviously done this before."

Arnie didn't bother to cool himself down; he let his blood rush as it pleased. "Done *what* before?!"

The detective hesitated, perhaps out of embarrassment, and scratched behind his neck. "Well, you were out cold. I didn't want to wake you."

"Johnstone, out with it!" Arnie's finger tremored.

"She escaped. Bruce Brogan's missing. They found his patrol car sittin' in his driveway at home. His wife's gone all frantic. They figure she pulled a fast one on him, holdin' him hostage somewhere. Everyone's on alert. They're lookin' for him now."

"Looking for *him?* They should be looking for my son. They should be looking for a little boy, not some grown, bumbling fool."

The hum of the car suddenly disconnected from its wheels, skidding into the side of the road before coming to a complete stop. The detective had stepped hard on the brake and was furious. "Some bumbling fool?" he shouted. "Bruce is a fine lawman and a dear friend. The only reason I haven't turned around to help look for 'im is on account of you tellin' me I owe you!"

Arnie talked himself off a ledge: *Calm, get calm, be reasonable, apologize; it's the right thing to do,* he thought. But, "Thank you for driving me," was all he could muster, biting back what he was really thinking.

While the detective exchanged the brake for the gas and directed his car back onto the highway, his eyes remained fixed on Arnie.

The look caused Arnie to wonder if he were being blamed for Bruce's disappearance. Rage flicked and toppled his tipping point. "You're all bumbling idiots. Everyone in Havensight thinks that. You couldn't find a stone if it sat in the middle of a clear, shallow stream." No matter how hard he tried, Arnie couldn't think straight right now. He realized his last comment, one he thought was simply a knee-jerk comeback in his head, must not have been so silent because the detective slammed on the brakes again, this time not even pulling over. Late at night, the narrow country road was not a busy one, thankfully.

The detective pointed. "See that sign up ahead? Moorelingville. Now get out."

It was barely distinguishable, but he was right. The rural town's boundary was a hundred yards or so away. Arnie wondered if apologizing would do any good, but the detective's stone face and gnarly scowl strongly suggested not. He got out of the car. Flashing law enforcement lights abruptly lit the sky as the detective made a three-point turn for the opposite direction and quickly faded out of view, leaving Arnie in a swath of black and standing motionless.

A mere moment later, headlights came fast. The honks of warning were loud, and tires squealed sharply just as Arnie leaped out of the car's path. Arnie rolled headfirst along a gravel edge, ending up in a ravine. Shallow mud had softened any blows he could have otherwise suffered from the tumble. Even the taillights of the car that nearly hit him had also disappeared down the road, out of sight.

I can't help my own son. I'm a failure. Consumed with overwhelming hopelessness, a hollow pit for a soul, he raised a fist to his King, the one he trusted. Always trusted. The one he coaxed others to believe in. "What are you doing? Why? Get down here right now, fix this! If you love me, fix this!" His demand was loud and came from deep within, but the only reply was an aggravating and chirpy orchestra of field crickets.

Arnie crawled to a dryer patch of land and sat leaning against a tree. Not able to see or even care that its bark was infested with insects, he wept.

Something rustled a few feet away. It didn't sound natural, although as someone who didn't normally hang out in the woods alone in the middle of the night, Arnie couldn't be sure what sounds would be natural, anyway. His palms already clammy, he wiped them again down the front of his slacks and stood up as quietly as he could, legs shaking from stresses beyond any danger this sound could pose. Peering into the darkness, he pried his tight lips apart. "Who's there?" he pushed out.

"Dad."

Dad? It had been his son's voice. Could that even be possible? *Have I become so unhinged?* "Joppha?"

"Dad. I'm okay." The rustling moved closer to Arnie until he could see the outline of his son in clear view. A transparent, glowing outline.

A comforting wash came over Arnie, a feeling of contentment and peace beyond his own comprehension. He didn't reach out to clasp his son; he knew there was no use. There would be nothing substantial to hold. But it was him. All him. All he was. And he was fine.

Joppha grinned. "I have to go now."

Arnie surprised himself with his own return dialogue. "I know, son. Don't be scared. It'll be alright. You will be well taken care of, better than I could even imagine. And I'll see you soon. One day, and that day will be grand."

Joppha started to turn away but paused. "It's nobody's fault."

Neither had to say he loved the other. It was implied. Neither had to say goodbye. The separation would be temporary. Neither cried, at least not at this moment. Arnie would save his tears for later.

The flashing lights of Detective Johnstone's patrol car appeared again, stealing Arnie's attention from his son. Coming to a complete halt, Arnie could see the detective leaning over to push open the passenger door.

"Shots were reported, coming from the bog near here. *Get in!*"

Arnie looked at the spot where he had just conversed with his son. Nothing. Nothing there but darkness, a reflection from the patrol car's flashing light shed upon a narrow bush about his son's size. Rain started to fall. Heavily.

"Get in. We have a shooter. Could have something to do with yer son," the detective shouted.

Arnie jumped into the detective's car. As Detective Johnstone rattled off the details, Arnie was full-on consumed with some kind of miracle: he had just seen his son. Such a glorious vision. *Curious that he'd be holding a scrolled-up magazine of all things.* Nevertheless, Arnie reveled in the amazing peace of knowing his son was *okay.*

"My son just passed," Arnie whispered and offered up nothing else to explain.

CHAPTER FIFTY
RUN

At the Bog of Moorelingville

THE LANDING HAD been gentle, but then one of her eagle couriers instructed her to run.

"Run?" Pipiera asked, startled by the command.

"Yes, get going. Up there." The other pointed to a slight hill that looked much higher than it really was because of its extra-tall trees.

Another shot was fired, and that's when Pipiera realized Bruce Brogan was now aiming at her.

"Now would be a good idea, honey," the first eagle courier pointed out, while the second gave further instructions. "When you get there, just stay put."

"Get there…*w-h-e-r-e?*" Pipiera wanted more details, but her eagle couriers calmly flew off without providing any further details; she could see they had already commenced regular chit-chat with each other. "Humpf." Seeing Bruce coming at her pretty hard, she took a sprint in the opposite direction. Mud kicked off the heels of her shoes and up the back of her calves as she splashed through the swamp. There was no graceful way forward until, after several hundred yards, the ground inclined and the earth hardened. She scrambled up a short but steep hill with plenty of bare roots to use for leverage. The thick and almost tangible darkness among the rows and rows of tree trunks became her refuge. She could hear Bruce's threatening words, though it didn't sound like he was still chasing her. Walking cautiously a few yards in, she still wondered where exactly was the 'there' she was to run to. But once she laid squinted eyes upon a very old cottonwood tree beside a small cave, her instincts spoke loud and clear. *That* was the place.

Exploring the scene, she sensed it: Jophiel's sword and a battle of wills, the finishing, telling tale lingered in the air, likely trapped by the dark. It was a mixture of the familiar sweet and swirling trace of Kingdom aroma with a stagnant stench of sulfur, sure to be Kasartha's. They had fought here, and she was certain of it.

She curled herself up outside the cave, sure that little Joppha's body lay within. She didn't bother to enter and check. And why would she? He wasn't really there; she knew that much. He was *home*. Safe, loved. A deep sigh produced a slight lift to the sides of her mouth.

A voice other than Bruce Brogan's hollered in the distance, and her ears perked.

"Oh, father," she whispered.

The voice belonged to Charles, a distraught Charles. She needed to see for herself that he was alright. *Well, of course he wouldn't be,* she told herself, *not after a day like today!* She realized now that she never should have told him or let him believe who she really was. That was a mistake. *Aivy won't be pleased about that, either*, recalling the look Aivy gave her once Matthew revealed his knowledge about her. Well, now, at least, she and Matthew could use that knowing relationship as an advantage, she hoped.

Cautiously crawling toward the kerfuffle, she reached the edge of the woods and peered down into the clearing. There was Matthew partially sitting up and a flashlight shining straight into his face. He was using his elbows, attempting to sit all the way up. *Ah, I can see his drop-off was successful. I bet it was a nasty fall-in for him.* She thought about their conversation only seconds ago, in the Kingdom Courtyard. *Will he remember our agreement?* She counted on it. The thought brought to mind once again her challenger, Kasartha. Scanning the premises, she concluded there was no sight of that troublemaker. *'course, he's done his damage. It would be just like him to leave. No need to stick around.* Kasartha had caused so much havoc in so many lives, and she wondered if these attacks of his, these mind games, would ever stop.

Charles was accusing Bruce, and Bruce was yelling at Charles. More bright pinheads of light were coming toward them from the woods on their side of the clearing. *Three, four—no, five—of them, at least.* A law enforcement team, one man using a two-way radio and speaking practically the entire time, the rest flaring their flashlights anywhere they could. Two kneeled over Matthew while Bruce pointed them her way. The man with the radio held Charles back; it appeared he wanted to come with the two who were about to hunt her down.

Pipiera wanted to run and keep running, leave this whole business behind. But instructions rang deep in both of her ears: *get there and stay put.* She crawled back, not really sure why she was being sneaky about her movements because, after all, she would plant herself by the cave so she could be found. And arrested.

Oh, Serena. You and your schemes. Why do I listen?

CHAPTER FIFTY-ONE
SHE DID IT

On Route, Havensight to Moorelingville

THANK HEAVENS FOR Dr. Alexien's rental vehicle. With the unlimited miles and the flexible deadline for its return, Marnie could at least not stress about logistics. It was enough for Dr. Alexien to be so generous with her time and concern, to drive her straight away from Havensight to some large health center, a hospital nearby Moorelingville, one that could contend with gunshot wounds. Marnie had no idea how she'd repay Dr. Alexien, but now was not the time to worry about that.

"I just…I really…I don't know how to thank you. I don't know what I would have done had you not been there. And taking the time to drive me? And calm me down!" Marnie chuckled nervously.

At last, after a seemingly forever long drive through the night, the two women pulled into the Moorelingville Health Center's circular drive. It was early morning, and although darkness was beginning to lift, Marnie's tension was not. Several patrol vehicles were parked close to the emergency entrance, and she just knew they were there because of Matthew.

Matthew, my son. Shot.

Marnie pushed open the car door and eagerly stepped out, though she caught sight of a woman in the back of one of the patrol vehicles. Though her head was down, her arms held back and likely handcuffed, it was clear who she was.

"That Pippi girl, I knew it!" Marnie snarled.

Dr. Alexien grabbed Marnie gently and prodded her toward the emergency entrance. "We don't have the full story, Marnie. We shall not cast judgment just yet," she cautioned.

As Dr. Alexien strode across the lot with Marnie, Pipiera—who had, in fact, been arrested and had already sat locked in that back seat for several hours—glanced her way. The two caught each other's eyes, and, for the briefest of moments, a glimmer from the rising sun flashed its brilliance across the parking lot.

"Stay away from my family!" Marnie yelled, ignoring Dr. Alexien's words of advice.

"Sssh, come, Marnie. Calmly. It's going to be alright. We'll sort this out. Have a little more faith." Dr. Alexien pulled Marnie inside the building where they would locate Matthew and, hopefully, Charles.

The ladies were ushered into a curtained-off cubicle where Matthew lay in a half-sitting position, his leg all bandaged up. Marnie could see he truly was alright, not half or three-quarters or even the eleven-twelfths dead as she had feared might be the case the whole night long.

"We have to stop with the family meetings like this," she

said to him as relief washed over her face. Lowering her head to hide her tears, her head shook, not even wanting to count the times she ran to emergency rooms because something happened to him. "I love you," she whispered and wiped her wet face. Nearing him, she was careful to give him a hug across his shoulders.

"I'm sorry, mom. Really," he chuckled. "It's been quite a night. I don't mean to scare you all the time." He hugged her back. "I love you, too." His voice was strong, confident.

Even though he sounded well, Marnie could see the color was drained from his face and his hands were clammy. Dr. Alexien moved in closer and grabbed Matthew's left hand and Marnie's right from across the bed, and bowed her head. She spoke silently to her King, and the other two closed their eyes tight.

"You could have been killed, Matty." Marnie held her son.

"Joppha's gone," Matthew spoke dryly. "Dead, Mom, he's dead."

As though to protect her brain from the news, Marnie's hands grabbed both sides of her head. This was breaking news, and her mind calculated away. *Then was Matty right, was his nightmare about Joppha real and trying to tell him something? Oh my gosh, poor Arnie and Cilia.* She looked at Matthew. "I am so, so sorry, son."

Matthew broke into a sobbing snippet, then regained his composure just as quickly. Marnie wondered how he would get through this. *He was so close to Joppha, like a brother. Oh, and dear Karo, I won't even be there when she learns of this!*

"That Pippi girl, I hope they hang her," Marnie spoke firmly.

"Mother!" exclaimed Matthew. At the same time, Dr. Alexien cried, "Marnie!"

"You mustn't have an accusing heart," Dr. Alexien scolded.

"Mom, she didn't do it! How could you think that? She was trying to help; can't you see that?"

Marnie's body went rigid. *Matty, you are wrong; just wait and see.* She carefully restrained her prediction.

Matthew took notice of the concern on Dr. Alexien's face. He hadn't seen her for quite some time now and had come to appreciate her words of advice over the years. He appeared thankful that she was here, albeit mysteriously, to support and guide his mother.

"Then who shot you?" Marnie snapped.

"Not her," Matthew replied calmly. "Bruce Brogan. He thought I harmed Joppha. And he thinks I schemed with… Pippi. He was just doing his job."

Marnie's eyes grew wild. "*Just* doing his *job?*"

Just then, Charles sauntered in, leaning heavily on his cane. He had just finished a series of interviews with various detectives from Moorelingville and Havensight. Law enforcement was crawling throughout the hospital hallways, and one stood guard by Matthew's curtained-off treatment room.

Marnie was horrified by her own preoccupation with Matthew. *How could I have forgotten Charles?* She pulled over a chair. "Dad, come, sit here." He obeyed, wanting to share and relieve some of the burden that had collected over the past twenty-four hours and which sat heavily in his chest.

"They don't believe me," and he looked at Matthew. "They're gonna lock her up, treatin' her like a killer! Matty, you gotta speak up." Matthew looked the other way, his lips tightened.

"What?" Marnie begged. "Speak up about what?"

"She's my daughter." At that, Charles banged the shiny

cement floor with the end of his cane. "Believe it or not. Maggie went home and sent her to me. Penney came back to take care of me."

No one spoke.

Marnie needed to add this new clue into the picture. *Charles actually believes this Pippi is his long-gone daughter? Wow, she really is quite a master of all things, particularly deceit.*

CHAPTER FIFTY-TWO
DOESN'T MATTER

In the City of Moorelingville

YOU'D THINK A *health center this size could have provided me with a space more private,* Arnie growled within. Wanting to sob, scream, hold himself and rock, anything. Instead, Arnie was left alone with a wood and metal stacking chair at the end of a hallway outside the so-called Family Room #1, which was used for Moorelingville police interrogations, while across the hallway, Family Room #2 was occupied for Havensight's own unofficial police interrogations. It seemed the two forces had many differences of opinion, none of which mattered to Arnie. He was still processing the worst possible news. Joppha was *gone.* The vision of his young son in the wee hours of that morning provided Arnie with some kind of magical comfort to survive each moment that passed. For the time being, anyway.

The door to Family Room #1 opened wide for the first time in a solid two hours. A weary Bruce Brogan stepped out and was eagerly met by Detective Johnstone, who comforted Bruce and ushered him quickly into Family Room #2. A rather tall, thin man in a double-breasted suit and tightly laced oxfords no one could miss because of the shine stepped out of the first room and tucked numerous papers into a folder as he practically ran down the hall boasting a grin that rivaled his shoes.

This is a circus, Arnie thought. *What on Earth was Bruce Brogan doing there in that bog? What made him think shooting at Matthew would solve anything? I bet Moorelingville had the same questions, and Havensight's trying to defend the guy. It doesn't really matter*, Arnie concluded. *Nothing will bring my son back.*

The tall, thin-suited, perfect-shoes man came back and stopped in front of Arnie, kneeling down so they could be face-to-face. "Arnie," he started. "Just a few more minutes. I'm really sorry to keep you this long. I cannot imagine what this is like for you. One of *our* men will drive you back to Havensight."

Arnie felt the emphasis on his use of 'our.' The Moorelingville authorities versus the Havensight authorities will ensure he gets home to his family. "And Joppha?" Logistics were a priority and needed to be dealt with. "Will he come with us?"

The man shook his head, "We need to do an autopsy, Arnie."

"No! Why? Please, I wish you wouldn't; he's gone through enough. Leave him, I beg you." The very thought of it made Arnie feel cut apart himself. It was amazing how he stayed so strong.

The man shook his head some more. "Arnie, there were

no exterior signs of foul play, no apparent method of harming your boy. No marks on that tree where Matthew Mackenzie claims he saw him. No strange footprints, no sightings of any man or any animal or anyone else in those woods. Excepting of course, that Bruce Brogan, that older gentleman, and our own law enforcement team. Plus, of course that woman and, well, that doesn't all line up, either. We need to find out how your son…" He lowered his head, not wanting to say the word. That *final* word.

"So, what's next?" Arnie asked.

"Well, we are going to hold that woman, Pippi—of no fixed address, by the way—at least until the autopsy is completed. We'll take it from there."

"And Bruce?" Arnie was curious. Might he have had something to do with his son's demise?

"Well, that's entirely separate from your son's case. Bruce Brogan shot a man. Without reason. Without any apparent justification. We're not sure what we're going to do with him just yet. He's cooperating and has agreed to remain in our custody and come to the station for more questioning until we decide whether he'll be charged or what with."

Arnie nodded—though wondering how there could possibly *not* be a connection—and, as he did, he caught a glimpse of Marnie standing down the hall, watching them. It appeared she was waiting, wanting to talk to him.

"One more thing," Mr. Suit and Shoes continued, "We're not arresting Matthew Mackenzie, but he is a person of interest. Havensight authorities have not cleared him, either; they're chomping at the bit to put him away. If we find any other evidence, we'll pass it on to them directly. That's about it. Can you wait thirty minutes? Someone can drive you home then."

He stepped away, slipping into that first room and shutting the door abruptly.

Arnie nodded, not really feeling he had any choice in the matter nor anything to add to this whole interrogation business. He returned to his default position, a new one he had practiced all night: keeping a head that weighed heavily in his sweaty hands from slipping, and balancing angry elbows as they pressed and knifed their way into his knees. He wanted to go home to his family, but *I won't go without Joppha.*

He noticed her shoes, Marnie's. They had crept quietly over, bringing her along with them, no doubt. Arnie wasn't sure if he could face anyone familiar, not just yet.

Marnie touched his shoulder. "Arnie, I am so…so sorry. I just heard. Matty told me." She shifted her weight and paused before switching the topic to her son. "He was…well, he was shot. But I guess you know that." Arnie motioned for her to grab a chair, pointing to a stack of them just up the hall. By the time she returned, he had had the chance for a few more deep breaths.

She had barely sat down when she raised what seemed to shock her most. "You know they thought Matty was responsible for all this!"

Arnie paused, then nodded, "I know him better than that." He heard Marnie let out a deep exhale. Relief, no doubt. *So, your son is fine. Mine is not. Glad you're happy.* He couldn't help it: terrible thoughts coursed through his veins and settled in his brain. He was thankful he hadn't spoken them out loud. He realized her facts needed some correction. "Havensight authorities *still* think he's a suspect. You know that, right? You didn't notice the guard in front of that there curtain?"

Marnie's chin dropped, "That's not for protection?"

Arnie chortled, "Huh, they couldn't protect a dog from a flea."

A period of quiet ensued as they both watched feet scuffling to and fro. Finally, Arnie asked, "How is he?" referring to Matthew.

"He's fine. We'll be taking him home." Marnie said the words delicately. She was the lucky one; she could take her son home. Arnie simply nodded.

"Karo?" Marnie asked, still gentle and with much concern in her tone.

"She's with Cilia and the twins. Laura stayed with them the night. They must be suffering and wondering, too."

"We'll have to work together, to get her through this," she whispered, he nodded.

It seemed the pleasantries were over. Arnie needed to ask a hard question. "Who exactly is this Pippi?" Anger accompanied each word. "Your son *insists* she's innocent. Yet no one knows anything about her. What's up with that, Marnie?"

"I don't..." Marnie couldn't answer; Arnie was on a roll.

"And Charles, for Pete's sake, the guy walked up and down this hall all night long claiming her to be his daughter who *died*? *What* daughter? Has he gone insane? What was he doing in that bog last night? Do you not keep track of him? He's in his nineties, for Pete's sake, Marnie!"

"Late seventies, but yes, you're right. I've no excuses." Marnie said quietly.

Mr. Suit and Shoes came out of the family room, possibly to hear what the commotion was. Looking at Arnie, he held up a finger, "Just another thirty minutes, Arnie." And he slipped back into the room. The sound of that door shutting irritated Arnie, as it had all night.

"Arnie, I'm sorry. I wish this day never happened. I wish it could be a page someone could rip right out of a book. We're heading back today, fingers crossed. Would you like to come with us?"

"Nah, thanks. I need to stay here with Joppha. They're doing an autopsy." He rubbed both sides of his head with sweaty palms. "When I can bring *him* back to Havensight, then I will come home. Then we'll make…" His voice trailed off. The idea of making funeral arrangements was simply too much. He looked up at Marnie, who was already standing and ready to go. "I'm sorry, Marnie. Safe drive. I know you'll comfort Karo. Please check on Cilia and the twins, too."

"I will. I promise."

Arnie watched her slip down the hall, and he wished, too, for this page to be torn out of his book. It had been the worst day of his life.

CHAPTER FIFTY-THREE

WHAT DO YOU THINK?

"I THOUGHT I WAS going to die," Matthew told Dr. Alexien when she asked him how he was doing. "At first, I didn't feel anything, and then—well, then my thigh started burning. Like it was on fire. It was then I realized the bugger had shot me. Sorry," He apologized for his language. "Bruce. I guess I should say that's when I realized Bruce Brogan shot me."

"And then?" Dr. Alexien gently urged Matthew to continue. "What happened next? Can you recall?"

Matthew studied her face for a moment. *She knows. I bet she's one of them,* he thought. *It makes sense. She was always prodding me about those times when I blacked out.* He answered cautiously, "Then, the pain came."

"Anything else?" she really seemed to want more.

Matthew tightened his lips and decided he'd test her. "Yeah, *Pipiera* and *Jophiel* and I took a little jaunt upstairs." He used a casual tone with emphasis on the Kingdom-version of names, then watched as Dr. Alexien's eyebrows elevated.

Busted. He crossed his arms. "Just *who* are you?" Matthew demanded.

Marnie's arrival back to their little sectioned-off cubicle caused a disruption and allowed Dr. Alexien to avoid a response. Marnie had left to seek out Arnie, to speak with him and convey their condolences. "Oh, what a nightmare, poor Arnie. I just cannot imagine." She noticed her son and very helpful friend having a stare-down. "What's going on here with you two?"

Dr. Alexien smiled and spoke to Marnie, "Oh, Matthew here was just telling me how the shot to his leg has changed him." Gazing back at Matthew, she continued, "He's had a spiritual awakening. He's tuned in to a higher power: a King, might you say, Matthew?"

Okay, she's on the same side as Pipiera and Jophiel, so it seems, Matthew concluded. "Yes, you could say that," he responded, keeping his eyes fixed on Dr. Alexien's face.

Dr. Alexien continued as a doctor with a prescription warning, "Don't be surprised, Marnie. He's likely to do a great deal of soul-searching. Figuring out his purpose in life sort of thing."

Marnie chuckled, "He's a grown man; he's been doing that for years now."

A nurse arrived and interrupted, waving some papers in the air. "Discharge time, mister!" She gently shoved a white paper bag full of medical supplies toward Marnie, "Here, I suspect you're gonna be nurse?" Marnie smiled broadly and happily grabbed the bag along with a sheet of instructions for care. He was lucky his injury was non-life-threatening, the wound superficial.

When Marnie slipped back out to find a wheelchair,

Dr. Alexien leaned in close to Matthew. "Tell grandfather to stop claiming *Pippi* as his daughter. That's not going to help her cause any. Plus…*they'll think he's crazy.*" She motioned circles around her ear to accentuate *c-r-a-z-y.*

Now she's making demands of me? It was true, she was, and she wasn't finished.

"And tell your mom you want to stay here. Stay with Arnie while he waits. It'll be good. You can do your thing."

Do my thing? He recalled Aivy's words: he was to be there to support Arnie, or something like that. Matthew nodded. He was beginning to feel special, someone who really mattered and could make a difference. Someone being called upon. *A mission of my own,* he chuckled to himself.

Steering an empty wheelchair, Marnie returned and maneuvered it close to her son's bedside, eager and ready to roll him away. The two women discussed the best way to keep Matthew comfortable for the long drive home and where to grab a good, hot breakfast before hitting the road.

All Matthew could think about was that he lived in two worlds now, or so it seemed. Would it be possible to reconcile them when they are so far apart in so many ways? He wasn't sure how to do it, but whatever *his thing* was, he might as well start now.

"Mom," Matthew said. "You two go ahead. I think Arnie could use a friend. I'm going to stay back. I'm pretty sure he'll help with my wound and me getting around and stuff."

"Oh, don't be silly, Matty, Arnie could be days, he told me so. He won't leave without…Joppha and they plan on doing an autopsy."

Matthew shifted uncomfortably. *An autopsy! What's next?* He caught Dr. Alexien's glare. "Well, it may not take that long.

But all the more important that I stay. With him." He hoped his mom would understand and accept his decision.

But the idea was not agreeable to Marnie. She explained that it was she who had all that was needed to take care of his wound, thanks to the nurses, and she was perfectly capable and willing to be his errand girl for a few days. She made note of the special time it would be for Charles if they made the journey home together. Then, she begged. She had to get back, she still had much to deal with—Maggie's funeral and all, so much planning still to do—and she would appreciate his input, needed him there. Finally, she played the guilt card, "Karo needs you. Really, Matthew, think about how she must be coping with all this."

But Matthew was no longer a child, and, in the end, the decision was his. Marnie would have to return to Havensight without him, but not before Dr. Alexien could sneak in a wink and a whisper for Matthew's ears only. "You have a higher calling now."

Matthew saluted the women as Dr. Alexien whisked Marnie away, pulling her along by her elbow. He could tell his mom wasn't pleased. They would find Charles, who was again wandering the halls, and then they would head home without him.

CHAPTER FIFTY-FOUR

THE MOORELINGVILLE BOND

"MOVE ON OVER." A stocky, uniformed officer instructed Pipiera to make room in the back seat for a cohort: Bruce Brogan.

"Arrested. *You?*" Pipiera asked, her wide eyes blinking. *Now I didn't see that coming. Boy, nothing seems to go as I think it will around here.* She shuffled over awkwardly, given her cuffed hands. An undesirable odor reeked from his shirt, soaked under his armpits. Chomping on gum, he stopped once he noticed Pipiera. *I'm guessing they found him guilty of shooting off that gun of his,* she figured. *He could have killed Matthew. This day could have been even worse than it already was.*

The arresting officer guided Bruce's head, keeping it low to avoid any contact with the roof as he willingly submitted to the back seat. He didn't answer Pipiera, though he did manage a scowl, and she noticed the deep red in sunken eye sockets and a glistening shine on his forehead. To Pipiera, he appeared more horrified than angry. She imagined all this business— Joppha's death and him nearly killing another boy—must bring back memories of his own son's passing. How could it not? When she eyed him cautiously, he told her to 'keep her lookin' to herself.

"You never did tell me how Marcus died," she said casually, as if they were still friends, still working together for a common purpose. He looked straight ahead and tight-lipped to avoid her. Pipiera did what she did best: continued to pry. "This must be difficult for you." She employed deep sincerity. "Such a void takes years, changes a soul." She watched his chest exhale a frumpy frustration, then heave from a large intake of new air. "You could be a comfort to Joppha's dad." She leaned toward him and with a quiet whisper, she added, "*You* get it."

Thanks to the reflection in the window, Pipiera could see Bruce's nose twitch, and he snuffled it up in silence. He asked her to please just shut up.

At least he said please, she thought. That was a start. The pair sat quietly as they were driven away from the hospital and headed for the Moorelingville Police Station. They entered the lot, parked, and the driving officer exited the car. His boots crunching the gravel as he walked away gave Pipiera a hollow feeling, reminding her she was not free by Earth's standards. She turned to Bruce for knowledge. "So, what happens now?" In return, she received the back of his head and, in the car window's reflection, rolling eyes. *He's obviously been told not to talk to me, I'm guessing. Or he doesn't like me. That's more likely. Could he really think me guilty? 'course, he did see me float. He's afraid of me. I wonder if he dared tell his colleagues that?*

Yet another Moorelingville officer arrived and ushered Bruce out of the car, and Havensight's Detective Johnstone joined them, slapping Bruce on the back. Pipiera could overhear the detective's promise to get him out of this ridiculous mess and bring him home in no time. "You won't be here long, I can promise you that," the detective said while tossing a nasty glare at the chuckling Moorelingville officer. The three of them disappeared into the sprawling brick building, which was considerable in size despite having only one level above ground. She hoped the cells where she was certain they would place her were not in the basement. She was growing a dislike for that level: it always seemed to be a place of chaos and confusion, not to mention loneliness.

Thirty minutes passed. Pipiera was incredibly sleepy, her head getting too heavy to hold and her stomach gnarling an angry tune. *Did they forget about me?* She wondered. *They must have. Seriously?* Then five men exited the building and chatted in a circle in front of the doors. She watched from her seat in the back of the patrol car. Animated discussions, some hand-shaking, and some back-slapping. Bruce Brogan was leaving with that Detective Johnstone. It appeared they couldn't get out of the parking lot fast enough.

Guess that detective made good on his promise, Pipiera thought. *But if Bruce is going back to Havensight, how am I to free him?* As their car brushed past hers, Pipiera caught Bruce's gaze. It was a direct stare, and for the first time since the shooting, he didn't give her his angry face.

Two of the three men left in the parking lot headed directly toward her. The third tucked himself back inside the building.

"Oh, here it comes. Help me, King, tell me how to answer their questions," she was nervous; neither looked friendly. *'course, why would they? They think I schemed to harm a young child.*

The first officer opened the back door and crouched, his

facial features an intrusion on her personal space. "C'mon, honey. Your turn," was all he said. He held the door open as she wiggled and struggled to get her body, which felt heavier than ever before, out of the vehicle. He assisted her final maneuver. Had her hands not been cuffed behind her, she could have done it without him. He led her to the building's entrance like a farmer leading an old cow, the other officer walking along beside her. *As if I'm gonna run*, she mused, then giggled at the notion she harbored inside. *What would you do if I simply floated away?*

"Something funny?" the officer walking alongside her asked as the other yanked her elbow abruptly.

"No," Pipiera responded quietly. The gravel crunched beneath their feet, the officers' steps in unison. The sound alone brought memories of the Dragon's army when they had encircled her years ago and led her to the rebel courtyard. Tricked, imprisoned and alone. Sickened with the familiarity, she wanted to ask questions, like what will she be charged with, or why did they think she did it, or what on Earth did they possibly think she would gain by carrying out such an act? But she decided it was best to stay mum. *I was just sitting there, next to Joppha's body, so suddenly I'm a criminal.*

Before entering, one officer asked Pipiera to kick her feet and shake off the caked mud from her shoes. *Who wears platform shoes into a bog? Oh, uh, that would be me.* Layers of dried mud had covered up a large portion of her ankles and calves. A rag hadn't been offered, so with her hands still locked behind her, she kicked the building and rubbed her legs against the brick until the other officer indicated that was enough; go in, already.

As the men opened the doors wide for Pipiera to enter, she

encouraged herself: *this is not the Rebel gate. I am not making an informed choice.* Turning around to scan the parking lot, she implored, *Papah Megs, I really need you. Where are you?* She felt a push and a yank and heard the double doors clang as they closed behind her, and she knew she had just been swallowed by a building of Earthly authority. Now at its mercy, she wondered if there would be any.

CHAPTER FIFTY-FIVE
SO, NOW WHAT?

In the Outer Courtyard of the Kingdom

"ARE YOU SURE you got this?" Megalos strode gigantic steps by the picnic table where Serena, Aivy and Jophiel sat, directing his question to Aivy specifically. "I got this feeling she needs me." Back and forth he went.

Megalos was sure he felt Pipiera's call to him. *Not a call of danger, just angst. Nevertheless, we need to check on her. And that was hardly the reunion she'd been waiting for with Maggie.* Megalos anticipated Pipiera to be more vulnerable than ever right now.

Aivy stood and appeared impatient, though she took a thoughtful moment, perhaps thinking about how Megalos must feel. He would be worried for his Pipiera, but she needed to be truthful. Gentle but truthful. "No, Megs. You know what happens down there; it's not *our* doing. Plus, Megs, that's not my job." Getting a little defensive, hands on her hips, she looked up sternly to catch his eyes, "You *know* that!"

Ignoring Aivy, Megalos continued to pace, rubbing his chin and stopping only to sigh and reverse direction frequently.

"This is my fault." Jophiel claimed responsibility for Pipiera's present dilemma. He sat tall, now a full citizen of the Kingdom; he could still hardly believe it. Following his processing and orientation, he chose his age. "I wanna be the same as Pipiera!" he had told the King, who laughed joyously and granted him his desire.

He stood.

"Shall I go take a little trip, hmmm?" His eyebrows high under a groomed mop of golden hair, mischief danced wildly in his eyes. "It would be fun," he joked. "I'll get to jab her in jail; now, that would be a hoot." His deep, warm chuckle made even Megalos smile.

Though she laughed, Aivy didn't waste any time shutting the idea down. "No, no, Jophiel. Too risky. You're still in that emotional memory stage. More days must pass before you can even think about taking on a mission."

"Okay," he said. "Not a mission. How about a *visit?* A simple, little, short, itsy-bitsy visit."

Serena had been quiet, listening to the discussions of her comrades. She snickered, likely calculating just how long it would take for Jophiel to wear Aivy down with his boyish charm.

Crossing her arms as she often did, Aivy shook her head. "Nope. Jophiel, I know you! There'll be no *itsy-bitsy* visit, as you say. You stay put. Hear me?"

"I won't intervene. I promise. I'll just be present. Watch. Give her some encouragement, perhaps. I could remind her, like, of just how easy it is to forget about the grand picture when one is stuck in the mud down there." He wiggled his buttocks and his shoulders, now free of the powerful and heavy wings once attached.

Serena broke out laughing, "Is that your new signature dance?"

"Nope," he said. "Guess again." He stopped wiggling around and made large stepping motions with his feet, pulling on his knees as if each step upward needed help.

Aivy cocked her head and spoke with sarcasm, "*Now* he wants to play charades?"

Serena jumped up and clapped, excited to play along with Jophiel. "Your legs are heavy."

Jophiel shook his head and kept up his faux stepping motions.

"You're in wet cement!" Serena called out, hoping this guess was closer, and Jophiel motioned that it was.

Megalos caught on. "Mud. You are stepping in thick muck. You're stuck." Jophiel clapped; that was it. Then he started to make swimming motions with his hands. "Ah, of course," Megalos understood his game. "You want to help Pipiera get out of the mud and swim to the crystal stream." Megalos turned to Serena. "He's mimicking an Earth-journey stone."

"Oh, I get it! Fun. Can we do another one?" Serena hopped in her seat.

"No!" Aivy butted in. "Jophiel, that would not be a *simple* visit, that would be an *intervention*."

Jophiel plugged his nose, held one hand up high, and wiggled downward as if he were going underwater, drowning. Serena howled, and Megalos chuckled. The new Jophiel was such an entertaining part of their Kingdom community now. Then he got on his knees so he'd be closer to Aivy's height and clasped his hands as if to beg, *pleeeze.* By now, Megalos was howling along with Serena. Though all kidding aside, Megalos dearly hoped Aivy would agree to take Jophiel's request to the Authoritarians for blessing. *It would make me feel so much better if I thought Jophiel could be there with her, even if it ended up being a simple, non-communicative presence,* he admitted to himself.

"Jophiel. You must know you do not have the same capabilities you once had. You, yourself, would need an escort." She smiled sweetly at him. He humbly nodded back.

"So, how do we help her? I feel it. She needs us." Megalos didn't dare offer to go himself. It's not that he wouldn't, because he would in a heartbeat. He was still feeling the heat from his recent escapade, where he made an unsanctioned deal with the leader of the rebels—a deal he later learned that the King had skillfully adjusted. *I'd best not push it,* he figured.

"Is there anything *I* can do?" It was Serena who came forward this time.

Aivy faced the three of them, Jophiel, Megalos and Serena, all desperate to help their friend, great-granddaughter, and great-niece. "Okay, okay, I'll put in a request. But don't anyone do anything until you hear back from me. Got it?!"

"Got it," Megalos and Serena said in unison. Aivy's index finger specifically acknowledged Megalos's response.

Then she turned to Jophiel. "Joph-i-*el?*" Her face was telling. She needed to hear it from him.

"Yeah, got it," he said.

Oh dear, Megalos thought when he saw Jophiel cross his fingers behind his back. *This could be trouble.*

CHAPTER FIFTY-SIX

BASEMENT THINKING

In the City of Moorelingville
Three days later

MOONLIGHT STROKED THROUGH two slits up by the ceiling, eerily reminding Pipiera of the Dragon's eyes. She couldn't believe this was the plan. *Something's gone wrong. I'm sure of it.* She was in prison, alright, but it wasn't Bruce Brogan's cell or anywhere near him.

"Some popcorn tonight?" Ronaldo, the night guard, was the jolly one of all her captors. Said she reminded him of his own little Pipeeta, who she assumed was his daughter, so he called her that. "Gotta good one tonight, *Smokey and the Bandit*. Sally Fields." He held up the video cover. "Don't go getting any ideas, no runnin' from the law, though," he chortled heartily. When she didn't laugh back, he encouraged her some more. "Ah, come on, Pipeeta, I told ya, I gotta good feeling. Just be patient; they're sortin' it all out."

Pipiera had spent three nights locked in this room. Though,

after spending a few hours in that holding cell in Havensight, this one in Moorelingville she much preferred. Heck, it was better than the room she had at Mrs. Damien's place. A private washroom complete with a shower, fresh towels daily, soap that smelled like green apples, a cushy couch she could lounge on, an assortment of books on a shelf, and a bed—although it was narrow and the mattress thin. She was careful not to put her dirty shoes on its cover. And Ronaldo stayed close, got her tea when she wanted, brought a snack each night, and they watched great movies. Pipiera would snooze most of the day-light away; the day guards didn't pay much attention to her. So, her nights were not so bad, but she was growing weary in her thoughts. *Had they arrested Matthew, too? He had shouted that Joppha was dead, and it was his fault. Bruce was a witness, and Bruce had gone free. Might Matthew be in another room in this building? Or is he still in the hospital?* She wondered how he was making out with his mission. *I hope better than me.* And she ached for Arnie. *How could he possibly understand?* She hoped his faith was strong enough to get him through—and his family.

More than a few times, Pipiera had the temptation to lift and float near the ceiling. Just the thought gave her a giggle. Maybe they'd be so afraid they'd let her go free. But misuse of her capabilities would have severe consequences on so many fronts. In fact, her lifting herself in the bog is what got her in jail, might have even been the cause of Bruce shooting Matthew. Besides, she wouldn't get far: her capabilities were not enough to leave the planet. So, she plodded forward.

"Sure, I'd love some popcorn, thank you, Ronaldo," she said, and he passed the buttery bag through the bars.

The theme song played loud at the end of the movie,

credits rolling and Ronaldo snoring. Pipiera squealed in alarm and jumped to one side. Someone had jabbed her from behind.

"Jophiel!" She exclaimed. "Is that really you? Look at you, you're…you're…"

"All growed up?"

She laughed, "Yeah, all *growed* up." There were no words she could find to express the wonder of seeing him in this form: a man, a citizen of the Kingdom. *This was his dream,* she thought, so pleased and proud of him.

"Not a bad little pad you got here," he grinned and looked around.

Pipiera quickly glanced at Ronaldo. Thankfully, he was out cold, sound asleep and snoring loudly.

"Don't worry; he can't see me or hear me. Just you!" Jophiel chuckled.

Oh, not this again, Pipiera mused. She whispered as quietly as she could, "Am I happy to see you!"

"I know," he replied, grinning. She punched him, her arm going through his body, and they both laughed.

She noticed a light globe in the ceiling's corner. "What's that?" she asked.

"Ya mean, *who's* that. My escort." He turned his back to Pipiera, "See, no more wings."

"He's not going to show himself?" Pipiera was curious about his escort. She was still learning new things about Kingdom ways.

"Yeah, I told him to shut himself off."

"Ha ha, you mean I could have told you to shut yourself off when we were in that closet of Matthew's years ago?"

"Good thing you didn't know. We wouldn't be the friends we are right now, would we?"

She just laughed and nodded; a tear slipped. "Yup, sometimes not knowing stuff is best," she said. Another quick glance at Ronaldo. Still fast asleep. *Whew.* "I'm surprised to see you, Jophiel; I would have thought you'd still be in orientation. Surely, the emotional heaviness is still far too risky." She stopped suddenly, her breath caught in her throat. "You didn't come here unsanctioned, did you?!"

Jophiel scratched his head and laughed heartily, "Uh, no, little girl. Only you would do something like *that.*" She punched him again, straight through the chest, and the two laughed some more. Pipiera stole another quick glance at Ronaldo. She didn't need him reporting to the other guards that she was a crazy woman, talking to the walls all night as if a real person were there. That wouldn't help her cause; she was sure of that.

Jophiel, still taller, but not by nearly as much as when he was a Kingdom escort, looked down at her with deeply sincere and caring eyes. "Don't worry, Pip, he's out for the night. We can talk freely."

Another tear slipped. Her friend had taken a risky trip and arranged for the guard to sleep deeply so they could have a visit. She was truly thankful. "You came just in time, Jophiel. I was beginning to lose faith." He explained to her that he wanted to come earlier, but it took some convincing for Aivy and the Authoritarians to agree. She didn't doubt that at all and mused at her own phrase: *just in time.* Everything done by the King was always *just in time.*

"It's tough down here. It's not been so simple," she released.

"Ah, c'mon. Look around: ya got a nice couch, somewhere

to wash, looks like a comfy pillow and—ah, look at those popcorn kernels. I bet you could reach your arm through those bars over there and pour yourself a cup of water from that there cooler. What more do you want?" he teased.

"Don't need those bars."

"That's not what imprisons you, Pipiera. You know that."

He was right. She knew that. But three days locked in a basement room, her only contact with guards, had worn her down. The two sat on her bed. He bounced a bit, noting it was not nearly as soft as the couch appeared. "Crushing pressure," he said as he continued to pounce the mattress, "unlike this bed of yours, can make you sink. Sink down till you're stuck, good and deep in mud. Mind if I give you a little advice?"

She nodded willingly, waiting to hear something profound.

"If I were you, I'd sleep over there," he said, pointing to the couch.

"Is that all you got? Nothin' better?"

"Still working on some new material, need some new stuff to joke around."

She shrugged and got serious, "Sometimes everything is so difficult."

"So. Triumph," he instructed. He made it all sound so simple.

She remained quiet. *I shouldn't have let myself get worn down. If I hadn't, Jophiel wouldn't have had to take such a risk to come.* She looked at him admiringly, *but I'm glad he did.*

"So, why me? Why did I have to take this mission? Serena and Alexien were so adamant, but I am so confused now. You know, basement thinking."

Jophiel crossed his knees, his hands gesturing to emphasize his explanation, "Here's what I picked up hanging around up there. Arnie *was* a leaning post. But now, Arnie *needs* a leaning post. *And,* Matthew must learn *to be* a leaning post."

"It's not that simple, Jophiel."

His hands continued to gesture wide with flowing movements, "Yeah, it is. All this other stuff? Just fluff."

"Just. Fluff." She needed more.

He looked at her quizzically, then spelled it out. "You are here to show Matthew *how* to be that leaning post."

Pipiera blinked, waiting for more.

"So that Arnie can go back to *being* a leaning post," he added.

"And Matthew?" She asked. "He'll become one, too, I take it."

Jophiel paused. "We need Matthew, Pipiera. He's the planned head gatekeeper for the times of later. He'll be more, so much more, than just another leaning post. He is to become a pillar, a protecting pillar of light." Ensuring he had her attention, he reaffirmed what he had already told her, "He's got a lot of character building to get through."

She twisted her mouth, paused thoughtfully. "And how does Bruce fit into all this?"

"Matthew has to forgive Bruce in order to move forward on his path."

Pipiera was starting to get it. The pieces were falling into place, almost. "But freeing Bruce, that's not necessary for Matthew's sake."

"Indirectly, yeah, sure it is. I can't tell ya everything 'bout the future."

"Matthew, our next Head Gatekeeper," Pipiera imagined him in the place of Megalos. She shook her head and chuckled;

then nodded and grinned. *Kingdom ways are so chaotic, creative and curious. Never ceases to amaze!*

Uncrossing his legs, Jophiel shifted uncomfortably on the plank bed and sat taller. "Thanks to you, he made it through yet another training session."

Her frown suggested she didn't get it.

"C'mon, let me spell it out. Boy goes missing. Mystery woman comes to town. Accusations fly." He chuckled a bit, jabbed her, then continued. "But Matthew? No, he refused to accuse the mystery woman. Sure, he was suspicious, but rather than eating up the loud voices around him, he opted to seek the truth."

She let that soak in for a minute. *Mining for nuggets of truth, huh.*

"That, my dear Pip, was a critical pass. He kept those accusing rumours out…so he could seek for himself and protect the truth. *Like*…a good gatekeeper would." He tightened his lips, though, as if there were more but he couldn't dare release it.

"Hmm. Okay, then, I get it." Still a little bewildered, she asked, "So, am I done here? Can I go home? Because I'm ready to be done here." She knew full well she had more to do.

He took her hand in his. "Aivy wants you to take care of one more thing while you are here."

"I know, I know. Free Bruce Brogan from his emotional prison. Like, how do I do *that?*" The temptation for sarcasm got the best of her. "Is mister shoot'em-up-bang-bang supposed to be a leaning post, too?"

"No," he laughed. "And just be yourself. I think you drive them crazy upstairs; you should see them scramble to work around you!" His shoulder pushed hers, another way to jab.

"Any advice?" She hoped he would give her some words she could act upon.

"As a matter of fact, yeah. Next time Mr. Ronaldo over there tells you he thinks everything's gonna be fine for you, agree with him. Tell him thanks; you believe that too. Tell him you are confident in and thrive by the truth; that you know the truth will free you. Then you believe it yourself. And, my dear Pip," he tapped the end of her nose. "Call on the King, perhaps? You haven't the whole time since arriving in this here basement." His eyes studied hers.

"Yeah, but…" She wondered, was he right?

"You've called Megalos; you've called Serena. But, my dear, you haven't called upon the King."

Oh my gosh, he is right.

CHAPTER FIFTY-SEVEN
NO VACATION

In the City of Moorelingville

MATTHEW DISCOVERED QUICKLY after his mother, Granddad and Dr. Alexien left him in that Moorelingville emergency cubicle that, although he was discharged for medical reasons, he was clearly not free to go for law enforcement reasons. In suspicion of harming, actually *killing* Joppha, given his burst of guilt, all according to Bruce Brogan's statement, Matthew was advised he could not leave Moorelingville. *So, it didn't really matter what that Dr. A. wanted. Me, on a special mission, yeah right.*

Bouts of shivers attacked Matthew's core. Every other hour, there'd be another uncontrollable shake. Nothing he thought a good long hot shower couldn't take care of once his wound was healed enough. Being shot, and the luck the bullet hadn't harmed him more than it did, was the repairable part. The wounds of being accused of something so unthinkable, and worst of all, losing Joppha in the first place, he wasn't so sure would heal. Guilt ate at him ferociously, worsening each day. Little by little, his Kingdom visit felt less and less real, rather more and more like a wishful dream. After all, he had been unconscious for a while. Who could really say what happens to one's mind in such a state?

Arnie and Matthew were sharing a room at the Shady Bog Motel, a Triple A-rated spot complete with in-ground pool, plenty of hot water and free coffee each morning. Arnie resisted adamantly at first when Matthew asked if he'd consider sharing the room. They barely spoke. Matthew clung to Arnie's robotic movements, anything that suggested their relationship could stay intact, acknowledging full well, Arnie would have preferred he not be around in such close quarters. Not at a time like this. It would have been easier for the two to walk away from each other.

"Ow," Matthew jerked. Arnie was not as gentle as his mother would have been when it came to ripping bandages off one's leg with a bullet wound.

"Hold still." Arnie's instruction was sharp. They were the only words Arnie had spoken to Matthew all morning; he had been on the phone the entire time with Cilia. Practically the entire night before that, too.

"Today?" Matthew asked, knowing Arnie had been told that the results of the autopsy should come in just a few days, and that was three days ago. Cilia was holding back on planning a service in honor of their beloved Joppha, and Marnie was pushing back the date for Maggie's funeral, as well. All of Havensight was on hold, an entire community shocked. Arnie was firm: he wouldn't go home until he could bring his son's body with him. And Matthew wouldn't be released as a person of suspicion until that ominous report was delivered. Surely, they would discover he had nothing to do with harming his young friend. And they would apologize.

Car doors slamming in the parking lot, followed by firm crunches in the gravel, came before a loud knock at the door. *This is it.* Matthew was sure of it. Arnie's hand shook as he employed sharp, sterile scissors to cut short the new bandage on Matthew's leg. Matthew grabbed the scissors, insisting he'd finish, and pointed to the door for Arnie to get it. "I'm here for you," Matthew whispered. He had never seen Arnie so distraught, ever. *This is not getting better by the day, it's getting worse.* Matthew choked on the realization—the suffering from this nightmare wasn't over, rather, it was only the beginning for the Decker family. It won't even matter what the results of this report might be.

Two Moorelingville officers came into their small room and sat down on the loveseat. It crossed Matthew's mind that it looked a little odd for the two fully uniformed men to be sitting so close to each other, but there were no other options. Matthew sat in his underwear, T-shirt and bare legs—one bandaged up—at the end of one bed. Arnie stood in his suit, the same one he'd been wearing now for several days, his face unshaven and a little scary looking, in front of the other bed.

"Please, Mr. Decker, have a seat." But Arnie refused and said nothing. Though his facial expression was blank, it spoke volumes.

The other officer slipped into the washroom and grabbed a towel, tossing it to Matthew, who then spread it across his lap.

Okay, can we get on with this? Matthew kept his impatient thoughts to himself. This was, first and foremost, Arnie's news. Whether this news would free Matthew came second.

"Arnie," the officer switched off the formalities. "Did you know your son had a defective heart?" That caused Arnie to sit down, but still, no words came from his mouth, although it opened wide.

"Your son died of natural causes. Again, our condolences. This cannot be easy for you. But perhaps knowing there are no signs of foul play…perhaps, well maybe, that might bring some relief for you."

Arnie seemed to have drifted into another world. *He obviously didn't know that. I didn't know that. I think he would have told me.* Matthew was sure of it and stayed quiet, waiting for more.

The other officer spoke, "Can you think of any reason why your son would have been so far from home and in the middle of a bog, no less? Any reason at all?"

Arnie shook his head and glanced at Matthew.

As if I know the answer to that?

Both officers gave Matthew an annoyed look. The first one continued, "We know he got on that bus to get here." Holding a glare at Matthew, "He wasn't being watched very well."

Stab. That was worse than being shot. Matthew glared back in defiance.

The other officer chimed in, "Laura Bing's purse was found dumped and abandoned. But there was no man. No one seen at the terminal. That one witness was pretty much a flake and the other, well, no fixed address. Can't locate him. Can't confirm anything." Motioning a stern nod Matthew's way, "Then this guy's chatter about some nightmare giving a vision of being all tied to a tree…" He shook his head while the other chimed in, "Nothing verifies that. Just a nightmare. That there bog's a lunar tidal swamp. His shoes and feet—heck, his pants right up to his waist—would have had a salty residue, at least something to suggest he was in water. Bone dry he was."

The men had just made Matthew appear to be some kind of crazy.

"Then how'd you know he was there?" Matthew was defending himself. He didn't enjoy being dismissed this way. He wondered how much that gas station attendant back in Havensight had overheard, misinterpreted and reported.

"If Bruce hadn't shot off his gun, we wouldn't have discovered him so quickly."

Oh, so Bruce is the hero. Matthew was having trouble keeping his thoughts quiet. "Then how do you explain me being there? How did *I* know to be there?"

Both officers glared at Matthew. "Something we'd like to know, too."

Matthew realized he wasn't helping his own cause and became silent. This was clearly not the time nor place to discuss Kasartha and the Kingdom world he'd been drawn into. Many things still needed answering in his own mind, like what's real and what's not.

The two officers stood. "We'll arrange transportation for you and your son back to Havensight today." Arnie stood, teary-eyed, and shook both their hands. "Talk to your doctor, see if there were any signs he might have missed." Arnie nodded. He would do that, but it wouldn't be his first priority.

"Oh, almost forgot." Out of his vest, the first officer pulled a ragged magazine, scrolled up tight and visibly worn around the edges. Then out of his pocket, he pulled two plastic, green toy soldiers and passed the lot to Arnie. "Found these items with your son, those little soldier guys were clutched in … in his fists. Thought…thought, you might like to have 'em."

That magazine! Matthew recalled it—a vivid memory of a transparent Joppha coming to him when he was down and out in the bog. *He was holding that, I recognize it, I remember it! What gives?* he wondered. *That means seeing him wasn't just my imagination after all.*

He noticed Arnie's face, so astonished and curious as he unrolled the scroll of worn pages and stared at the cover, mouth gapping. Following a pause, his arm nervously stretched out, his hand shook to receive the toy soldiers. Matthew remembered Joppha playing with them in the back seat of the car, insisting they would guard and protect him no matter what all the way to the bus station that fateful day. Arnie passed one of the plastic figurines to Matthew.

How generous, I don't deserve this, but I'm honored to have it. "Thank you," was all Matthew could choke out. Arnie and Matthew had a moment, imagining the pain each had inside.

"Am I free to go?" Matthew asked quietly, to which the officers nodded.

"Yeah, you're free to go."

Whew. Matthew fell back onto the bed.

The officers left, and Arnie directed Matthew to hurry up and get dressed if he wanted a ride.

Pipiera! Matthew had a sudden, urgent thought. She had been arrested, so this must mean she was free to go as well. He ran into the parking lot, hopping gingerly given the sharp stones on his bare feet. "Wait!"

He couldn't read their expressions since both officers had placed their sunglasses on already.

"Pipiera. I mean Penney. I mean Pippi…is she free to go, too?"

The first officer smirked, and Matthew realized why. *Ah, shoot, not dressed yet.*

"Yeah, she'll be released next, going there now. Get some clothes on, would'ja?"

The other added, "And maybe git yourself some *psychiatric counseling?*"

Matthew grinned. *They think I'm crazy. If they only knew the bigger picture!* He hoped Arnie wouldn't mind arranging for Pipiera to go back to Havensight with them.

All he could do was ask.

CHAPTER FIFTY-EIGHT
STARS ABOUND

In the Town of Havensight
Eight weeks later

PIPIERA SHOOK THE blanket and waved it in the air a few times, allowing it to snap before a graceful fall onto the cool grass. Matthew had invited her over to gaze at the night's sky. It was an evening when shooting stars would deliver up quite a show if conditions allowed. Amazed Pipiera was that Marnie actually wanted her to join them. A welcome signal that their relationship had made a definite turn and was heading in the right direction. All thanks to Matthew.

Matthew had spent the better part of the afternoon setting up his father's telescope and reading its manual. A super-sized set of binoculars strapped around his neck, he claimed they were ready. He looked proud and excited, the first time she had seen him crack a smile since that dreaded day when Joppha went missing—the day all were forced to carve a new pathway so they might carry on without him.

Both funerals were well behind them. Healing for Charles was slow but nothing compared to the healing journey Arnie and Cilia would endure.

Matthew and Pipiera shot the breeze, so to speak, waiting for more darkness to fall.

"Emerson called me today," Matthew announced. "Says it's not working out. He's coming home right after the long weekend." Matthew hadn't been surprised and nearly blurted out a criticism, given that he felt his friend had abandoned him at the time when he needed him most. But having memory of such crazy, out-there incredible experiences, ones he dared not share—including a recollection from years back; some hummingbird creature writing down all the thoughts and words from his head directly into an official, gold-rimmed book somewhere, up there, beyond the stars—he bit his tongue, and instead chose to applaud Emerson on giving it a try.

Oh, good timing, Pipiera thought. With Emerson out of the picture, she had been Matthew's bestie for the summer. But she knew she'd have to leave soon, so the news that Emerson was returning was good. *A sign,* she figured. Matthew hadn't seen him since the day his dad flew them to Moorelingville and then strong-armed him into taking a job at his company. *Maybe that's why he's smiling,* Pipiera thought. *His friend is coming back.*

"I think you've missed him," she said.

"Yeah, I miss the guy," he laughed. "I've got a proposal for him."

"Really, what?"

"Well, Mr. Hurley's retiring, selling his sports shop. I'm

thinking he and I could run it. If we could work out some kind of payment plan with Mr. Hurley, of course. We could do it. We know our stuff; can't be that hard."

"A big commitment, a lot of work," Pipiera cautioned. "You'll be tied to the community."

"Yeah, I was thinking about that. But I'm in. This is my hometown. I'm here to stay, put some roots down." Taking a deep breath, he spoke quietly, "Arnie needs me. Mom needs me."

"And Laura?" Pipiera asked, thinking she knew the answer already. Matthew and Laura had several discussions over the summer about their futures, and Matthew had confided to Pipiera. Their plans were far apart. Once she finished this summer dance school and year-end show, she'd be heading back to the big city. She was excited about the prospect of joining a more prestigious dance school and branding her whole 'Miss Laura' presence while continuing her studies at university, and she hoped Matthew would come along, get a more *professional-like* job and live close by. She didn't care much to return to Havensight except for brief visits to see parents and such. There was a time when Matthew thought if he could ever leave Havensight, he'd be free of whatever darkness loomed and could be quite content. But things change. He verbalized them to Pipiera. In the end, Matthew had given Laura that ring anyway, but not in light of securing his future—as he once thought that would satisfy a void— but rather, he gave her the ring to celebrate their friendship. He hoped they could always be friends, and though he delicately communicated there was not a future for them, she had grinned and reminded him that we never know what our tomorrows will bring.

"She's leaving next week," he said. Pipiera simply nodded. Matthew had been through a lot this summer, and it seemed some things were clearer now for him. "When I meet the right woman, I'll know it. I won't have to *secure* her." He chuckled at himself.

Pipiera realized that Jophiel had been right. Matthew could have fallen hard into a deep darkness this summer if it had not been for her own walk alongside him, pulling him up out of those hungry, swirling waters. She smiled at him, "You're doing well, Matthew."

He nodded, an acknowledgment of the very tough summer.

Marnie came out bearing a full tray of snacks and accompanied by a sidekick.

Karo, too? What a night! Pipiera was pleased. "Karo, I'm so happy to see you. How are you?"

Karo nodded sheepishly and sat quickly, cross-legged on the blanket. Shyly, she rubbed the angel-winged pearl pendant hanging on a chain around her neck, the special piece of jewelry that had belonged to her grandmother, as though somehow she was thanking Pipiera for it. Marnie began to pass out plastic plates for each and opened three Tupperware bowls of snacks. Cheezies, potato chips with dip, and some late-harvest strawberries. Then she waved a packet of 'half moon' cakes, laughing, "Look what else I've got."

Pipiera had never felt such a warm and fuzzy feeling since taking on this mission and couldn't help but smile. She did her best to hide the happy tears that threatened. She had Matthew to thank. All summer he'd suffered, and all summer she helped him, discussion after discussion. He boasted his thankfulness for Pipiera's friendship to his mother and sister and Arnie, for that matter. *They must have seen how much he leaned on me,* she figured. *And how much I cared for Charles, taking him for walks around the neighborhood to keep up his strength and to settle his mind.* Pipiera had encouraged Charles to not get tossed around by the winds of the world, and she had overheard him counseling Marnie with the same words. *That domino effect. So great.*

Marnie and Karo were, in fact, embarrassed by how terribly they had treated Pipiera, accusing her without facts, not wanting to know who she really was as a person. Pipiera had been so gracious and forgiving in return, hoping eventually they would come around. And tonight was signal enough that they had.

As they settled, out came Charles, hobbling hopelessly on one foot, dragging along a lawn chair.

"Dad!" Marnie exclaimed. "What are you doing up?" She ran to grab him, while Pipiera ran over to grab the lawn chair.

"Think I'm gonna miss this? My Maggie's up there. If she's gonna put on a show, I wanna see it!"

They all laughed. Darkness fell, and the show began. Pipiera mouthed 'thank you, thank you, thank you' to her King over and over.

CHAPTER FIFTY-NINE
THE TICKET MAN

PIPIERA CAME ALONG for the drive. Matthew wanted to stop by his place of work, Hurley's Sports, to see if he could corner Mr. Hurley to arrange a meeting. He invited Pipiera for a bit of encouragement. Sitting in old Betsy's front seat while Matthew entered the shop, she happened to notice Bruce Brogan writing a parking ticket for some spiffy automobile, sure to belong to a tourist, one block down. She still hadn't figured out how to 'free' him, so to speak. Up to this point, he would have nothing to do with her. *No doubt he's afraid of me, but he must know I'm innocent.*

Stepping out of the car, she headed his way, her brain scrambling for answers. *What shall I say to him? After all, he had seen her float. It seemed he had told no one, thankfully.*

"Bruce?" As if she had run into an old friend.

He looked at her and blinked a few times. His head dropped and he scratched the back of his neck; then, as though it took all his might, he lifted it back up.

Yeah? His eyes might have said, but not his tongue.

"I hope you'll forgive me for all the chaos you went through. It must have been a challenge. For that, I am sorry."

He blinked some more and scratched behind his ear.

"I really did appreciate meeting you and your sharing all that stuff with me about Marcus."

He removed his hat to scratch the top of his head.

"Anyway, that's all I wanted to say. I wish you well. Take care." She started back to Matthew's car, thinking this was just too awkward.

"Wait!" He hollered after her. She froze and turned, wondering where his mind was. *How will he be toward her?*

He said nothing, though, just that same blank look. She turned again, facing the direction of Betsy.

"Wait!" He hollered again. "You from…up there?"

Oh dear, Pipiera thought, and remained tight-lipped.

"Did Marcus send ya?"

Oh boy, how do I answer this? She toed the sidewalk and shook her head slowly. *Serena warned me not to break the rules. Ripple effect, not good. She was right.*

He played with the rim of his hat. "I reckon I owe you an apology. So, I'm sorry. I'm sorry to Matthew, too. Tell him for me?"

Whew, movement, she thought. "He's just at the sports shop, you could tell him. He'll understand, Bruce. Really." Then she escaped, walked briskly to Betsy, climbed in and took a deep breath.

Bruce didn't take the bite and continued down the main street in the opposite direction of Hurley's Sports.

But the very next day, Bruce Brogan tagged behind his wife, bearing a bowl of homemade chili, a big lettuce salad and a loaf of homemade bread to Marnie's house. Marnie surprised even herself by inviting them in and called Matthew and Karo to the kitchen. Together, the group shared the meal, Marnie marveling at how it would have been easier to go on being angry and admiring the strength of the Brogans' desire to make amends.

Upon hearing this news, Pipiera knew that her time in Havensight would be up. Soon, she would be called home.

CHAPTER SIXTY

GOODBYE AUNTIE

AT THE SIDE of the road north of town, Matthew pushed gravel around lazily with the toe of his runners while Pipiera leaned against Betsy, face toward the cloudless sky. She was enjoying the mid-morning sun and the somewhat cooled breeze of late August. He didn't want her to go, but she said this phase had ended. It was time.

"So this is where you arrived," he chuckled and scanned the sea of golden wheat, tall and gracefully dancing in harmonious waves like a corps de ballet. "It's a shame to cut it." That was Matthew's way of describing its beauty. They had both noticed the harvesting combine on their drive past the field, stopping short of the town's border, the Moon River.

Dressed in the same outfit she had arrived in earlier that Spring, including those three-inch-platform shoes she grew to dislike and the fedora hat that she never wore, she had no suitcase. "I'm going home with many riches," she smiled. "And knowing that you, my dear nephew, are going to be just fine."

Matthew smiled back but wondered, *I'm not as sure about*

that as you are. Life was bleak, given the tragic summer, and he still had a hard time believing he was worthy of any future. As she instructed, he watched out for and held on to the wonderful wisps of sun as they came. Like how his mother became more curious about all things of faith and asked questions that stumped him, such as does *belief* come first or taking a plunge to *belong?* She actually admitted to a deep longing, even though she couldn't understand it.

Or like how Karo had softened up this summer once he gently made her aware of a strong accusatory nature she had latched on to. Matthew was particularly concerned, knowing how Kasartha's power to plant his thoughts into unsuspecting minds worked. Karo was vulnerable, as he had been.

He cherished his daily chats with Charles. They were no longer a burden as they once were, simply to keep him busy so Marnie could make dinner in peace.

He liked how Bruce Brogan comes around now, albeit sheepishly. Always peeking around corners and staring up at the ceiling, asking if Pippi was around somewhere.

But most of all, what he held onto the most, was that hint of a smile in Arnie's eyes when Matthew would visit Cilia and him daily to bring them and the twins something he'd hoped would be helpful. Danishes, muffins, lavender bunches, magazines, a stew made by his mom, or even just a couple of takeaway coffees.

Without Pipiera's elbowing, Matthew may have never practiced the art of being aware and hanging on to what is good. He toed the gravel some more, this time a thick pile. It had been a dry summer, and a cloud of dust swirled from the pile.

"Hey, look!" Pipiera stooped to pick up a crystal she spied

under his foot and held it up proudly. Not much larger than an inch long, the one-of-a-kind stone had many cuts, none with any sort of blemish. She tossed it in the air and caught it with the same hand, and they both laughed. She handed it to Matthew, "Here. For you. When things down here get tough, just pull this out of your pocket and remember the bigger picture. Find the clear waters, flow with it. You're never alone. That'll help you remember what really matters."

Accepting the stone, he clutched it safely in his right hand. "What really matters," he repeated and couldn't help but smile at her.

"*And...,*" Pipiera teased, "best of all, you shall remember me when you look at it!"

Matthew tucked it safely in his pants pocket along with Joppha's toy soldier, "*Kalos,*" he whispered quietly. That was the nickname for the King. It meant *the Beautiful One*. Pipiera was so pleased Matthew had established that connection. He pulled her in for a big bear hug. "I'll miss you...*my Auntie Pip!*"

They laughed one more time, and she reminded him this was not goodbye. Holding her hat, she headed into the field of wheat and walked deep into its midst until all Matthew could see was that uncharacteristic peach fedora hat bouncing around and a ruffling of mature spikelets in its wake.

Matthew waited. He wasn't sure for what until a fierce, circular breeze caught his breath. The fedora hat blew high in circles back toward the road and slammed into his chest. A minutiae of a glimmer, and he swore he saw a single train whistling upward, then vanish.

He rubbed the crystal stone in his pocket, then placed her fedora hat squarely on his head and patted it securely. She had taught him to stand firm in the midst of uncertainty, so he sucked in and stood tall.

"I once had such a need to feel loved, but now? Now, I have such a need to give it. Thanks to you, Auntie." And he whispered a goodbye, a temporary one.

CHAPTER SIXTY-ONE

HOME AGAIN

In the Outer Courtyard of the Kingdom

"GOT IT?" JOPHIEL was carrying on with a happy skip, while Serena and Alexien carried a long, beautifully carved tray and laid it down carefully on the picnic table, right in the center. "Ah, so perfect," he thanked them and checked the rest of the table. Buttered popcorn, peanut butter toast, shepherd's pie and an egg salad sandwich all displayed carefully around the platter. "Hmm, what else? I know! Got anything like a 'half-moon' pie?"

"A what?" Serena asked. Alexien laughed.

Pipiera was due back today, and Jophiel wanted to surprise her in his way, a way to surely make her laugh. "All these foods have special memories for her," he joked. "But she will love your cherry strudel, Serena."

"Thank you," Serena took a bow. "Happy to oblige," she giggled.

Aivy came running out, not wanting to miss the party.

Plus, she needed to make sure that Maggie would finally enter the gate! Apparently, she had been driving Megalos crazy.

As scheduled and expected, Pipiera arrived following a wild and spinning train excursion with two eagle couriers. Not much fanfare, though. She wasn't a new Arrival, just merely coming back from a mission afar. Still, a pretty big deal to those who knew where she had been and what she had faced.

Jophiel's face beamed. He took her hand and led her over to the picnic table, the one decorated especially for her return. "You done good, kid." He still loved to tease her, and she seemed to enjoy it.

Megalos ran over to put his fatherly arm around her and kissed her forehead. He had missed her dearly and worried about her greatly. "I'm so proud of you," he said.

After Serena scolded her for not reporting back daily or ever at all, she, Alexien, and Aivy all took turns hugging Pipiera. They all chatted busily, asking questions about her experiences and expressing their thankfulness that she was finally back. At one point, Aivy had to console Pipiera, reminding her that weeping on Earth may last for a night, sometimes even a season, but will inevitably be followed by joy. There were appointed times for every matter, and she assured her that she hadn't left her family and friends to be alone.

Someone tapped on Pipiera's shoulders from behind. It was Maggie. Pipiera felt her lips quiver. "Mother," she whispered. Maggie grabbed Pipiera and held her tight, rocking her child back and forth as they stood, almost as one, the embrace was so tight. "I've waited so long…"

"Hush," Maggie consoled her daughter, stroking her hair, still rocking slowly. "We've so much to catch up on. You need to know how very proud I am of you. You were all anyone here talked about. My dearest love, my daughter."

Pipiera's teeth chattered. *Is this real?* "Are we really together? I wanted to be the one to welcome you!"

"I know, dear. It's okay, we're both here now."

Pipiera nodded, barely able to see through her tears.

Roly hollered over to the party, interrupting their special moment. With a grin, he pointed to the horizon.

Maggie clasped her mouth, "Oh my. Charles!" She ran, jumping over the waves like she was sixteen again.

Aivy, Serena and Alexien clamored around Pipiera, giving her a group hug, while Megalos stood by, admiring these special women. Pipiera smiled at Megalos. He nodded a grin in return.

Another surprise Pipiera hadn't anticipated! All was truly well.

As the entire party moved to greet Charles, Jophiel grabbed and linked into Pipiera's right arm as Megalos linked into the other.

"Our rose...," Jophiel started. "...between two thorns," Megalos ended. She laughed and wanted to stay still for a moment, watching both her parents. Both had arrived; they could enter as a family.

"You know something?" Pipiera said. "You two are my family, just as much."

"Yeah, we know," Jophiel smirked.

"Jophiel?" Pipiera had a question. It had been plaguing her mind for some time now. "Did you intend to enter rebel territory when you got on that bus?"

He tossed his head slightly and sang out, "Like a sheep to be slaughtered."

"So, am I right, then? You trapped Kasartha, and the attacks are done with?" Pipiera had had all summer to figure it out. That must have been Jophiel's assignment—the reason he was so keen to do an Earth-tour, and in Havensight of all places. Only someone like Jophiel could have pulled it off. Curious, creative chaos—events that no-one could ever understand! She hoped it had worked.

"Nah," Megalos injected, not offering any reasoning.

"So, then, the curse continues?" she asked.

"With even more vengeance," Jophiel advised.

She turned her head to scan the horizon where the cosmic waves came up over the edge. Sweet this moment was, even better than anything she had hoped for: escorting both her earthly parents into the Kingdom, surrounded by the dearest of ancestors and friends. Safe. Content. Divine. Stirring far below was anything but. Interferences. Storms. Deceit.

"This war is not over yet," she declared.

The End.

Awards for *The Gatekeeper's Descendants*, Book #1 in A Lifeline Fantasy Series by Johanna Frank

2021 – In the Beginning Award – Unpublished Authors, The Word Guild, Canada
2021 – Book Cover Award – BIBA (Best Indie Book Award), International
2022 – Honorary Mention – Young Adult Religious Theme, Readers' Favorite, International
2022 – Finalist – Best Published Novel - Young Adult Fiction, General Market, The Word Guild, Canada
2022 – Finalist – Best Published Novel - Speculative Fiction, Christian Market, The Word Guild, Canada
2022 – Finalist – Book Cover Award, The Word Guild, Canada

The Gatekeeper's Descendants is also available in audio.
Visit www.JohannaFrankAuthor.com
for an audio sample and more information.

Coming next: A Lifeline Fantasy Series Book #3

KASARTHA'S TOUR
Working title

Care to be notified once it's available?
Stay tuned and keep in touch at:
www.JohannaFrankAuthor.com

www.ingramcontent.com/pod-product-compliance
Lightning Source LLC
Chambersburg PA
CBHW030756210726

48290CB00002B/296